DAYLIGHT

Girl from the Stars

Book 2

Daylight

By Cheree L. Alsop

ISBN: 9781523208630
Cover Design by Andy Hair
Editing by Sue Player
www.ChereeAlsop.com

To the joy of a life of writing-
Writing is like watching a young bird jump from its
nest.
It struggles and flaps and fights not to hit the ground,
Then there's that moment where its wings catch the
wind
And it soars above the trees,
Taking you on one of the best rides of your life.

I love to write, and I love my readers.
I am so grateful for a family that supports me with so
much love,
And for the ability to share the adventures in my head
And give the others the chance to escape
To worlds unseen, yet filled with hopes and dreams
Just waiting to be explored.

Beware of the chenowik.

DAYLIGHT

ALSO BY CHEREE ALSOP

The Silver Series-
Silver
Black
Crimson
Violet
Azure
Hunter
Silver Moon

The Werewolf Academy Series-
Book One: Strays
Book Two: Hunted
Book Three: Instinct
Book Four: Taken
Book Five: Lost
Book Six: Vengeance
Book Seven: Chosen

Heart of the Wolf Part One
Heart of the Wolf Part Two

The Galdoni Series-
Galdoni
Galdoni 2: Into the Storm
Galdoni 3: Out of Darkness

The Small Town Superheroes Series- (Through
Stonehouse Ink)
Small Town Superhero
Small Town Superhero II
Small Town Superhero III

Keeper of the Wolves
Stolen
The Million Dollar Gift
Thief Prince
When Death Loved an Angel

The Shadows Series- (Through Stonehouse Ink)
Shadows- Book One in the World of Shadows
Mist- Book Two in the World of Shadows
Dusk- Book Three in the World of Shadows

The Monster Asylum Series
Book One- The Fangs of Bloodhaven
Book Two- The Scales of Drakenfall

Girl from the Stars
Book 1- Daybreak
Book 2- Daylight
Book 3- Day's End

CHEREE ALSOP

DAYLIGHT

Chapter 1

Liora and Tariq reached the Calypsan's Tin Sparrow and collapsed as soon as they made it inside. The sounds from the circus tents and vendor stalls of planet Luptos followed them into the small ship.

"I'll get the med kit," Tariq offered.

"Don't even think about it," Liora replied. "I've got it. You've moved far too much already."

"I think my knee's okay. The bullet went higher than he meant it to. It's embedded somewhere in my thigh."

"You know that's not very reassuring," Liora pointed

out as she lugged the medical kit one-handed to his side.

Tariq gave her a pained smile. "I'm a positive person."

"Since when?"

He gave an actual laugh, the first she remembered hearing. "Since this moment. I figure it can only go uphill from here."

"Hang around with me long enough and we'll prove that wrong," Liora shot back, winning another laugh from him. Liora tried several times to secure a bandage around his wound so he could work on her, but the blade in her hand made it impossible. She knew better than to pull it free without something to apply pressure, but she worried about Tariq passing out from blood loss before she could bandage him.

Tariq sat up gingerly and caught her fingers.

"Easy," he said at her wince of pain. "Let's take care of this first. Do you want an injection? I could numb it."

She shook her head. "I won't be able to get the bullet out if you do. I need to be able to move my fingers. It just shouldn't hurt as bad as it does." She tried not to think about what was going to happen.

"You mean getting a knife shoved through your hand should be easy?"

"Easier," she answered. Her voice tightened when he carefully grabbed the blade.

"Maybe we should tell Obruo not to stab his daughter."

Liora glared at Tariq. At that moment, he eased the blade from the wound. She held back a cry of pain and instead bit her lip so hard she tasted blood.

"It's alright," he said, his voice gentle. He concentrated on cleaning and bandaging the wound. "The hard part's over. I won't be able to check for damage until we reach the Kratos, but your fingers still work. That's a good sign."

Liora blinked quickly to hold back tears. "I'm glad you think that's good," she said, her voice wavering.

Tariq looked at her closely. "Liora, I can numb this."

She shook her head. "I need to be able to use it. I'll be fine."

He finished wrapping the bandage around it and tied the gauze off. He was careful to tuck the ends of the bandage beneath the other layers so they wouldn't snag on anything.

"You've done this before," Liora said.

Tariq gave her a half-smile. "A few times."

She sat up, careful not to put weight on her injured hand. "Alright, it's your turn."

"Is this payback?" he asked. "I tried to be gentle."

"Don't expect the same from me."

He settled on the floor with a worried expression. "I'm not sure I like the sound of that."

"Trust me," Liora told him. "I've removed bullets before. This is going to be easy."

She carefully cut his pant leg where the bullet had gone through. Tariq was right. Instead of breaking bones, the bullet had lodged in the muscles of his thigh. She rinsed the surgical instruments with disinfectant and willed her heart to slow. She had removed bullets before. Ironically, Tariq was the last person she had performed such a procedure on. Somehow, the knowledge that she could do it didn't help the nerves of actually performing the surgery.

She injected a local anesthetic into the wound.

"I could do without that," Tariq protested.

She gave him a flat look. "I need a copilot, and if you pass out from the pain and something goes wrong with this junk heap of a ship, we're both dead."

Tariq sat back. "You've got a point."

Liora put a rag below the wound to keep the blood somewhat contained. She took a steeling breath, then slowly sliced into the hole where the bullet had entered. Fresh blood welled up and spilled from the incision. Liora picked up a pair of forceps and slid them carefully into the hole.

"So Chief Obruo doesn't want to kill you." Tariq's words were tight as the forceps grated against the bullet. "Why do you think he's after you?"

"I'm not sure." Liora's brow creased as she concentrated on sliding the ends of the forceps around the slug. "It doesn't make any sense."

"The only reason that sadistic Damaclan wouldn't kill you is because he can gain something by keeping you alive."

Liora glanced at him. "What could he possibly gain?"

"That's what I can't figure out." Tariq sucked in a breath when she grasped the bullet and pulled it free. "You must be worth something to him," he finished, his voice tight.

Liora flushed the wound to reduce the chance of infection. "You mean besides being the illegitimate daughter of his Damaclan wife and the human she actually loved?"

Tariq winced when she pressed bandages against the wound tighter than she intended.

"Liora," he protested.

She caught herself. "Sorry." She wrapped bandages around his leg to hold the others in place. "It just doesn't make sense. What could I possibly be worth to him?"

Tariq was quiet for a moment. He glanced at her as if wondering if he should voice what he was thinking aloud. He let out a breath and said, "Liora, do you know who your father is?"

She gave him a searching look. "No. Why?"

Tariq lifted a shoulder. "Maybe he has something to do with it."

"He probably has no idea I exist," Liora told him with a shake of her head. "All I know is that Day is his last name and he's human. No matter how I asked, my mother would never tell me more than that."

"Maybe she was protecting you," Tariq mused.

Liora kept silent. She had long ago accepted that knowing who her mother was would be enough for her life. She didn't need a father when she was younger, and she sure didn't have a use for one now. The thought that Obruo's attack was in any way related seemed farfetched.

Tariq sat up when she was done tying off the bandages. She could tell by the pallor of his face that the loss of blood was catching up to him.

"Why don't you grab a bit of sleep?" she suggested. "I'll head toward the transporter and wake you when we're close."

He gave her injured hand a meaningful look. "Are you sure you can fly?"

She smiled. "I can fly this wreck blindfolded and still land it better than Hyrin. Just don't tell him I said that."

Tariq gave a quiet chuckle. "Oh, I'm telling him."

She stood and held out her good hand. "Only if you survive to the Kratos. You need to rest that leg."

He gave a grunt of pain as she helped him to his feet.

"All I know is that I can't wait to get back to the ship

and figure out what to do with the Omne Occasus. It makes me nervous that there's a galaxy imploder aboard the Kratos." He limped with her help. "The sooner we can get back to regular missions, the better."

Liora helped him to the bed the Calypsan who owned the ship had fashioned out of storage containers in the back. "Are you sure they'll let you continue with Coalition missions? Running with the imploder has made everyone rebels, hasn't it?"

Tariq's eyebrows pulled together. "You heard Shathryn. We're Coalition through and through. It's what we know. I'm not sure how Dev and the others would react if the Coalition doesn't pardon us after this."

He settled gingerly on the burlap sacks of taliper rice. It was a Calypsan staple and made the entire back half of the Tin Sparrow smell like sulfur. Liora returned to the front of the ship grateful she wasn't the one who had to use it as a bed.

She programmed the coordinates for the Diamond Albatross into the Sparrow's computer before lifting away from planet Luptos. Her final glimpse of the SS Kirkos that had been her prison for so many years was of the ship's hull upside-down and smoldering in the Luptos' swamp. A hint of gratitude for Obruo's thoroughness sparked unfamiliarly in her chest. In his efforts to destroy everything she knew, he had actually done her one favor. She would be happier if she never had to look at the Kirkos again.

The planet's atmosphere obscured the tents and circus ships from view. Liora guided the spacecraft across the Maffei One Galaxy intent on the Oregon transporter near the far edge. As she flew, the reality of what had happened circled over and over again in her mind.

Malivian was dead. Obruo was trying to kill her.

Liora knew better than to think the chief would give up. No matter what his reason for trying to find her, with him on her trail, nobody would be out of his reach. The Kratos crew might be safer sticking together against the Coalition and everyone else out to get their hands on the Omne Occasus, but Liora was the one bringing them the most danger. She wasn't sure how to come to terms with that.

When the Oregon transporter drew near, she heard Tariq limp forward from the passage.

"Are you alright?" he asked.

She nodded. "Are you?"

He eased into the copilot chair and stuck his leg out at an angle. "Sure. I don't know when I fell asleep."

"It hasn't been too long," Liora told him. "We're almost to the transporter."

"Thank goodness," Tariq replied. "I'm not sure how much longer we can stay on this Sparrow. Calypsans pack way too much grass for my stomach."

"I've never acquired the taste," she replied.

Tariq watched out the huge glass windows for a moment before he said, "So what have you been contemplating? Do I want to know?"

She glanced at him, debating how much to tell. "I'm not sure." She was silent for a moment. Nobody had ever asked her what she thought about. The memories and images that occupied her mind probably made that a good thing; however, thinking about the most recent events troubled her far greater. She took a chance.

"Obruo's the reason I was caged."

"I heard that." Tariq's voice was gentle with empathy. "I didn't realize it."

"I didn't either until he told Malivian he was supposed to keep me under control." She shook her head. "Obruo's been controlling me this whole time."

Tariq settled back in his seat. "Liora, if I know you at all, nobody controls you."

"Not anymore," she said firmly.

He nodded as if he appreciated the words. "Good. I'm glad to hear it."

A silver object drew near on the screen.

"There's the Oregon transporter."

"I can't wait to get back to a real medical bay."

At Liora's surprised look, Tariq shrugged with a hint of embarrassment. "Do you know how pathetic those tools are back there? Mine make the Calypsan's pale in comparison. You might even have stitches right now."

He raised his eyebrows invitingly.

Liora fought back the urge to smile. "As fun as that sounds, I think I'll stick with bandages."

Tariq guided the toggle toward the transporter. As soon as it coupled, he hit the button for the jump.

Liora sat back in the pilot's seat. The pulling sensation felt like cold water spilling over her from head to toe. Before she could decide if it was unpleasant, the sensation was gone.

"That's not the Atlas." Tariq sat up straight.

Liora's heart skipped a beat. In the exact coordinates where they were supposed to find the Coalition's lost Diamond Albatross and the Starship Kratos, a different Coalition starship waited. The Iron Falcon bore the name SS Cerberus along the hull.

"Incoming," Tariq said. He pushed the receiver.

Colonel Lefkin's face appeared on the screen.

"Hello, Officer Tariq. What a pleasant surprise." His

gaze took in Liora. "And a Damaclan." His eyes narrowed. "As far as I'm aware, there are no Damaclans in the Coalition." He pursed his lips. "Unless, of course, Captain Devren had reason to make an exception. I'm sure I'll find his reasoning adequate." The Colonel gave a humorless smile. "I invite you both to come aboard my ship."

Liora and Tariq exchanged a glance. The invitation was a thinly-cloaked order. Colonel Lefkin knew exactly what Devren carried aboard his Iron Falcon. Given the number of Coalition ships and mercenaries the Colonel had put on their trail, he would do whatever he could to ensure the Omne Occasus became his.

"This is what I get for being positive," Tariq muttered as he pushed gingerly to his feet.

Liora turned her head so the Colonel couldn't see her speak. "We could always run for it," she whispered.

"You're insane," Tariq replied.

"I'm part Damaclan," Liora reminded him.

Tariq watched her for a moment. The slightest hint of a smile twitched at the corner of his mouth. He glanced at the screen, then back at her.

"I'm putting my money on the Damaclan."

Chapter 2

Liora looked at Tariq. "You're serious about this?"

The wide doors to the landing bay of the SS Cerberus opened.

"Better than imprisonment on a Coalition ship. I don't like the idea of being tortured for information," Tariq replied. He glanced at the screen in front of him. "What's the status of the transporter?"

Liora hit a button. "The solar sails are still out. It'll take a few more minutes for the charge to complete."

"My officers are ready for your arrival," Colonel

Lefkin said. His tone was firm.

"On our way," Tariq replied. He turned the ship toward the Cerberus. "Ready the guns," he whispered.

Adrenaline rushed through Liora's veins. She pulled up the weapons' system on her screen and directed power to the ship's cannons while Tariq maneuvered the spacecraft slowly.

"Is there something wrong with your ship?" Colonel Lefkin demanded. "My grandmother could fly faster."

Tariq nodded. "Yes, Colonel. Our thrusters have only half power. We've been limping along to this point."

The colonel's jaw clenched as though their lack of haste annoyed him to no end.

Liora checked her other screen. "The sails are folding. The transporter's charged," she reported quietly.

"Good. Shoot the landing bay."

Liora stared at him. "What?"

Tariq glanced at the colonel, but the man had apparently lost patience at their slow approach and was looking at something off-screen.

"Shoot the landing bay," he said. "That Eagle's a lot faster than this Sparrow, but if we damage the landing bay, they won't be able to close the airlock, so their thrusters will be disabled."

Liora locked onto the left side of the door.

"Wait for my go," Tariq whispered. He maneuvered the Sparrow closer to the Cerberus. They could see officers waiting in two tight rows along the landing strip inside. There was no way their welcome was going to be a friendly one.

Tariq kept his gaze locked on Colonel Lefkin as he directed power to the thrusters. Liora barely dared to breathe; her good hand hovered over the fire command.

Pain shot up her arm and it took her a moment to realize she had clenched her injured hand into a fist. She opened it slowly.

"Ready?" Tariq whispered.

"Ready," Liora replied.

"Even at half-thrusters," Colonel Lefkin began, his tone one of complete exasperation.

Whatever else he was going to say was cut off when Tariq shouted, "Now!"

Liora blasted the loading bay doors at the same time that Tariq fired the thrusters. The Sparrow shot toward the Oregon transporter.

"What on…Officer Tariq!" Colonel Lefkin yelled.

Tariq slammed his palm on the console and the colonel's face disappeared. They reached the transporter and Tariq maneuvered the docking arm into the transporter's link. Precious seconds went by as Tariq attempted to lock the toggle in place.

When it slipped a third time, Liora set a hand on his arm.

"Let me."

Tariq nodded and climbed carefully from his chair. Liora took the pilot's seat and willed her nerves to steady. She pushed away all worry of the Coalition ship behind them and the fear that perhaps the colonel would be able to maneuver his ship to fire. If they were captured at this point, they would be hung as traitors.

Liora's heartbeat pounded in her ears. Using her Damaclan training, she settled her breathing and focused on the screen. With a few light touches, she maneuvered the toggle to the center of the link and connected it to the transporter.

"Done," she said quietly.

"Go," Tariq replied.

Liora activated the transporter. A moment later, they were back in the Maffei One Galaxy with the Coalition starship far behind.

"I'm going to shoot the sails to give us some time," Tariq told her.

"The Coalition's really going to be upset if we disable every transporter we use," Liora replied. The thought of leaving the colonel and his ship in the middle of space made a small smile touch her lips. "But I'm all for it."

As soon as the silver sails unfurled from the Oregon transporter, Tariq tore them to pieces with the Sparrow's cannons. The tattered sails fell away, leaving the transporter unable to charge with the light from the surrounding stars.

Tariq sat back in his seat with a satisfied nod. "That'll handle them for a while. I imagine it'll take the colonel some time to rally his ships after us when he has no idea where we're going."

The thought bothered Liora. "Where are we going? We have no idea where the Atlas might be."

Tariq studied the screen in front of them. "I think I might know how to find them," he said. There was something to his tone as if he wasn't sure he liked his idea.

"Anything is better than drifting along in this ship," Liora said.

Tariq nodded. "That's for sure." He let out a breath. "Head for the Cas One Galaxy."

Liora glanced at him. "Will they be there?"

Tariq shook his head. "I doubt it, but I have a feeling Dev will leave us a message."

Liora typed in the coordinates. "Why Cas One?"

When she looked at him, the expression on Tariq's face was torn between a smile and a look of trepidation.

"It was home once, a long time ago."

The silence that settled between them was one of relief. From what Liora knew about the Coalition, they had just escaped a near brush with what would have been a painful and certain death. The Coalition had no time for traitors, and given their role in helping Devren's crew obtain the Omne Occasus, they would have been sent to Titus for imprisonment. No one had ever escaped from Titus.

Chills ran down Liora's arms at the thought of being held captive in another cell. Her time as Malivian's circus freak mind pusher was one she would never repeat.

"You look tired."

She glanced at Tariq.

His gaze was on her hand. "And you're bleeding again. We need to rebandage that."

She gave the hand a critical look. Her fingers still moved, though there was definitely swelling beneath the bandages. Her fingertips remained a good color, and even though blood showed where the knife had gone through her palm, it hadn't soaked the gauze completely.

"I'll survive," she told him. "It'll heal better if I leave it alone." She couldn't quite stifle a yawn. The last time she had slept was before they landed at the last Gaulded. "I think I'll take a turn on that bed, though."

"Enjoy," Tariq said. "It smells like an entire Calypsan army back there."

Liora sighed. "I guess it could be worse."

"Could it?"

She grimaced. "It could smell like a Gaul army."

Tariq's quiet chuckle followed her to the back of the

ship. She sat on the rice bags and tried not to notice the odor that wafted from them. When she settled back, another smell touched her nose. It took her a moment to recognize that the subtle scent was Tariq's. It contained a hint of the red planet's sands and darker tones of metal and gunpowder. The thought that he had slept there sent tiny tingles running beneath Liora's skin. She couldn't decide how she felt about that.

Liora rolled onto her side and rested her injured hand carefully on the rice sack beside her. While she tried to maintain a tough front, the ache that ran up her arm made it hard to close her eyes. She wondered if she should let Tariq numb the wound, but the effort it would take to make her way back to the front of the small ship seemed like way too much. Just having the time to rest felt like a gift after all they had been through.

Liora closed her eyes and lingered in the place between sleep and awake. Concern for Devren and his crew remained foremost in her mind. She couldn't remember the last time she had worried about someone else. Perhaps leaving them at the Gaulded to hunt for Obruo had been a mistake. If they were in trouble and she wasn't there, Liora didn't know how she would forgive herself.

The thought brought a smile to her lips. The crew of the SS Kratos had survived for a very long time without her. Why she suddenly felt like they needed her to continue baffled her. Perhaps it was the want to be needed by someone other than herself? Liora rubbed her eyes. The thoughts were far beyond her exhausted mental state. For the moment, it was enough to accept that she felt she belonged somewhere. Whether they made it back to the Kratos was left to be seen.

Liora's thoughts drifted to a memory made more real for the sleep haze that filled her mind.

After the death of her clan by the hands of the nameless ones, she had wandered the land for days until her feet bled and her throat was so dry she couldn't make a sound. The whispers of the nameless ones haunted her, driving her further away from the family she had been unable to protect. At age twelve, she was clanless, motherless, and without anybody in the Macrocosm who cared about her fate.

"Let her go," a shadow hissed.

"She'll bleed planets dry," another whispered.

"More for us," the first said. "Souls are not long for this universe."

"Give her a blade."

"Show her the way."

"She'll be the key to the end of it all, the girl from the stars. The girl without a soul."

Liora's tears had dried long ago. She couldn't feel the pain of her feet or the ache of the fresh tattoos down her neck and along her arms. She couldn't feel anything at all.

Something hovered in the sky above her, blocking out the stagnant sunshine that lit the world around her without touching her skin. A soft hum filled the air, then she was inside a black room. It took several minutes for her sun-blind eyes to focus. During her state of shock, manacles were clasped around her wrists and ankles. Another was locked around her throat. Her clothing was sliced by a practiced hand and she was shoved into a circle of light in the center of the room.

"Damaclan," a voice said. Other words followed in a language she didn't understand.

The voice paused as though waiting for her to answer

a question, but she didn't know what the question was, nor did she care. She wanted to go back to wandering aimlessly through the desert until the nameless ones were forced to take her, too. It was the only thing that made sense, the only fate she deserved.

Several more words were spoken before rough hands grabbed her and shoved her into another room.

The smell hit her nose first. Unwashed bodies from various planets had been crammed into the tiny space.

Collectors.

The word struck her mind with a tingle of fear. Damaclan mothers warned their children about collectors to keep them from wandering too far from the clan. Mortalkind from across the Macrocosm paid money for various species to add to their collections. It was a body trade, a form of slavery in which the captives had no rights. Now, Liora was a part of that trade.

Too numb after all she had experienced to argue about her plight like many of the others in the room, Liora didn't speak. She ate what was handed to her without tasting it and her thirst was quenched, but the cacophony of hundreds of voices and languages battered unheard against her ears. She wished the nameless ones would take her, but in their ironic pity, they had left her to her fate.

"What do you do?"

The phrase was repeated several times before Liora realized the words were in her language. She blinked and her mind adjusted slowly to the meaning behind the words. She turned her head and found an elderly woman with white hair, dark skin, and three arms waiting patiently for her answer. The race Artidus came to Liora's mind from her mother's teachings.

"What do you do?" the woman asked again in the Damaclan tongue.

Liora wasn't sure how to respond. She didn't trust her tongue to speak clearly, so she limited her answer to one word. "Destroy."

The Artidus woman's wrinkled brow creased despite the smile that touched her lips. "It can't be that bad," she said, her words soft. "I know of your kind and your training, but good comes from every race as well as evil. Surely…"

The woman's words died away when Liora pushed at her with her mind in the way that used to infuriate Chief Obruo. She wanted the woman to understand and needed her to. It felt so important that someone know what had happened and why she deserved to be set adrift once more on the empty planet from which she had been taken.

She watched the woman's eyes widen at the memory of Obruo sending her out as a sacrifice to the nameless ones. It was the only way to save their clan. She was the last, their only remaining hope.

The nameless ones had been offended at her mixed blood and left her there to watch as they decimated Obruo's clan down to the last woman and child. Liora's heart clenched away from the memory of finding her mother dead in the doorway to their home.

"That's enough," the Artidus woman said. She drew back, breaking the push in a way no one else had been able. She blinked and her hazy blue eyes cleared. Before Liora could say anything, the woman wrapped her in a hug.

Liora closed her eyes. The gentle touch was something so rare in her life that she barely knew how to take it. The woman's three arms held her tight, removing some of the pain without Liora understanding how.

When Liora couldn't handle the kindness any longer and backed away, the woman's expression was filled with concern.

"Don't push at someone like that again, especially here," she said. She lowered her voice. "If they know you can do that, you'll be taken to places far worse than any these collectors can touch. Pushers are rare in the Macrocosm. A pusher who is also a trained Damaclan would be a rare and dangerous slave indeed."

The woman looked her over. Before Liora could draw back, the woman's third arm that came from the middle of her chest brushed Liora's messy brown hair away from her face.

Her eyes showed pity when she said, "You are as beautiful as your race is deadly. Let's hope we have time to teach you other skills so that purchasers will see past your attractiveness. The last thing we need is for you to be sold into a system to system harem where you will be used and cast aside when your appeal has been beaten and stolen from you." Her voice carried the burden of someone who knew what that felt like all too clearly.

"How?" Liora forced herself to ask.

The Artidus woman pulled a charcoal pencil and a pad of paper from the tattered bag at her side. "Collectors never rush lest they miss the opportunity for another valuable haul. I've been on this ship for six months and we've yet to dock. My skills lie in healing and languages. If luck is on our side, we'll have you reading and speaking the common tongue and able to save lives on the brink of death. Perhaps they'll find those skills to be worth more than a beautiful body."

With nothing else to do, Liora focused on learning. The Artidus woman, Shegare, turned out to be an apt teacher, and Liora found that applying herself to languages left little time to think about her past or what was to come. By the time they landed, Liora's skills had far surpassed even Shegare's hopes. She had learned not only the common tongue, but could read and write the root languages of Zamarian, Ventican, and Galian, along with speak several of the older languages she had picked up from other captives aboard the collectors' ship.

"Let's hope it's enough," Shegare said as they were led from the ship to a strange globe that looked as though it was made of old starships and random chunks of metal and debris welded together.

Liora awoke with Shegare's words lingering in her mind. She pushed away the pain of thinking about the woman who had shown her more kindness than anyone else in her life. Liora wished the memories would stay locked in the far recesses of her mind, but she didn't know how to keep them from assailing her when her guard was down.

Chapter 3

Liora made her way to the front of the Sparrow again. She realized when she looked at the monitor that she had slept longer than she thought.

"Is that the Cas One Galaxy?" she asked in amazement.

Tariq gave an appreciative nod. "Incredible, isn't it?"

Liora slid into the copilot's seat with her eyes locked on the screen. "I've never seen anything like it."

Long stretches of lightning arched around the planets in the Cas One system. Each planet was illuminated with a different color of lightning. Blasts of orange, green, magenta, and yellow surged out into space before striking back at the charged atmospheres in colorful explosions.

Massive ships with strange circular voids in the middle orbited the planets in the opposite direction of the lightning. The collectors sucked the jagged light into the voids where it was redirected by mirrors into holding cells.

"That's home," Tariq said. He nodded toward the fourth planet from the Cas One sun.

Liora caught the strange tone that hinted in his voice. "Has it been a long time since you've been back?"

Tariq was quiet for a moment. The green lightning from the planet reflected in his gaze when he said, "My reasons for being there are long gone."

Liora wondered how the ship was supposed to fly through the lightning that circled the planet. Tariq steered the ship toward two of the lightning collectors. When they drew near, he switched the radio on.

"This is Tariq Donovan requesting entrance to Verdan."

"Tariq, you dog!" the answering pilot responded. "How long has it been? I thought the Scavs had killed you by now!"

A slight smile tugged at the corner of Tariq's lips. "I'm harder to kill than that, Josen. You ought to remember."

Liora fought back a smile at the hint of the Cas One accent that appeared in Tariq's voice.

"There's a price on your head," the second pilot said. "Maybe we should turn you in."

Silence filled the airwaves for a moment. Liora glanced at Tariq, wondering if she should be worried. Tariq merely watched the dials and monitors in front of him; the slight tightening of his eyes was the only sign of emotion.

Josen burst out laughing. "Mrs. Metis would kill us," he said. "We know better than to get on her bad side. Open it up, Fray."

"Doing it now," Fray reported.

The two ships tipped the massive circles where the lightning was collected. As soon as the mirrors were pointed at each other, the lightning struck in the middle and arced, creating a hole.

"You've got ten seconds," Fray reported.

"Unless we close it early," Josen said.

"I only need five," Tariq told them.

Both pilots burst out laughing over the radio as if they shared an inside joke.

Tariq steered the ship toward the hole, hit the thrusters, and they were through before the lightning closed. Liora glanced at the monitor that showed the view behind them. The ships turned their massive circles and began collecting the lightning once more. The jagged streaks of green light covered the atmosphere, then disappeared from view the lower they flew. Darkness closed in from all sides. Liora missed the glow from the stars. She never realized how much she took it for granted.

"Is it dark like this all the time?" she asked.

Tariq nodded. "The atmosphere is too thick for the sun to shine through. The planet is lit from the inside instead of out."

A glance at the surfaced showed the truth of Tariq's statement. The ground that neared was covered in what looked like yellow glowing grass. Orange light flowed through the small shrub-like trees. Houses with small yards had softly glowing glass windows. Animals with iridescent horns that caught the light from the surrounding plants scattered as Tariq lowered the spacecraft to the ground.

When the engines whined to a stop, a woman burst from the nearby house.

"Don't even think about leaving that machine on my property," Liora could hear her scolding before Tariq opened the door.

"I'll shoot however many of you are hiding on that wreck of a ship, so help me," the woman continued. "I'm tired of squatters thinking they can land wherever they please without regard to those they're infringing upon."

Tariq didn't appear the least bit phased by her words. He hit the panel for the door to open, and a rare smile touched his lips.

"Mark my words, I'll fill your hide so full of…"

The woman's voice paused, and her tone changed completely. "Tariq! Oh my lands, it is you!"

Before he had even set a foot on the ground, he was wrapped in a tight hug.

Liora stifled a smile.

"Hello, Mrs. M," he managed to get out.

"Hello?" she repeated. She stepped back to look him up and down. "It's been eight years, and all you can say is hello?"

Tariq shrugged and the woman laughed. Her brown eyes creased at the corners and the lines on her face deepened. Her gaze shifted to Liora.

"And who's this? I don't remember a Damaclan on your crew."

Her tone was warm despite the tattoos her gaze lingered on.

"Liora's a recent addition," Tariq said. He motioned for her to come forward. "She could use a bit of your tending to. She's been keeping me running up to now." He nodded at her. "Liora, this is Mrs. Metis."

"It's a pleasure to meet you," Liora told her. "Captain Metis is a good man."

"Yes, he is," she said with a proud smile. She gestured to the house. "Come inside and get some food. You could use some fattening up. What have you been eating out there this whole time? Boiled ganthum?"

"With zanderbin hide," Tariq replied with a grin as if it was a shared joke.

Mrs. Metis shook her head and the gray curls that cascaded down her back bounced with the motion. "It's a wonder you guys are still ticking on Coalition rations. Come in and tell me what Rius and Devren are up to."

Tariq's shoulders tightened. "You didn't hear?"

Liora's heart slowed at the tone of his voice.

Mrs. Metis glanced back over her shoulder with a hand on the door of the small brown house. The windows were filled with golden light that cascaded onto the glowing yellow grass. "Hear what, dear?"

Tariq's gaze flickered to Liora and she saw the loss in them. She didn't know what she could say or do to make what was coming any easier.

"We'd better go inside," he told Mrs. Metis, his tone gentle. "We have some things to talk about."

Liora shut the door behind her. A small, fuzzy creature with a big nose and glowing curled horns sniffed her boots as she followed Tariq into the main room. A warm, spiced scent made Liora's stomach growl when she walked past the warmly lit kitchen.

Pictures and drawings lined the brightly colored walls.

35

A glance at one showed a younger Mrs. Metis with a man at her side Liora assumed was Rius. Two small children carried armfuls of flowering plants. Devren's dark eyes and smile were unmistakable next to his younger sister.

Mrs. Metis motioned for them to take a seat.

"Let me get you something refreshing before we talk," she said.

Tariq shook his head. "No, thank you. We're fine." He caught her hand and helped her sit on the chair near the couch.

There was a look of reluctance on Mrs. Metis' face as if she guessed what he was about to say, but didn't want to hear it.

"Maybe I should get you some tea," she said, moving to rise again.

Tariq shook his head.

"Mrs. M, I don't know how else to say this." He blinked and his eyes shone brightly. He took a steeling breath and said, "Captain Metis was killed by Revolutionaries."

Mrs. Metis shook her head. "I heard from him two weeks ago, and your friend said he is a good man." She gave Liora an imploring look.

Liora wished she could take the woman's pain away. She said gently, "I was talking about your son."

Mrs. Metis' gaze lowered to the floor. A tear trailed down her weathered cheek. "Devren's a captain," she said quietly. She gave a wavering smile. "Rius would be proud."

"Would be?"

Everyone looked up at the young woman who stood in the doorway opposite the one through which they had entered.

"Kiari?" Tariq said in surprise.

"Hello, Tariq," she said with a shy smile. Her eyebrows pulled together. "Why is my mother crying?"

"Your father passed away," Tariq told her, his words gentle.

Kiari's face paled and she covered her mouth with one hand.

"What about Devren?" Mrs. Metis asked.

"He's alright; at least he was the last time I saw him," Tariq told her. "We got separated. I was hoping he left news of his whereabouts with you."

"We haven't heard from him," she replied, her gaze distant as though she saw memories instead of the people in front of her. "You should stay a few days in case we do."

"That's very kind of you," Tariq replied. "We'll give you some space. I'm so sorry for your loss."

Tariq and Liora left the room. The sight of Mrs. Metis and her daughter holding each other with tears streaming down their cheeks stayed in Liora's mind. She followed Tariq out the front door and down a stone street lined with glowing plants.

Tariq didn't say a word. He merely limped through the small, strangely lit town to a long building with a short roof. A blast of hot air along with low talking and the scent of brewed barley hit Liora when she followed him inside.

He sat at a table in the corner and motioned for two cups of the pub's house ale. Liora nursed hers in silence, letting him cope with his pain however he felt best. People came and went from the pub; only a few glanced at the pair in the corner. Liora, with her back to the wall, eyed each of them. She didn't know if the population of

Verdan was querulous or calm. It seemed to be made of mostly humans, though a few Venticans and a Talastan ate at a round table across the room.

"They should have told her."

Tariq's quiet words caught Liora's attention. He kept his gaze on the worn wood of the table in front of him, his eyes searching as if answers could be found in the scratches and scuffs that marred the surface.

"Why wouldn't they tell her?" he mused. "The colonel swore Devren in himself. It was a priority. Unless his priority was having the ship manned to find the Omne Occasus instead of honoring Captain Metis."

Tariq's grip on his mug tightened to the point that Liora thought the goblet would break. She searched for something to say. Helping others cope in difficult situations wasn't a strong point of hers. She would rather fight than talk. Comforting someone else in obvious emotional pain wasn't something she had ever really done.

She could offer to cover his pain as she had once done for Devren; but Tariq didn't know the extent of what she could really do. She preferred it that way for the mere fact that he still spoke to her even though she was a Damaclan. Being raised by the clan that was responsible for the death of his wife and child didn't exactly bode well for friendship of any sort. While Liora didn't have anyone she would call a friend, she cared for the crew of the Kratos more than anyone else in the Macrocosm. She hated to admit that the man in front of her came at the foremost of that caring despite his repulsion to her.

"Maybe Mrs. Metis preferred that you be the one to tell her."

Tariq blinked, and his eyes focused slowly on Liora.

She wished she hadn't spoken when she saw the depths of emotion in his gaze.

"He was my father." Tariq paused, rubbed his eyes, and started again, his words slurring a bit. "What I mean is, he was like a father to me. My pop," his lips twisted slightly at the word as though he hated forming it, "He was a drunkard who felt that beating me every night was his duty as a father." He let out a breath and said, "Sometimes he got a bit carried away. He had a cruel streak, and he liked to cause the kind of injuries that would linger."

A tremor of empathy ran down Liora's spine. She knew exactly what Tariq spoke of.

A sharp light came to his eyes that chased away a portion of the drunkenness and he nodded. "I know. I really do. When you were poisoned and I sent your body through the analysis machine, I saw the same kind of injuries on your body. Scars, broken bones that hadn't been set correctly, burn marks, and tissue buildup from years of abuse." He tipped his head as though he hadn't just laid Liora bare with his words. "Your Damaclan gods are as cruel as my father's. Do you suppose they merely watch while their worshippers torture children, or do they laugh along with those we were supposed to look to for safety?"

Liora didn't know what to say. His analysis of her past struck like a fresh iron. She glanced away and saw several humans at a nearby table studying them with marked interest.

Tariq shook his head, his eyes glazed from the drink in his hands. "Kindness was foreign to my pop. Whatever he'd had once had fled when my mother died. I guess he couldn't quite forgive the child that killed her by being born."

Tariq leaned his face in a hand. His black hair fell in front of his eyes, hiding them from view. The humans from the table behind him spoke animatedly. Liora kept them at the corner of her gaze.

"When I met Dev and we found out we lived close by, I used to hang out at their house until Pop fell asleep. The times he caught me before I went over left marks I couldn't hide no matter how hard I tried. Mrs. M and the Captain noticed. They started inviting me over for nights, then weeks. I practically lived at the Metises. They fed me, got me to school, made sure I had somewhere to go at night. Devren always talked about joining the Coalition so he could be like his dad." He opened a hand as if freeing something. "I naturally followed. It made my pop upset, so it was my instinctive course of action. An insult he couldn't dodge."

Tariq lifted his drink, his head tipped to one side as he studied the golden liquid inside the goblet. "And now look what I run to when I can't take it anymore. Like father, like son."

Several humans rose from the table. Liora's hand slid to her knife and she stood silently.

Tariq took a deep drink of the contents. When finished, he slammed the mug onto the table and wiped his mouth with the back of his hand. A bit of froth clung to the stubble on his chin.

"Tariq Donovan. Is that you, you yellow-bellied Terrarian?"

Instead of anger, Liora saw another emotion cross Tariq's face. It looked like relief.

His gaze locked on hers. "Stay out of this fight no matter what."

He spun and slammed his goblet into the side of the first human's head. Another slugged him in the stomach. He bent over only long enough to gain his bearings, then he came up swinging.

Liora leaned against the wall and watched the fight with a touch of amusement. It was obvious the men weren't trying to kill each other. The brawl looked like ten brothers fighting over the last cookie, if brothers did that sort of thing. The other patrons at the pub merely relocated to tables further from the scuffle and continued their conversations as if the same thing happened every day.

Tariq clocked one man on the jaw hard enough to spin him around before he hit the ground. His other fist connected with a bear of a man who merely grunted with the impact.

"You had to bring Granson," Tariq muttered.

The big man's face split into a grin. Tariq's fist smashed the man's lips. He ducked under Granson's grab and spun, nailing the man in the groin with an undercut. The man gasped and stumbled backwards.

Two men tackled Tariq to the ground. He rolled to the right and threw the first into a table. The second punched Tariq in the face, splitting his eyebrow. Tariq blocked a second punch. He hooked the man's leg with his own and tripped him. Tariq was back up before the man hit the ground. He glanced at the men who still stood. Everyone bore bruises that would hurt the next morning.

The red-haired man who had called Tariq a yellow-bellied Terrarian glared at him. "You were always trouble, Tariq."

"And you were always ugly, Sveth," Tariq replied.

Liora wondered if they would brawl again. The bruised members of the group looked from Tariq to Sveth as if unsure of what to do.

The red-head's answering laugh shattered the mood. Tariq joined him.

"It's good to have you home," Sveth said, holding out a hand.

"It's good to be back," Tariq replied. He shook the man's hand.

They both pulled Granson to his feet.

"Have you been living on rocks with that Coalition crew?" Granson asked as he stood gingerly. "I haven't been hit like that in years."

Tariq grinned. "We only eat asteroids in the Coalition. You know the saying."

Sveth chuckled. "An asteroid a day keeps the scavies away."

Tariq nodded. "I'm hoping Dev shows up here sooner rather than later. He's going to have to up his intake of asteroids to keep them off his tail with our last haul."

Tariq's friends seemed to know better than to ask what it was.

"Care for a drink?" a man with a fat lip asked.

"Love one," Tariq replied.

Chapter 4

Liora slipped out of the pub unnoticed. She hadn't been in many towns by herself away from the hustle of the circus crowd. The quiet houses lit from within beckoned to her with their warm windows and the glowing flowers that swayed around the small porches. Rocks that appeared illuminated from the inside lined the road and kept her on course.

Liora had no way of knowing what time it was. It had felt late when they landed on Verdan, but without a sun shining through the thick atmosphere, she could only guess by the hush of the town and the lack of civilians visible that it was night.

Liora was torn between retreating to the Calypsan's ship and exploring the planet. It didn't feel right to wander through a town while the inhabitants slept, though she had dealt with enough of mortalkind in the past few days to want to avoid a rush of people during the day.

Liora reached the end of the cobblestone road. The rocks continued on, lighting a dim path that led into a jungle. Liora took a few steps forward and brushed the branches of the first tree with her fingers. Instead of leaves like most sun-lit planets, the trees of Verdan had long strands of branches that curled and twisted to the ground of the jungle. The branches glowed with blue and green light that started from the trunk and flowed in a steady faint glow to the ends of the branches.

The tree swayed slightly back and forth. It branches brushed the ground, deepening grooves that had been marked by a lifetime of the gentle movements. It looked as though the tree was writing on the dark ground. Strange scorch marks showed along the outside of the grooves.

There wasn't a breeze. Curious about how the tree moved by itself, Liora stepped beneath the branches and put her hand on the trunk. Her fingers picked up a slight vibration. Liora glanced around to ensure that she was alone; she then put the side of her head against the bark.

A humming sound murmured in her ear. The note was low and pulsing in time with the movement of the tree. When Liora stood back, she could no longer hear it, but the swaying of the branches continued. Liora stepped away from the tree. The other trees of the jungle moved, branches drifting along the ground with the barest hint of a whisper across the dirt. The effect was eerie; the entire jungle swayed as if it was an animal that slept in the half-light.

Liora's attention was caught by a small tube embedded in the side of the tree she stood closest to. Whenever the light pulsed, fainting light flowed down the tube. A glance at the other trees showed the same system. The tubes linked together, leading through the trees away from the town.

Lightning crackled across the dark sky. A few seconds later, thunder followed with a surge of intensity that made the ground rumble. The hair stood up on the back of Liora's neck as light sparked through the jungle. The tree branches flashed and static coursed to the ground in flickers, charring the grooves in the dirt. The jungle looked alive, filled with swaying, crackling branches. Light flooded through the tubes attached to the trees, pulsing across the underbrush and into the darkness.

A brighter crack of lightning turned Liora's head. The light struck a tall post in the middle of town. A horn sounded, long and low, reverberating against the houses and road. A moment later, doors opened and men and women flooded the street. They held staves with glowing tips and walked together toward Liora.

Liora stepped into the shadows that had returned beneath the tree branches and let the people pass. A familiar voice caught her ear from the last group of men.

"You're selling volts to the Hennonites now?" Tariq asked.

"Do you have a problem with Hennonites?" Sveth replied.

"I've had a few run-ins with them. They're not my

favorite race," Tariq replied.

"Ours, either," another man answered. "But desperate times and all that."

"Yeah," Sveth seconded. "With the shortage up top, we've had to make up for it wherever we can. The scavengers are getting greedy. They've intercepted three Ospreys loaded with volts. We can't afford to lose another. The Belanites won't be forgiving if we don't deliver to the Gaulded soon."

Liora walked on silent feet through the jungle, tailing the group. Lightning flashed and thunder rumbled, sending static through the trees and into the tubes the citizens followed. With each flash of light, Liora ducked behind a trunk to avoid being seen.

"You need guards," Tariq said.

"We've thought of that," Sveth replied. "But mercs are expensive and you never know which way they'll fly when it comes down to it. We can't trust the Gauls after last time, and the Belanites refuse to send their own escort. What we need is you."

"Me?" Tariq's tone said he had guessed where Sveth was going.

"Yes, you. You've flown in enough battle missions to know how to handle a convoy, and it sounds like you and Devren are on the outs with the Coalition anyway. Why not stick around?"

"I'm a medic, not a pilot, and I'm hoping things with the Coalition will smooth over given time," Tariq answered, though his tone bore far less assurance than his words.

"Are you saying you haven't missed the quieter life here?" another of the men asked.

"If you call that quiet," a third called out after an

exceptionally loud rumble of thunder sent sparks of light through the tubes.

"I've missed it," Tariq said. His voice was so quiet Liora barely heard him.

"Someone else has missed you," Sveth told him. The man elbowed Tariq. "Kiari isn't so little anymore."

Tariq shook his head. "She's Dev's little sister, and she'll always be Dev's little sister."

"She's the most beautiful girl in Echo," Granson said, his voice a deep rumble.

Tariq glanced back. "Then why don't you go after her?"

Sveth snorted. "She won't give any of us the time of day. She's been pining after her one true love. The evasive Tariq Donavan."

Tariq shoved him. The red-headed man laughed.

"It's true," Granson said. "None of us can get anywhere with that girl. She treats us like garbage."

"And that sounds like the girl for me?" Tariq questioned.

"You're already garbage," Sveth said. "You can skip her scorn."

Sveth ducked out of the way before Tariq could put him in a headlock.

Liora paused at the edge of the clearing they reached. Most of the citizens from Echo were human, but there were several green-skinned Roonites in the mix. The men pulled gloves from their pockets. Sveth tossed an extra pair to Tariq. The citizens fitted round canisters onto a giant metal-worked box. The tubes from the trees behind Liora and many more in front joined at the box and several others scattered throughout the clearing. As soon as the top of one canister flashed white, another was put in its place. The full canisters were stacked carefully on a cart near the tracks until Liora lost count of how many they collected.

When the lightning and thunder died away about fifteen minutes later, the collectors nodded happily at each other.

"Good haul," one woman said. "That should keep us in the silver for a week or so."

"It'll keep the Belanites off our backs for a while at least," another commented.

"As long as we can get it to them safely," a Roonite woman said.

The women walked past Liora unaware of her presence. The men secured the canisters on the cart and steered it onto the track. A man walked next to it with a remote in one hand to control the cart's speed. The rest of the Echo citizens followed behind looking exhausted but happy.

"I'm telling you," a woman said to a man near the end of the crew. "As soon as I send Tenson to bed, the lightning hits. It's uncanny."

"He'll be a lot of help when he gets older," the man replied.

The woman laughed. "If we can get him out of bed. That boy sleeps like a Folian."

"Don't say that to Merilee," a younger woman said, catching up to them. "She's sweet on that Folian from Gaulded Two Zero Seven."

"Is that right?" the first woman replied.

Their voices died away as they followed the men and cart through the trees.

Liora hesitated. She was torn between returning to Echo to sleep in the Calypsan's ship or continuing her exploration of the jungle. She knew enough by the creatures Malivian had collected to realize that dangerous beasts could lurk beneath the trees. The jungle was dim once more now that the lightning and thunder had passed. Without Tariq, she had no way of knowing what to expect once she entered the foliage.

Liora took a step toward Echo. A sound to the left caught her attention. She paused. The sound repeated. A surge of adrenaline ran through her body. The cry was a low yowl that ended in a yip. Whatever made it sounded desperate. Whether it was hungry or in trouble, Liora had no way of knowing.

She had seen plenty of creatures come through Malivian's circus to know not all animals were what they seemed. Some could mimic the sounds of a baby crying; others appeared sweet and innocent until prey neared, then they turned into spitting, clawing, deadly-spiked creatures that carried poison in their veins. No matter where the animals came from, it seemed every planet had their share of lethal beasts.

Liora didn't know if years in a cage had given her empathy for the helpless, or if sheer curiosity with an edge of recklessness at being alone and able to choose her own fate sent her through the trees. Either way, Liora's senses thrummed with potential danger. Creatures moved within the shadows. Strange, thorny bugs and small animals with protruding teeth and needle-like claws scurried away from her. A bigger animal crouched beneath the dimly glowing vines and blinked glowing eyes that narrowed at her appearance as though it viewed her as prey instead of a predator. A chill ran down her spine and she hurried on.

Her ears caught every yowl along with a few static

pops from trees that carried lingering volts from the electric storm. Her keen eyes searched the shadows cast by the dim greens and blues of the drained trees. Each footstep was taken with great care not to disturb the underbrush of thorny bushes and purple-leafed plants with glowing orange berries.

A scent similar to sulfur touched her nose. The yowl came from the other side of the trees. Liora's right hand closed around the knife strapped to her thigh. She winced and glanced down. The bloody bandages around her palm reminded her that she had a weakness she would have to hide if whatever lay beyond the trees attacked. Liora gingerly drew the knife and switched it to her left hand. The weight was reassuring.

She peered through the branches. A yellow, murky bog that seemed out of place in the glowing jungle bubbled in the foggy clearing. A scent of decay emanated from the bodies half-submerged in the thick liquid. As Liora watched, a bubble rose and grew until it was the size of a Gaul's head. It shuddered, then exploded. Liora winced at the horrible stench that assailed her nose.

Movement caught the corner of her eye. Near the far edge of the bog, a form struggled. Glowing claws reached through the thick liquid. The animal looked feline and almost as long as Liora was tall. The creature tried to pull itself on top of another floating form, but the body tipped, dumping the creature back into the bog. Fangs flashed in the darkness and the yowl of pain sounded again.

Liora made her way around the edge of the clearing, careful to stay within the cover of the trees. Aware that the animal's desperate cries may have attracted other creatures, Liora scanned the ground between the animal and the trees. It appeared as though she was alone. Liora's grip on her knife tightened and she stepped from the foliage.

The animal's gaze locked on her immediately. Glowing green eyes narrowed into slits. Every muscle stilled as the creature held onto the carcass beneath it. Liora realized that the animal it gripped looked fresher than the rest of the bodies in the bog. She wondered if the cat creature had chased its prey into the bog, only to realize its mistake when it was too late.

Liora glanced around the clearing. Instinct warned that if she saved the animal, there was nothing but her knife to keep it from attacking her after it was free. She should leave such a large predator to its fate; yet empathy whispered in her chest. She knew what it was like to be trapped without a chance of escape.

Liora shook her head. The thought that empathy might be her downfall made her bite back a smile. If only Chief Obruo could read her thoughts, he would have killed her the moment she was born. No child with Damaclan blood should ever harbor empathy for any other living creature. It was a kill or be killed life. Compassion had no place in the warrior lifestyle. It would serve her right if it was truly the cause of her death.

Despite her combatant thoughts, Liora sheathed her knife and reached for a fallen branch from one of the trees. She edged closer to the bog, her gaze switching from the trapped animal to the jungle in case she was attacked while her back was turned.

The cat creature bared its fangs when she drew near. Its huge claws, each of which were the length of her hand, sunk deeper into the dead furred, horned animal beneath it. The short gray ruff around the cat's neck bristled. Its fur was clumpy and weighed down with the thick liquid of the bog.

When Liora reached the edge of the dirt, the creature backed away. The movement upended the animal it held onto and the cat was thrown into the bog once more. It gave a yowl of pain as it scrambled back onto its slain prey. The creature bared its teeth at her. The heat that pushed against Liora let her know the source of the animal's agony. It was nearly unbearable just to be standing near the bog, let alone be covered in the boiling yellow goop.

Liora didn't know what to do. If the creature wouldn't let her help it, and if it kept dumping itself into the hot liquid out of fear every time she drew near, it would be drowned or be boiled to death before she could get it to shore. Yet the pain in its glowing green eyes wouldn't let her leave it in such a hopeless situation.

"Fine," Liora said aloud to center her thoughts. "Let's try something else."

She closed her eyes and pushed toward the cat creature.

Liora had never tried to share thoughts with an animal. She wasn't sure how it would respond. There was no reason to send words; Liora settled for pushing a calm, encouraging feeling toward the creature. She then took a breath and changed the feeling to one of hope and trust.

It took a moment for her to realize that the animal's low hiss had stopped. Liora opened her eyes. The creature's lips had lowered, relaxing from the snarl. It watched her warily, but the fear in its gaze had lessened. It shifted slightly and its claws sunk deeper into the animal beneath it.

Liora slid the branch forward. The splayed end

touched the dead horned animal along with another carcass too eroded for Liora to make out what it had once been. The cat creature reached out a clawed paw and set it on the branch. When it pushed its weight down, the carcass tipped and the branch dipped into the bog.

Liora shoved it further until only just enough remained that she could hold it down with her weight. The heavier part of the branch rested on the horned animal. The added burden pushed the body further beneath the boiling yellow liquid. The cat scrambled to stay up. Its paws dipped into the bog. A yowl of pain escaped it. The creature gathered its feet beneath it. The shifting weight shoved the prey under further. The animal's tufted ears flattened at the pain. Its muscles bunched and it sprang.

The motion shoved the carcass down, robbing the creature of some of its momentum. Liora knew it wouldn't make the jump. She yanked the branch back to give the animal something to land on. When it hit, the impact of its weight threw her toward the bog. She rolled to dirt at the edge of the steaming liquid and latched onto the animal's thick ruff. With the help of its claws scrambling madly along the branch, she pulled backwards with all of her strength. Liora's efforts were rewarded when the creature's claws sunk into the thick, glowing grass at the edge of the bog and it climbed free.

She collapsed onto her back and sucked in huge gulps of air. Her hand throbbed. She closed it and held it against her chest as she fought to calm her thundering heart.

A low huff sounded. Liora turned her head and looked directly into the cat creature's steely green gaze.

Chapter 5

Liora's muscles tensed. She was halfway on her side with her knife pinned beneath her. She wondered if she would be able to reach the blade before the animal attacked. She inched her hand downward.

The creature's eyes narrowed. Its chin lowered and its tufted ears flattened against its skull. She wondered if it was about to attack. It raised one paw tipped with lethal looking, blue glowing claws. Liora felt the branch along her right side. If she rolled, she could pull it above her and thwart the creature's attack. The movement would free her knife and give her a fighting chance against its claws and fangs. She watched for the animal's next move.

To her surprise, it raised its claws to its mouth and licked them with a long, forked purple tongue.

Liora pushed herself up slowly. Besides the twitch of a tufted ear and a sideways glance of its green eyes, the creature appeared unruffled by her actions. Liora reached a sitting position and watched it.

The animal had similar characteristics to several big Earthling cats Malivian used to have in his cages. It had the same feline face, long tail, and sleek body, but that's where the similarities stopped. The claws didn't retract, and the fangs fit outside of its muzzle when it closed its mouth. The gray ruff that surrounded its neck smoothed down so that it was barely visible above the rest of its fur when the animal was calm.

As it cleaned itself of the yellow liquid from the bog, a glowing blue light ran beneath its skin. Liora realized it was an outline of the creature's skeletal system. The cleaner the animal got, the more of its bones she could make out through its sleek gray coat.

Liora's hand ached. A glance at it showed that the knife wound had bled through the gauze, and the gauze itself was covered in the yellow liquid of the bog. She needed to change the wrap before the wound became infected.

Liora rose slowly with her gaze on the creature. The cat merely flicked an ear and continued cleaning its fur. Liora checked her knife to ensure the sheath was secure, then made her way back toward Echo. The jungle appeared less volatile than before. Without the thunder sparking the electric reaction through the vines and bushes, the faint glow of green and blue was almost comforting, but Liora refused to accept the false sense of security.

When she made her way through a stand of thick trees, the yellow glow of a creature wrapped around a trunk stood out. Liora drew cautiously near and the animal uncoiled. A hiss sounded and its head rose to her height. Green hues flashed down its spiked spine. When it opened its mouth, yellow liquid like that from the bog dripped onto the jungle floor. Steam rose from the moss.

Liora stepped carefully to the left, and another head lifted. This one had a purple hue with glowing red fangs. A glance behind showed several others, their attention drawn by the hissing of their companions.

Adrenaline pulsed through Liora's body. Out of the corner of her eye, she saw the first snake creature's coils loosen in preparation to strike. Its head drew back. Liora's muscles tensed.

Liora met its slit gaze before it lunged. She had a flashback of Malivian watching her in the same predatory way. The snake's head darted forward.

Liora dropped into a crouch and stabbed upward with her knife. It embedded deep into the snake's huge head. She tried to rip the blade free, but the blood-soaked bandage on her hand made her grip slide. She spun in time to knock the second snake to the side, and she heard the hiss of another behind her. Before fangs embedded into her back, the snake's hiss was cut short. Liora looked over her shoulder.

The cat had sunk its teeth into the snake; it broke the glowing snake's neck with a sharp shake of the head. Another snake attempted to strike while the cat was occupied. Liora grabbed up a broken branch and drove it sideways into the snake's open mouth. She slammed the snake's head into the closest tree trunk and twisted the branch to the left, snapping the creature's jaw.

When she turned back around, the cat creature had finished the last snake. It licked its claws with a forked tongue and a low purr rumbled through the trees. Liora crossed to the first snake she had slain and pulled her knife free. She wiped the blade in the glowing moss before she sheathed it. A glance at the cat showed it tearing into the flesh of the snake it had killed. Yellow venom dripped from the cat's mouth. It didn't appear to feel the effects that made the grass smoke below.

Wary from the attack, Liora studied each tree before she passed. She wasn't about to let herself get surrounded again, and she had no idea what else waited in the darkness. She stepped through the trees close to the Metis house and paused.

Two forms stood in the shadows near the front door. A closer look revealed Tariq with Devren's sister Kiari. Kiari had one hand on Tariq's arm and the fingers of her other hand trailed slowly through his dark hair. Tariq's eyes were closed.

Liora's heart thumped strangely in her chest. She took a step backwards. Tariq's head jerked in her direction and his eyes flew open. His gaze locked on hers. Liora took another step back toward the jungle.

"Liora, don't move," Tariq barked.

His gun was suddenly out of the sheath at his side and aimed at her. Liora stared at him.

Kiari's eyes widened. "It's a felis!"

Liora glanced behind her. The cat creature she had rescued from the bog stood at the edge of the jungle. Its green eyes reflected the light from the Metis home, and the blue glow of its bones through its fur made it look like a phantom in the darkness.

"Don't shoot it," Liora said.

"Are you insane?" Tariq replied. "Step to the right so I have a shot."

Liora shook her head. "Lower the gun."

Tariq stared at her. "Liora, the felis is going to kill you. Move away."

Liora turned her back on the humans, careful not to move right or left so as to cover Tariq's shot. She heard Tariq curse as she walked toward the felis.

"Liora, don't!" Kiari called.

Liora ignored her. She reached the big cat and crouched so that they were eye to eye. The felis watched her; she saw her reflection in its gaze. Her heart thundered in her chest. She knew she was taking a chance, but showing Tariq the creature wouldn't harm her would be the only way to keep him from shooting it. She had seen the human in action enough times to know that the felis was dead the moment the bullet left his gun.

Liora raised her hand.

"Liora," she heard Tariq say quietly, his tone tight with exasperation.

The felis drew back slightly. Liora pushed a feeling of calm and trust toward it. She could only hope it would be enough.

The big cat's eyes narrowed, then shut. It reached its head forward and her palm rested in the soft fur of its forehead. The felis's tufted ears wavered between up and straight back. Its tail twitched with uncertainty.

As Liora watched, the blue of its skull began to glow brighter beneath its fur. The bright light flowed down its neck and through the bones of its body. A low rumble reached her. Liora realized with a start that the animal was purring with contentment. She drew back her hand with a smile.

The felis opened its eyes and sneezed. It gave a wide, toothy yawn that ended in a yowl. Liora rose. The felis turned and padded back into the jungle. A moment later, it was gone.

Liora looked back to see that Tariq and Kiari had drawn closer.

"That was ridiculous," Tariq said.

"That was amazing," Kiari countered. "I've never seen anyone touch a felis without losing a limb."

Liora reached them with slight misgiving. At Tariq's steely, questioning gaze, she felt the need to explain. It was a feeling she wasn't used to.

"It was stuck in a bog."

"You saved it." Tariq's reply wasn't a question, but a statement filled with disgust.

"I couldn't leave it there to die," she replied, attempting to move past him.

Tariq grabbed her arm. "You should have left it there. You're lucky it didn't kill you."

She met his gaze, her own fierce. "I can take care of myself."

"Can you?" he asked.

Liora was very aware of Kiari watching them both. The young woman looked surprised at Tariq's reaction. He seemed to realize she was there at the same time. He dropped his hand. Liora shoved past him toward the house. She heard them fall in behind her.

She put a hand to the door.

"You need to rewrap that wound," Tariq said, his voice level.

"I'll take care of it," Liora replied. She stepped inside

and shut the door behind her.

"I was hoping you'd be back soon," Mrs. Metis called from the kitchen. "I wasn't a very good host earlier. Tariq's news caught me off guard." She sniffed. "You never really prepare for something like that." Mrs. Metis appeared in the doorway and wiped her eyes on her striped apron. She gave Liora a kind smile. "You need to eat, and if Tariq's leg was any indication, you're in need of medical care as well." Her gaze rested on Liora's hand. She gave a motherly smile. "Let's get some food in your stomach while I take care of that."

Liora followed her into the kitchen. A single settling complete with a matching ceramic bowl, plate, and cup, real silverware, and a maroon cloth napkin waited at the table. At Mrs. Metis' gesture, Liora took a seat. She couldn't remember the last time she had eaten on a setting so nice.

"I know Coalition food isn't always the greatest," Mrs. Metis said as she ladled thick broth into the bowl. "I made Tariq's favorite, creamy tarlon soup, pickled cavern beets, and braised pulon. It's a traditional Verdan founding feast."

"It smells amazing," Liora said. Her stomach grumbled.

"Tariq said you've both been living on Calypsan rations from the Sparrow. He refused to tell me why you have a Calypsan craft or why you separated from Devren. I don't suppose I'll get the answers from you?"

Expectant silence filled the kitchen as Mrs. Metis set out gauze and antiseptic. Liora didn't know how to tell her that they had left Devren to protect the Omne Occasus on his own while she and Tariq chased down the Damaclan intent on killing her along with anyone else she cared about.

She finally went with, "I'm sorry."

Mrs. Metis nodded. "I expected as much. Rius never tells me what he's up to." She paused, then corrected herself in a quieter voice, "I mean, Rius never told me what he was up to."

Silence filled the room.

Liora broke it, her words gentle. "I'm sorry for your loss. Your husband was a great captain."

The older woman gave a wavering smile. "Thank you, dear. It's going to take me a while to accept that he's not going to walk in the door at any moment."

Liora nodded.

Mrs. Metis picked up a pair of scissors. "You need to eat. I'll take care of your hand if you can feed yourself with your left."

Liora lifted the spoon beside the plate. It was heavier than she expected. She took a sip of the soup as Mrs. Metis cut through the bandages around her right palm.

The soup had so much flavor Liora let it sit on her tongue as she tried to identify the various spices with the tarlon. The cream tasted fresh, and the herbs of the soup complimented the smooth texture.

"Amazing," she said to herself.

She realized Devren's mother had stopped her gentle movements. Liora glanced at her.

Mrs. Metis smiled. "I'm sorry. It's been a while since anyone has enjoyed my cooking so much."

"It tastes incredible," Liora said honestly. "I can't remember the last time I ate anything nearly so good."

A pleased expression crossed Mrs. Metis' face. "You can stay here as long as you'd like."

That brought a small laugh from Liora. "Thank you,"

she replied.

Mrs. Metis turned her attention to Liora's hand. Liora watched her cut the bandages carefully away.

"I'm not going to ask where this yellow fluid came from. It looks suspiciously like the bog not far from here." Mrs. Metis kept her eyes on the gauze. "The jungle is dangerous for those of us who have lived in Echo our entire lives, let alone a stranger unfamiliar with these parts."

"I don't avoid danger," Liora replied.

Mrs. Metis glanced at her. "I suppose that's why you're with the Coalition."

"I suppose," Liora answered, her tone carefully level.

Mrs. Metis finished cutting the gauze and pulled it gently from Liora's hand.

Fresh blood welled up from the knife wound.

"No stitches?" Mrs. Metis noted with a tone of surprise. "Tariq knows better than that."

Liora bit back a smile at the woman's words. "We didn't have time or the right equipment."

"I've taught that boy how to pull thread from a seam and make a needle out of a sterilized zanderbin bone shard. He should have taken care of this."

"I can see where Tariq got his start as a medic," Liora replied.

Mrs. Metis gave a small chuckle. "Devren had no patience for it. He would rather be off playing soldier. Tariq was always the one carting the med kit after them. I lost track of how many scrapes and gashes he fixed for his friends."

"It sounds like you gave him a good life here." Liora asked the question that bothered her. "What made you take him in? I know it's hard to take care of a family. Why add one more?"

Mrs. Metis carefully cleaned the wound with antiseptic. "He was Devren's best friend." She glanced at Liora. "I don't know how much he told you about his past."

"He told me his father was abusive."

Mrs. Metis nodded. "That's putting it lightly." She smoothed a cool gel over both sides of Liora's hand and the pain of the wound eased. "I set a few of his broken bones. After Edron dislocated one of Tariq's shoulders, we told him Tariq was going to live with us. Rius didn't let him put up a fight. A few days later, Edron left on one of the cargo ships."

"Wouldn't staying with Edron have made him stronger?" Liora asked.

Mrs. Metis paused her gentle work on Liora's hand. She met Liora's gaze, her brown eyes clear and searching. "Tariq told me a few things of your past; I hope you don't mind. From what I've heard, few Damaclan children survive the training process." Her forehead creased. "If you lived anywhere close to Verdan and we heard of how you were raised, Rius would have brought you home to live with us, too. Being strong isn't the only acceptable trait; we value compassion and empathy here."

Liora sat back. The thought that the stranger in front of her would have taken her into their family given different circumstances caught her off guard. She couldn't imagine being raised in such a home where smiles and kindness appeared abundant.

"It's a simple life, but a fulfilling one," Mrs. Metis continued. She smiled at Liora. "If you have any wish to give up the Coalition lifestyle, you're welcome to stay. Echo is a wonderful home for many people."

Liora forced a smile despite the way her chest tightened at the woman's words. "Thank you for the offer. I enjoy the stars far too much to settle in one place."

Mrs. Metis nodded. "My husband was the same way. He was always looking beyond, anxious to see the next galaxy, to send word of what lived near the following sun. He had a wandering heart."

"Do you regret letting him go?" Liora asked quietly.

Mrs. Metis wiped a stray tear from her cheek. "It was never my place to ask him to stay. He loved the Coalition and the cause; he loved his crew, and he loved exploring the Macrocosm. I have always considered myself fortunate that he chose me out of all the galaxies he has seen. He completed me, and no matter how many times he left, he always came back home."

The fact that he would never return again hung in the air between them.

Mrs. Metis turned her attention back to Liora's hand. "This has gone too long to be helped by stitches. We'll clean it out and close it up with bandages. It'll take longer to heal and you'll have to watch out for infections." She paused, then said, "I'm worried about the scarring. It's going to be a rough wound to heal."

"Scars mean you survived," Liora replied. It was something her mother used to say when she patched Liora up after many of Obruo's fiercer training sessions. "Without scars, we wouldn't be who we are."

A smile crossed Mrs. Metis's lips as she placed gauze over the wound. "You're right about that."

"Right about what?"

Liora hadn't heard Tariq walk in. She wondered how the human could be so stealthy without seeming to do so on purpose. Perhaps he really had learned a lot from the way his father had raised him.

"About scars making us who we are," Mrs. Metis replied. "Liora and I were just talking about surviving."

Tariq took the seat across from Liora with a noncommittal grunt. "Did she tell you she just survived an encounter with a felis?"

Mrs. Metis gave Liora a startled look. "Do you have other wounds I should be patching?"

"It didn't hurt me," Liora replied. She met Tariq's gaze with a flat look.

"It should have," Tariq told her. "Felis are dangerous."

"They are," Mrs. Metis agreed. "There's a bounty on their heads in Echo. Tell Tariq if you see it again. He knows how to deal with them."

"I noticed," Liora muttered.

"What was that?" Mrs. Metis asked.

"Nothing."

Liora could feel Tariq watching her. She refused to meet his light blue gaze. The human unnerved her, and she didn't like the way her emotions had responded to seeing him and Kiari so close. Liora knew it wasn't like anything could ever happen between her and the Kratos medic, and she thought she didn't care, but her heart betrayed her.

Mrs. Metis finished wrapping Liora's hand.

"Keep it dry," Mrs. Metis directed. "We'll change the dressing again tomorrow if it bleeds through. Wounds like this tend to be stubborn."

"Like someone else I know," Tariq said under his breath.

Mrs. Metis gave him a surprised look. "What was that,

Tariq?"

"Nothing," Tariq replied.

Liora rose. "Thank you for the bandages."

"You're very welcome, my dear," Mrs. Metis said. She set a worn hand on Liora's shoulder. "Let me know if there is anything else I can do for you."

"I think I'll catch some sleep on the Sparrow," Liora told her.

"You don't have to sleep on that old ship," Mrs. Metis replied. "I already have a room made up for you. It'll be much more comfortable. I'll show you the way."

Chapter 6

Liora awoke with a start. For a moment, she thought she was still on the Sparrow, but the handmade quilt and glowing orange flowers along the windowsill brought everything back. She squinted in the half-light, unsure what had awoken her.

"No."

Tariq's voice brought Liora up from her bed on the floor. She tossed the quilt back onto the mattress and padded on silent feet to the door. She glanced up the hall of the small house. Everything was still. She could hear

Kiari's quiet breathing from the room next to her own.

"Let him go."

Liora made her way further down the hall to Tariq's room. The door was open a crack. She pushed it and it swung inward on quiet hinges.

Tariq lay on the bed. The blankets had been thrown onto the floor and he clutched the pillow in one arm as though he held someone in a headlock. His eyes were closed tight and a sheen of sweat was visible on his bare chest.

"Tariq," Liora said quietly.

Tariq grimaced, showing clenched teeth.

"Don't do it," he said, his voice tight.

Liora crossed to his bed. She set a hand on his arm.

"Tariq, wake up."

Tariq moved faster than she was ready. Liora stumbled back, but he caught her arm and threw her against the wall. He landed on top of her and locked an arm around her neck. The pressure of his knee against the small of her back stole Liora's breath. She tried to struggle, but Tariq was stronger.

"You killed him," the human growled in her ear. "It's all your fault."

Black spots danced in Liora's vision. She elbowed him in the stomach, but his grip only tightened. She clawed at his arm, but he didn't seem to feel the pain. She felt herself blacking out.

Liora pushed at him. In her panic, she shoved her fear of being out of control, of being at the mercy of someone who was merciless, of being trapped without an escape.

Tariq froze.

"What's going on?" His words sounded clearer. His grip loosened.

Liora elbowed him in the stomach and ducked out of his grasp. She backed against the wall, ensuring that there was plenty of space between them if he tried to attack her again.

"Liora?" Tariq stared at her. Confusion filled his face. "I was dreaming. It was a nightmare. Someone killed Devren. I was fighting back, I…" His eyes widened. "I fought you."

Liora watched him warily. Her left side hurt where she had hit the wall, and breathing through a bruised throat wasn't her favorite thing, but she didn't let the pain show.

"I heard you having the nightmare; I tried to wake you up."

Tariq looked at the scratch marks along his arm. His words were quiet when he said, "I was choking you."

The confused regret in his voice ate at Liora. She crossed her arms and leaned against the wall to hide how much his attack had shaken her. "I shouldn't have touched you."

Tariq rose from the floor and took a seat on the edge of his bed. His bare chest heaved with the exertion of their fight. He rubbed his face with one hand.

Liora reached for the door. "I-I should go."

"Wait."

Tariq's quiet plea stopped her. Liora hesitated with one hand on the door latch.

"I'm sorry."

Liora shook her head. "You don't have to apologize. I shouldn't have been in your room, I just…." Her words died away.

"You just what?" Tariq asked, his voice barely above a whisper.

Liora didn't know how to phrase the way she felt. She settled with, "I just couldn't let you be afraid if I could stop it."

Tariq let out a breath. "Like the felis."

Liora made herself look at him. "What?"

He nodded. "That's why you saved it. You couldn't let it be trapped if you could do something to rescue it."

"Tariq, I don't—"

He cut her off. "I felt it, Liora. I felt whatever you did to me. It was like when you beckoned me the day you were dying from the thorn's poison. I felt it instead of heard it. You spoke inside me." His voice lowered. "I've never been so full of despair. I don't know what you did just then, but in order to project those emotions onto another person, you had to have felt them first."

His words hit too close to home. Liora didn't know what to say. She wanted to build walls around her heart, to trap him out. There was concern in his eyes when he looked at her; she couldn't take empathy, not from him.

"When I said sorry before, it wasn't for attacking you." Tariq paused and a wry smile touched his lips. "I mean, of course I feel bad about that and I am sorry, but I was apologizing for the way I treated you before, when you were first aboard the Kratos."

"You're part of the reason I was freed," Liora replied, watching him.

Tariq shook his head. "Devren's the one who got you out, not me."

"But you knew he would go back, and you could have stopped him."

Tariq looked as though he was about to deny it, but he hesitated. His eyebrows drew together and he conceded, "You might be right about that."

Liora couldn't help a small smile at his concession. "I know that was hard to say."

That brought an answering smile from him. "A bit."

Liora lifted her shoulders in a small shrug. "I know Devren well enough to know that he wouldn't have gone against you if you had strictly forbidden him to free me."

Tariq shook his head. "I don't forbid him to do anything. Devren's his own man."

Liora conceded, "But you're also his best friend. He trusts you, like you trust him. It must be nice to have someone to rely on like that."

Tariq nodded. "It is, and if he'd show up, we would know what he's going to do next. Now, it's a waiting game." His hands clenched, letting her know how much he hated not knowing if Devren and the crew of the Kratos were alright.

"I'm sorry I made you leave him."

"I'm also my own man," Tariq said with the hint of another wry smile. "And I wasn't about to let you go alone. I don't have any regrets."

"Not any?" Liora asked.

Tariq opened a hand as if granting her that much. "I regret not killing Obruo. The next time I see him will be his last."

Liora knew exactly how he felt. "I have a feeling we won't have long to wait," she said quietly.

"Your entire home was destroyed?"

Liora nodded. "I saw it with my own eyes. I don't know why he's still alive. It makes no sense."

"If he had died…." Tariq's voice died away.

Liora finished his unspoken words. "He wouldn't have been there to kill your wife and child."

Silence filled the air between them. She wanted to

change the subject, to chase away the pain in his eyes. She nodded to indicate the house. "Verdan is nice. I understand why you came back here."

"A planet of darkness where even the vegetation rebels against our terraforming and everything, including the lightning and thunder, is out to kill you?" Tariq replied. There was a hint of amusement in his voice. "Yeah, it's home."

"Are you going to stay?"

Tariq studied her. "Why would you ask that?"

Liora didn't want to admit that she had overheard their conversation in the jungle. "I just noticed the way you look, that's all."

Tariq's eyebrows drew together a bit. "How do I look?"

"More at peace," she replied honestly. "You look like you belong here, like you can relax here. You're not like that on the Kratos."

"It's a bit hard when every other ship in the Macrocosm is out to kill you," Tariq admitted. "I never know if I'll be patching up crew members or sending ashes into the void. It keeps a person a bit on edge."

"So which do you prefer?"

Tariq ran a hand through his hair to push it back from his eyes before he glanced at her again. "Forward, aren't you?"

Liora realized she might have crossed a line. "You don't have to answer," she said. "Maybe I should go."

"No." His reluctant tone stopped her hand on the door. "I guess I don't know, myself. I didn't think it would feel like this."

"Like what?" she asked softly.

After a moment, he replied, "Like home." He fell

silent for a few more seconds before he said, "I didn't know if I would ever feel that again. It hit me a bit harder than I thought."

"It's been a long time."

Tariq nodded. "Maybe I was avoiding it because I was afraid it would feel like this." He looked at the floor beneath his bare feet. "I told myself that when Dannan was killed, I wouldn't live a normal life. I didn't want to, not without her." His voice dropped to almost a whisper. "She was my everything. I lost my sanity when I lost her. Instead of living, I was surviving."

"Is there a difference?" Liora asked without looking at him.

"There's a huge difference," Tariq replied.

Liora made herself ask into the following silence, "So what about Kiari?"

She could hear the begrudging smile in Tariq's voice when he answered, "It's that obvious, huh?"

"You looked pretty happy with her." The words tasted bad. She kept her face carefully expressionless.

"She's in love with who I used to be."

Liora thought about that. "Are you so different?"

Tariq let out a small breath. "You know that feeling when you kill someone and you watch the light fade from their eyes." He met her gaze. "You feel like a part of your soul dies with them."

Liora had told herself long ago that she had lost whatever part of herself had a soul when her clan was killed, but there was no denying the truth of Tariq's words. When she killed someone, anyone, there was a price. Obruo never understood that. Perhaps the Damaclan side had no conscience when it came to taking a life. It certainly appeared that way. Yet human kind had a history of killing without remorse. Perhaps it was all a front.

She realized Tariq was waiting for an answer. She nodded. "I know what you mean." Admitting it before she had received her tattoos would have been another nail in the coffin Obruo had created for her. She didn't know how she should feel about the answer. Not being impacted by the lives she took would have been much easier.

"Losing the person who completes you makes a hole inside so deep, I feel like there's no way out." He glanced at her and then lowered his gaze as though what he was about to say was difficult. "Is it bad that sometimes I relish killing because it makes me feel something, even if it that something is less than I was before?"

Liora knew exactly what he meant. The thought that someone else understood made her feel strange. She was used to thinking herself the only supposedly mindless killer with a conscience. It was unsettling.

"I have lost far too much of my soul to burden Kiari with a man who isn't whole." Tariq's words were quiet but firm as though he had made up his mind. "She might love the man I was when I lived here, but that man died when Dannan and Lissy were taken from me." He shook his head. "Home will never be mine to have."

Liora studied the bandages across her hand. Her wound hadn't bled through Mrs. Metis' careful work, yet she felt the pain of the gaping flesh beneath. It echoed how she felt when she looked at Tariq. He gave an outward appearance of being strong and whole, yet when he let down his walls and spoke to her away from the others, she saw the pain that simmered beneath the surface. They were more similar than she wanted to admit.

"Why does that happen?"

Liora looked up at Tariq's question.

He gave a shake of his head with an incredulous expression. "Why is it that you can break me down? You're the one person who reminds me of why I lost everything that was my life."

Liora sucked in a breath at his words to push down the pain they brought.

She barely heard him say, "So why do I trust you?"

She met his gaze. His light blue eyes searched her face. She forced a casual smile that felt foreign on her lips. "Keep your enemies close?"

Tariq chuckled. He tipped his head to one side and gave her a look she found unnerving.

"What about you, Liora. Could you be happy here?"

Surprised by his question, she shook her head. "I just got out of one cage. Why trade it for another?"

That brought a smile to Tariq's face. Liora found an answering one spreading across hers.

"So, a wanderer forever, then?" he asked.

"Something like that," she replied. "Endless stars to explore; bad guys to fight; a crew to protect. Not to mention dodging death at the hands of my psychotic father figure. It should keep me pretty busy."

He nodded. "Liora Day, the girl without a planet; the girl from the stars."

"The girl without a soul," a voice whispered in the back of her mind.

A chill ran down Liora's spine. She reached for the doorknob.

"Goodnight, Tariq."

"Goodnight, Liora."

She stepped through the door.

When she reached to pull it shut behind her, Tariq said, "Leave it open. Please."

Liora thought the request was odd, but she did so and walked back to her room, her footsteps quiet and mind filled with the whispered words of the nameless ones who had killed her clan and foreshadowed that she would be the one to end it all.

Chapter 7

At dinner the next evening, Liora was about to take a seat across from Tariq when the pub's door flew open. Officer Straham looked around, his eyes wide and chest heaving. His gaze locked on them.

"Oh, thank goodness," he gasped. "We need you. The Scavs and Coalition followed us. It's a war!"

"Count us in," Sveth said. The rest of Tariq's friends rose.

"It's about time the fight came to us," another man called.

"Why is the Coalition after you?" a woman with dreadlocks asked.

"There's a lot that I haven't told you," Tariq replied, heading toward the door with a look of anticipation on his face. "But I can guarantee one heck of a fight."

"Echo against the Macrocosm," the woman yelled.

"Echo against the Macrocosm," the others took up the shout.

Everyone rushed out the door after Liora and Tariq.

Liora drew her knife. Tariq held a pistol in each hand. They followed Straham to the Kratos' Gull sitting skewed in a swath cut from the jungle. Its sides were battered as though it had barely survived the landing. The crew fired at Coalition officers through the trees. Other, unmarked enemies shot from the south. Liora wondered how far away their ships had landed.

"If we can disable their crafts, they won't be able to retreat," she shouted at Tariq as they ran down the road.

"They'll be at our mercy," Tariq replied. He called over his shoulder, "Sveth, Gerand, head to the ships. We need to block their escape."

"My kind of fight," Sveth said with a light of reckless savagery in his gaze. He motioned to several of the men behind him. "Come with me."

Devren shot from the cover of two fallen trees. Nearby, Hyrin and Shathryn returned fire from behind a glowing boulder. Shathryn's purple hair was flattened on one side and she shot at Coalition officers with a continuous outburst of angry dialogue.

"Teach you to shoot at my friends," she shouted, clipping an officer in the shoulder. "What ever happened to manners and being innocent before proven guilty?" She shot another in the chest. "I thought we were all on the same side, and now I'm dodging metal like some merc caught up on the wrong side of a Zamarian's temper." She hit another in the face. "It's not right, I tell you! It's just not right!"

Closer to the Gull, O'Tule and Lieutenant Argyle protected each other's backs from a nest of salvagers. O'Tule's green skin had black grease stains across it as though she had been helping the Salamandon with repairs. The rest of the Kratos crew looked tattered and worn as they returned shot for shot, but they didn't give up in the face of the tremendous odds that fired upon them; nobody would ever say the crew of the Kratos contained cowards.

Tariq and Liora slid into cover on either side of Devren.

He stared at them. "Where did you come from?"

"We've been waiting for you," Tariq replied. He fired two shots and two salvagers fell. "Took you long enough."

"We were busy," Devren said dryly. He clipped an officer in the leg. Tariq finished the man with a shot to the chest. "We're in way over our heads here."

"That's alright," Tariq replied. "We brought you an army."

Devren glanced back and Liora followed his gaze. A smile touched her lips at the sight of the citizens of Echo storming the trees. Someone must have gone to rally the others. A sound caught her ears. She realized that the horn in the middle of Echo had been activated. Tariq really had brought an army.

An explosion sounded to the right. Cries of pain followed. Liora peered over the logs just long enough to confirm that the Coalition officers had brought cannons.

She made out four of the hovering machines through the trees. Another ball flew above them and landed with a blast of shrapnel that cut through trees and Echo citizens. Shots were returned, but nobody could fire through the shields that protected the cannons. Another missile soared through the air and a huge swath of ground exploded, sending Verdan body parts into the air.

"We'll have a chance if we can stop the cannons," Devren said. "Otherwise—Liora!"

Liora leaped the logs and ran through the trees. She ducked, dodging behind trunks and mossy rocks to avoid the bullets that followed her path. Part of her wondered with a separation unaffected by the battle if she could help the others without killing anyone. The other part of her watched with helpless rage when another cannon tore through Cason, one of Tariq's friends from the bar. A man nearby yelled his name. Sorrow and despair tightened the man's voice; he had just lost somebody he cared about.

The anger took over. Red colored Liora's vision and everything else fell away but the enemies in front of her. They sought to kill the Kratos crew and the citizens of Echo who had done nothing wrong except bravely risen to the call of battle protect their own. They didn't deserve to die.

Liora's grip on her knife tightened. She leaped a log and drove the blade into the heart of a Coalition officer. Ripping the knife free, Liora spun to the next man, a huge Gaul with blades attached to his horns. She jumped back before a sweep of the horns opened her stomach, then leaped forward and slammed the knife through the top of his skull.

Ordinary metal would have broken against the Gaul's

thick bones, but the knife Branson had given her from the Kratos' armory didn't falter. The Gaul slumped to the ground at her feet.

Two Arachnians with swords in each of their four hands barred her way. Liora flipped her knife over and threw it point first. It stuck deep into the first Arachnian's throat. He dropped his swords and clawed at the blade.

The second Arachnian charged with a growl. His swords moved so fast she could barely keep track of them. Each sweep of the blades she dodged cut through the air with an angry hiss. She had no way to block them. Her left foot slipped on a root and she twisted to the side. A sword tip sliced into her thigh before she could maneuver away. Liora grabbed a handful of moss and threw it at the Arachnian.

When he lifted a hand to shield his face from the debris, Liora dove and rolled up behind him. She pulled the blade from the other Arachnian's throat and spun in time to block two thrusts. The Arachnian's fast sword work demanded every grain of her skill. Liora blocked, stabbed, ducked, blocked again, and managed to nick the Arachnian's second left arm with her blade. He grimaced and doubled his efforts. It was exactly what Liora had anticipated.

She watched for the second right. His skill far surpassed hers, but like any swordsman, no matter how hard he had practiced, there was one hand with a slight lag behind the others. She countered each blow and barely felt the few times a blade made it past to mark her arms and once across her chest. She waited with the patience of a thousand Damaclan training bouts. Despite the chaos of bullets and screams around her, the explosions of the cannons that were her goal, and

Devren's orders to protect her advance, Liora kept her focus on the center of the Arachnian's chest and the slight lag of his lower right hand.

She saw it the moment the Arachnian pressed forward. He had successfully landed a sword across her cheek. She felt the warm blood coat her skin and knew pain would follow, but she didn't flinch or falter. Taking the blood as a sign of victory, the Arachnian gave a triumphant grin and pressed what he felt was his advantage.

His first right sword came up in a sideways sweep Liora knocked away with a blow of the knife that made her ears ring. His first left stabbed upward in an attempt to drive his blade through the base of her jaw to her brain. She countered with a block and spin just in time to catch the lower left's sweep for her stomach. Liora moved her knife with the direction of the sword, guiding it away just inches from her skin.

The lower right followed in a secondary sweep after the left. With the tilt of his hand, the Arachnian also stepped forward to maintain the balance of the sword. It was the step that threw him off. It slowed the sweep and also gave the slightest opening before he brought his upper right hand back up. It was Liora's only chance. She knew it was going to hurt, but pain meant survival; she would rather suffer pain than die at the hand of an Arachnian mercenary.

Liora lunged forward. Her knife sunk deep into the Arachnian's abdominal cavity where his heart throbbed. At the same time, his upper right sword stabbed deep into Liora's right arm where it met her shoulder. She bit back a gasp at the pain and pressed her advantage, shoving the knife through the Arachnian's exoskeleton and into the fleshy tissue beneath.

The Arachnian let out a scream of pain and tried to struggle. Liora stepped into the thrust. The sword cut deeper into her shoulder as she shoved and twisted her own blade in a mortal wound to her enemy.

The Arachnian's swords fell from his hands. He took a step back, dislodging her blade from his heart. His gaze searched hers with surprise and pain while he attempted to hold in the blood that spilled from his abdomen. His knees buckled and he fell backwards. Liora grabbed his sword carefully with both hands and pulled it free from her shoulder. She switched the knife to her left hand and reached the cannon with both blades swinging.

As soon as the three officers manning the machine fell to the ground, Liora ran to the next. Bullets peppered the trees around her, but Liora felt nothing as she opened throats and bellies to the vibrant forest floor. Thunder rumbled above and lights sparked all around. Green and blue flowed beneath her feet when she reached the third cannon and attacked. Light warred with darkness. Liora decapitated a Ventican soldier and sliced off the hand of a human who attempted to shoot her despite the close quarters. Liora finished him with a thrust angled upward from his stomach to his heart that ended his shouts of pain.

She glanced over her shoulder. With one cannon left, the Echo citizens and Kratos crew advanced on the mercenaries and Coalition troops. A missile hit a tree, sending shrapnel and wood into those who fought. A woman cried in pain. Others shouted for help.

Liora glanced over the final shield. Bullets sped past. They knew she was coming. She checked the sword. The grip was slick with blood from her shoulder wound. It would be more of a hindrance than a help. Liora tossed the sword to the ground. She spun the knife in her left hand so the weapon lay along her forearm with the blade outward.

Her plan was to vault the shield and dart for the left where the trees lay heaviest. Liora's hope was to reach the cannon before the bullets stopped her completely. She had to admit that it wasn't the best plan she had ever had, but Echo citizens were being killed and she would do everything in her power to keep the Coalition from the Omne Occasus. She set a hand on the shield.

"Liora, wait!"

Tariq's voice caught her attention. She glanced around the other side of the shield and stared at the sight of Devren and Tariq loading lightning canisters into a padded mat. The mat was tied with two lengths of stretched cord attached to separate trees. The men pulled the pouch back as far as they could, then let it fly. Just before the canisters hit the final shield, Tariq and Devren drew their pistols and fired.

The canisters exploded with a percussion that knocked everyone backwards. Liora's ears rang. She pushed to her feet and leaped the shield. The daze from the explosion made her stumble, but she kept her footing. She reached the cannon shield, vaulted it, and cut down the three lizard-like Hennonites before they could regain their senses enough to raise their guns.

The fourth, a Zamarian with metal rings in his gray and blue skin, raised two knives as long as his forearms. Bladed gauntlets protected his hands and arms. Thick black leather armor covered his neck and chest. His eyes narrowed. Liora raised her own blade. She gritted her teeth, prepared to fight for her life.

A yowl reverberated through the trees and a gray and blue form leaped over the shield. The gray felis she had saved tore into the throat of the Zamarian mercenary. The animal's long claws made quick work of the man's thick leather armor. The cat's fangs slashed, and the Zamarian's struggles stilled.

With the cannons down, the Echo citizens and Kratos crew members rushed forward. Liora and the felis led the charge through the trees. Each enemy they came to was ended swiftly and without mercy. They were threats, and as such, they deserved no mercy. Killing them protected the lives of the Echo citizens, people she had never met, but families with children, hopes, and plans for the future. Somehow, fighting for them felt more right than anything else she had ever done.

Liora fought until the scavengers and Coalition troops ran from both her and the felis in terror. She didn't know if the blood coating her body was theirs or her own. She ghosted through the trees like a wraith, slicing hamstrings and opening bowels to run onto the next threat while the felis ended those she dropped. The screams drove her own, pounding with her heartbeat, propelling her forward with a thirst that she could recall only seeing matched by the nameless ones who had slain her clan.

Four mercenaries huddled in a grove of trees. Bullets hit the ground at Liora's feet. She leaped a bush and spun. Her knife bit into the necks of two women armed with pulse machine guns and machetes. Liora ended the spindly Banthan on her left with a blade through the heart, grabbed the gun in his twitching hand, and pulled the trigger. The Salamandon on her right slumped to the ground. The felis appeared like a ghost and verified that the salvagers were dead.

The forest fell silent. A few moans and a cry of pain reached Liora ears, but the sounds of gunfire had vanished.

Sveth's voice tore Liora from her rage-induced haze. "No wonder you told her not to fight at the bar."

"Seriously," Granson said with awe in his deep voice. "That girl could kill us all."

Liora looked back at the four men who stood peering through the trees. The two who had spoken took a step back. Fear showed in their gazes. Liora couldn't decide if that was good or bad. Adrenaline still pounded through her veins. She knew the slain bodies around her were only a sliver of the number she had killed that day. Her hands itched with the need to keep doing what she had been raised to do. If she killed, she didn't have to stop and think about the lives she had taken. Stopping and the flood of regret that followed was the hardest. She wasn't ready to face it.

"Lieutenant Argyle, run a sweep from Echo to the Coalition and merc ships. We need to erase all signs of the enemy in order to keep Verdan from becoming a Coalition target," Devren instructed.

"Yes, Captain," Argyle replied.

"Tariq, have the wounded brought to the church house for treatment. I don't think the minister will mind if we turn it into a hospital until everyone has a chance to receive care."

"Jamste's the minister now," Tariq said. He kept his eyes on Liora.

She hadn't moved since killing the last four officers. She opened and closed her hand around the hilt of the knife. It kept her grounded, stable, or at least what she told herself was stable with lifeless eyes and blood-covered leaves burning images into her mind. The cat stood beside her, as silent as she, its fur unmarred by the battle, and its tufted ears twitching back and forth.

"Jamste?" Devren repeated. "No kidding? Let him know my mother will join us as soon as—"

"I'm on my way," Mrs. Metis called through the trees. "Kiari has my med kit. We'll meet you there."

Devren nodded. "Hyrin, we need a bead on whoever tracked the Kratos. The only way we can keep the Omne Occasus safe is if we can keep it hidden."

"Did you bring it here?" Tariq's voice revealed his trepidation at the thought.

Devren shook his head. "Of course not. It's hidden with the SS Atlas."

Tariq stared at him. "Where on earth did you hide a Diamond Albatross? And why aren't you with the Omne Occasus?"

Devren glanced at Sveth and Granson. "We'll talk later. For now, find Bonway and Sicily and have them start moving the bodies to the quarry."

"Will do, Cap," Sveth replied with a sideways salute that came off awkward enough to make both Tariq and Devren smile. Granson and Sveth hurried off through the trees.

Devren turned back to Tariq. "We need to hide our tracks. I'll meet you back at the church house."

Tariq lowered his voice. "What about Liora?"

The sound of her name made Liora realize she still had not moved. The blood on her hands was drying into a sticky mess. She wondered if the moss beneath the bodies around her felt the same way. She tried to center her thoughts, but to do so meant to accept the carnage. She wasn't ready for that. It was easier to listen to the crackle of the light that sparked through the trees.

"I've got her," Devren said, his voice gentle. "We'll meet you at the church. Mother's going to need your skills."

"You should have learned to heal," Tariq said. His footsteps crunched through the undergrowth. "It'd come in handy in these situations."

"I can't stitch worth a copper; you know that," Devren replied. "I'd rather people live."

"That makes two of us," Tariq replied over his shoulder. He disappeared between the trees.

Chapter 8

"Liora?"

She kept her gaze on a leaf that glowed gently in shades of red and purple. It pulsed like blood flowing through a human's veins. The effect was beckoning and calming. It slowed the adrenaline and loosened Liora's chest so she could breathe again.

"Liora."

Liora pulled her gaze from the leaf. Devren's dark eyes searched her face. His hand was raised halfway as though he had intended to brush back the hair that stuck to her cheek, but he wasn't sure if the action was a good idea. Liora didn't know, either.

There were a million things Devren could say. Though he kept the judgement from his gaze, Liora knew he had seen it again. The blood that coated her skin was merely a faint second to the eagerness of her blade and the way she had searched for the next enemy with relish.

She lowered her gaze.

"Don't do that," Devren said quietly. "Don't take on the guilt. You saved lives today, many lives."

"You saw me out there. I'm nothing more than a killing machine. It's what I know. It's what I do." She watched the glowing green moss at her feet. "They were right to be afraid. Once it hits me, I can't stop until every threat is dead. I'm not one of them; I'm not human. I'm a beast made to murder." She let her voice drop. "You shouldn't let me near your human family, your village, your ship, or your planet. Everything dies in my wake. I destroy life, not save it."

Devren's hand touched her shoulder. "Liora, look at me." When she refused, he spoke anyway. "There is nothing more human than protecting those you care about."

Liora shook her head, unwilling to let his words sink home. Her chest churned with emotion as she stared at the blood on her hands and arms. She didn't deserve his empathy. He should fear her like everyone else.

At her silence, Devren continued, "Why did I run to Verdan when I knew the Coalition was on our trail? It's because I know there's a village ready to fight at my back. I grew up here. I learned to fight beside my friends who were more like brothers and sisters to me. I knew they would join the battle on our side because we'll defend each other to our last dying breath. It's the human way." His voice quieted and he said, "I think you're more human than you know. You killed, and now the fact that you regret it means you're not some mindless creature made only to destroy." He touched her arm. "You don't have to hold it all inside."

His words undermined her carefully controlled calm, and when she looked at him, the compassion that burned in his dark gaze broke through the walls she had carefully built around her heart.

Tears burned in her eyes. She blinked quickly to keep them from falling.

"It's alright, Liora," he said softly. "You don't have to be strong all the time, especially in front of me."

His gentleness was something Liora wasn't used to. It made her walls crumble and the tears broke free. Devren pulled her to him and his arms wrapped around her, holding her close. Her tears soaked his shirt. She couldn't explain where the sadness came from, or why it felt like her heart was broken in two. But she felt safe in his arms, and when she stepped back and dried her cheeks, the understanding smile he gave her made her heart catch.

"You're easier to understand when you're not afraid to be vulnerable," he said.

She gave him a small smile. "It's not the fear of being vulnerable, it's that in the Damaclan world, weakness is death. I have a hard time showing weakness."

Devren nodded. "Maybe it's time you accept that being vulnerable can be a strength instead of a weakness."

Something soft brushed Liora's hand. Devren glanced down and his eyes widened. Liora found the felis' head beneath her fingertips, its green eyes dark and wild. Blood marked its whiskers from those it had slain at her side.

Liora crouched and ran a hand down its neck. The felis closed its eyes. The blue outline of its bones along its gray fur glowed brighter and the low rumbling purr vibrated from its chest.

She lowered her hand. The huge cat opened its eyes once more, its gaze on the jungle. Liora rose. The felis stalked silently back into the trees on clawed feet. It disappeared without looking back.

"Is there a reason that felis fought beside you?" Devren asked with a tone of confusion.

Liora glanced back and had to hide a smile at the trepidation on his face as though he feared the cat would come back and attack them.

"I saved its life and it saved mine," she told him.

"I never thought I'd see the day a felis would fight beside one of us instead of against us," Devren said.

Something about the way he said it chased the edge of bitterness from Liora's heart. She couldn't explain why the cat had gone against all its instincts to fight with her, but Devren was right. After everything, she was one of them rather than one of the enemy who lay slain at her feet.

"Maybe it felt it had to choose a side," she said.

"Maybe there wasn't a choice at all," Devren replied. He glanced at her. "Maybe it already knew where it belonged, it just had to accept it."

Liora shook her head at his statement, but she couldn't hide the begrudging smile that spread across her face at his words. "You're ridiculous."

"Maybe." Devren lifted his shoulders in a shrug; a teasing smile lifted one corner of his lips. "But you're the one who just pet Verdan's greatest predator." He looked at the blood on his fingertips, then back at her shoulder.

"You need to get fixed up."

"I can wait," she replied. "Let them tend to the others first."

Devren shook his head. "You're a member of my crew, and also, my mom would kill me if I didn't march you to the church to get treated."

That brought a ghost of a smile to Liora's face. "We wouldn't want that."

"No, we wouldn't," he agreed.

Liora walked beside him through the forest. The sight of Echo citizens working alongside the Kratos crew to clear away the bodies of the slain filled her with mixed emotions. She knew she was responsible for many of those they carried. Her ability to kill and not feel the consequences had scared her; what terrified her even more were the emotions that now threatened to overwhelm her. The only asset she brought to the Kratos crew was her ability to protect them. If she lost her edge, she might lose the only family she had.

Devren led the way into the church. Liora had never been inside a worship house before. It was different than she had expected. There weren't any chairs. Long, padded planks lined the floor at regularly spaced intervals. The pulpit at the end was made of glowing wood which detailed the carvings of lightning etched around the form of a man.

Blankets covered the ground and the moans and cries of pain from the men and women on top of them filled the air. Mrs. Metis and two other women worked on a man near the center of the room. He held his leg which lay in tatters below the knee. Liora saw Mrs. Metis pick up a bone saw. With a tight heart, Liora turned away from the man's protests. To the Damaclan, such an injury could be worse than death.

"Come this way," Devren said. He led her through a door to a small washroom.

"Are we supposed to be back here?" Liora asked. As much as she was glad to be away from the main room filled with people in pain, she wondered why nobody else used the small washroom at the back of the church.

"Jamste's a friend of mine," Devren replied. He turned on the faucet and waited for the water to grow warm. He glanced at Liora in the small mirror. "He owes me one."

He motioned for Liora to put her hands in the small stone-lined sink. Liora hid a wince at the bite of the warm water on the nicks across the backs of her hands from the battle and the bandaged gash in her palm that had been worn raw by the hilt of the knife.

"You don't have to pretend like it doesn't hurt," Devren said.

Liora looked up to find him watching her in the mirror. He gave her a small smile and picked up a rag and some soap.

"Actually, he owes me a few more than one," Devren continued.

He used the rag to gently wipe her hands. Liora felt strange standing there while someone else took care of her by doing things she was capable of doing for herself.

"We used to play a pretty rough game." A hint of embarrassment brushed Devren's cheeks with red. "Coalition against the Macrocosm. Tariq came up with it, and we played it every waking hour our parents would let us. We thought we were invincible."

The thought of the two men as boys running through the jungle playing war games cheered Liora. He moved the rag to her arms and she stilled.

"I can do that," she said, her voice soft.

Devren lifted a shoulder. "I'm not doing anything else right now."

She nodded past him toward the sounds of agony and the reassuring voices of Mrs. Metis and Tariq.

"They could use your help."

"So could you."

Devren put a clean rag to Liora's cheek where the blade had cut it open. Liora couldn't bring herself to meet his gaze. The gentleness of his touch was so foreign she had to fight back a fight or flight rush of adrenaline.

"I have a question for you," Devren said. There was a strange tone to his voice that caught her attention. "I've been debating whether to ask, but…."

His hesitation softened her fear over what he would ask.

"Go ahead," she said.

She watched his dark eyes as he carefully washed the wound on her cheek. They flicked to her and then back to what he was doing.

"When you were stabbed by the thorn the day we found the Omne Occasus, why did you call for Tariq instead of me?"

The question hung in the air between them. Liora didn't know how to respond. There was obvious disappointment in Devren's voice that he tried to hide. She didn't want to hurt him. The only thing she could think of was to go with the truth.

"I was dying," she said. The words were hard to admit. She had never been so weak; it was hard to think of that day. "It wasn't a conscious decision. I needed help, and I called for the first person that came to my mind." She let out a short breath and admitted, "I wasn't even sure Tariq would come. It didn't make sense that I called him. I can't explain it."

A slight noise caught Liora's attention. She turned to find Tariq standing in the doorway watching them. She couldn't read the expression on his face. His gaze traveled over her arms and the cheek Devren had mostly cleaned. His keen eyes rested on her shoulder where the Arachnian's sword had sunk through the dark fabric of her Ventican shirt.

His eyes narrowed. He put a hand to the wound. Liora winced at the gruffness of his touch.

Tariq drew his hand away and showed Devren the blood. "Have you learned nothing?" he demanded. Tariq's angry tone surprised both Liora and Devren. "You always tend to the most critical wound first."

"I though the blood was coming from her hand," Devren explain with regret in his tone. "I was only trying to—"

"Let her pass out when she loses enough blood?" Tariq spat. "Great plan. Your mother would be proud."

Liora saw the hurt on Devren's face.

"Tariq—" she began.

"Come on. I'll stitch you up," Tariq said.

"I can help her," Devren argued.

"You've done enough damage already," Tariq replied.

"You're the one who brought her here in the first place," Devren pointed out. "She wouldn't be injured if it wasn't for you."

Tariq's jaw clenched. "And you would be dead if it wasn't for me. You knew we would be here. That's why you came back!"

Devren's dark eyes flashed. "You're an officer of the

SS Kratos. You should have stayed with the ship in the first place."

"I was helping Liora," Tariq replied. He gestured at her shoulder. "Unlike you."

Liora couldn't stand it any longer. "I can take care of myself," she snapped. "Maybe you can stop fighting like a pack of heins and help those who sacrificed for you."

She snatched the small medical kit from Tariq's hand and stormed out of the washroom. Liora hurried past the wounded citizens being tended to by Mrs. Metis and her daughter, and pushed through the church doors. Someone called her name. Liora ducked behind the next house.

Grateful for the cover of darkness, Liora made her way to the Metis house and the starship beyond. The secondary lighting flickered on when she pushed the panel to trigger the door. She didn't think she would be glad to smell the grassy scent of the Calypsan's Tin Sparrow, but when she shut the door behind her, the silence and familiarity of the ship calmed her pounding heart.

Liora locked the door and took a seat on the shabby bed. Her shoulder ached, but not as much as her chest at the thought of Devren and Tariq at war with each other. She didn't want to be the reason their friendship was damaged.

The situation had escalated quickly; Liora still wasn't quite sure why Tariq had been so gruff when addressing them. Her experience with such social situations was limited. She hoped time might resolve things better than her interference.

Liora wrapped a bandage around her hand to keep the wound Devren had washed clean. As she tied off the cloth, she couldn't help remembering how gently he had bathed her skin, his fingers soft and careful as though he understood a life where every touch used to mean pain.

Liora shook her head to clear her thoughts and sorted through the small medical kit she had taken. She picked a curved bone needle and a length of waxed string. A small container labeled disinfectant filled the air with a tangy scent when she poured some on a clean cloth. She pulled her sleeve down to reveal the wound, and scooted to the end of the bed where she could see her reflection in the small window.

The disinfectant stung, then had the surprisingly welcome effect of numbing the wound. Liora had stitched plenty of her own injuries without painkillers and she had no qualms about doing so again, but stitching a wound with minimal pain seemed almost a luxury.

A closer look showed that while the wound had lost a lot of blood, it wasn't as deep as she had first feared. The Ventican cloth had protected her once again from an injury that could have been debilitating, and instead was merely an inconvenience.

As Liora worked the bone needle through her skin, her thoughts strayed to the kind Zamarian woman who had seen merely a young woman in need of help when others could see only her hated Damaclan tattoos and clan marks. Thanks to Chief Obruo, the woman had been killed along with her son and everyone else on Gaulded Zero Twenty-one. Her act of kindness in giving Liora the armored clothing may have proven her doom.

Liora thought of that encounter. The woman's son had been kind at first, showing empathy for a young woman whose face was bruised and bloody after her encounter with Malivian.

"You could use a place to clean up. No one should walk around the Gaulded like that. It'll mark you as a target."

"No, thank you," Liora had declined.

The Zamarian tipped his head to indicate the shop behind them. A variety of weapons and armored clothing hung from the walls. "You don't have to trust me. My mother's in there. She'll see that you're taken care of."

Liora had watched him closely, her guard up. "That sounds ominous."

The Zamarian grinned. "You don't trust anyone. Someone as beautiful as you is smart to be wary." His gaze had then shifted to the tattoos on her neck and his eyes widened in the way that she always expected. Fear was easy to predict. "But you wouldn't trust people, would you, Damaclan."

The word had been spoken as an accusation. She remembered the way the Zamarian's eyes had narrowed with suspicion; he lifted his hands as if expecting an attack.

"Leave her alone, Zran," his mother had called from the inside shop.

"Mother, she's a Damaclan," he stated with obvious distrust.

"She's a girl," his mother had replied; Liora remembered the hint of steel in her voice. "Treat her with respect."

Zran had shaken his head and backed away. "I value my life," he had muttered before leaving through the back of the shop.

Liora tied the end of the thread and used her teeth to sever the string. The thought that Zran had been right circled her mind, haunting her with other thoughts that threatened to overwhelm her when her guard was down.

"Liora?"

The light tap of knuckles on the Tin Sparrow's door broke her from her brooding thoughts.

"Can I come in?" Tariq asked.

Liora debated if she could stay silent and pretend she wasn't inside the starship. She pressed a square piece of bandage to the wound and wrapped it before pulling her sleeve back up.

"Your felis is waiting out here," Tariq said, his voice a bit tighter. "I know you're in there."

Liora sighed and pressed the lock release. The door clicked when Tariq pushed the panel from his side. It slid open to reveal a showdown that struck Liora as hilarious.

Tariq and the felis eyed each other with matching hostility. The cat's blue glow pulsed ominously, revealing the bones of its jaw and the caverns around its eyes. It looked as though it wouldn't allow Tariq to enter the ship.

"Why is it protecting me?" Liora asked.

"Don't ask me," Tariq replied, his gaze on the creature and muscles tense as though waiting for it to attack. "You're the one with the army."

"What does that mean?"

Liora followed Tariq's gesture toward the edge of the jungle. Her heart slowed. Other felis' stalked among the trees. Their yellow, orange, and blue glowing forms slipped in and out of the pulsing trees like silent wraiths.

"That makes no sense, unless…."

"Felis are pack animals," Tariq said, answering her unspoken question. "You saved one. The rest are here. Well done."

His words stung.

"I couldn't leave it to die," Liora retorted.

"Yes, you could have," Tariq said, his words sharp. "As I said before, you should have left it to die. Instead, you endangered yourself yet again to save something fate threw into that bog because it was supposed to die."

"Maybe you should have told Devren to leave me in that cage, then," Liora retorted.

That took some of the rage from Tariq's face. "I didn't mean it that way," he said.

Liora crossed her arms. "Did you come here for a reason?"

"Yes, to check on you," Tariq replied.

"I'm fine. You can leave."

She lifted a hand to the door panel. Tariq caught her wrist.

"Wait. Please."

She glanced at his hand on hers. He let her go.

His voice softened a bit. "Let me check your shoulder."

"I've already stitched it. It's fine."

"You say your fine a lot," Tariq replied, his eyes locked on hers. "Why don't I believe you?"

She turned her gaze to the felis near the door. Its lips were lifted in a silent snarl. If Tariq wasn't careful, he was going to lose a limb.

Tariq appeared to realize it at the same time. He took a step back and eyed the cat.

"Uh, can I come inside so your bodyguard doesn't decide to eat me for dinner?"

Liora debated whether to take pity on him or leave him to the felis' mercy. Tariq's eyes widened.

She hid a smile and took a step back. The felis' eyes narrowed as it watched the human step into the starship.

Liora was half-tempted to leave with the cats instead of continue her conversation, but she pressed her hand to the door and watched it close.

Chapter 9

"I'm sorry."

Tariq's apology sounded heartfelt. When Liora turned around, she found him leaning against the wall with his hands in his pockets and his head lowered.

"I don't know what came over me. I shouldn't have treated you or Devren like that."

"So why did you?"

Tariq was silent for so long Liora wondered whether he would answer. She fiddled with the bandages around her hand until she caught herself doing it. She had never been a fiddler. What was it about Tariq that threw her off so completely?

Tariq sucked in a breath and looked at her. "I guess I told myself that you called me on that ship because I was the one you wanted to come find you."

"That is why I called to you," Liora replied, confused by the direction of his thoughts.

Tariq shook his head and ran a hand through his mussed black hair to push it from his eyes.

"You told Devren it didn't make sense that you called me."

Liora watched him closely, trying to figure out why it bothered him so much. "Half the time I think you hate me because of what I am. The other half; I don't know. It's like..." She hesitated to say the words.

"What?" Tariq pressed.

Liora gave in. "It's like you don't know whether to strangle me or," her voice dropped to just above a whisper, "kiss me."

"Do you want me to kiss you?"

There was surprise in Tariq's voice along with something else that made Liora meet his eyes again. There was want in his piercing blue gaze when he looked at her. It was bare and bright. His hands clenched and unclenched as though he could barely hold himself back.

The pent-up emotions and frustration she read on his face gripped her so tight she could barely breathe.

"I-I don't know what I want."

Tariq's hand was in Liora's hair and his lips pressed against hers before she could draw another breath. The kiss was short and rough. When they parted, Liora's chest heaved as though she had run for miles. Tariq drew back and stared at her as if amazed at what he had done. He leaned forward to kiss her again when a knock sounded on the door.

"Tariq?"

Kiari's voice shattered the moment.

Tariq backed away from Liora. Her heart pounded and she fought to regain control of her thoughts.

"Tariq, are you in there?" Kiari asked.

"Uh, yeah, hold on," Tariq replied. He raised a hand to the door panel, hesitated with a glance at Liora, then pressed it. The door slid open.

"Mama said I would find you in here," Kiari told him. Her cheeks were bright and the smile that lit her features was difficult for Liora to ignore. "Are you hungry?" Kiari glanced at Liora as if just noticing she was there. "I mean, both of you. Temla and several of the others made food. They've set tables near the church so the wounded won't have to go far. I was sent to round you up." Her eyes sparkled when she said, "Like old times, right?"

"Like old times," Tariq repeated. He looked back at Liora, his expression unreadable. His brows pulled together and he nodded. "On my way."

"I'll walk with you, if you don't mind," Kiari said. "There's a lot of felis' about, and I don't seem to have Liora's way with them."

"Uh, right." Tariq cleared his throat and nodded. "Of course." He took a step toward the door and then seemed to remember Liora. He met her gaze. "Do you want to walk with us?"

Liora was still trying to come to terms with what had happened. She shook her head. "Go on. I'll be fine."

"Fine," Tariq repeated. He followed Kiari out of the door, his gaze vacant as if he didn't see what was ahead of him.

The door closed and Liora immediately felt his absence. The taste of his lips lingered on hers. Liora brought a hand to her mouth.

She had never been kissed before. It was both better and worse than she had imagined. His lips were soft, but the stubble from two days' growth of facial hair had prickled. His hand in her hair had sent tingles down her spine; she imagined she could still feel his fingers there. She had to admit that the kiss had been wonderful, but it had been short, cut off as if he had regretted it. Had he meant to kiss her, or done it as an impulse from his question? Had he forgotten she was a Damaclan, only to remember when it was already too late? Did he regret kissing her?

She tried to remind herself that he had almost kissed her again before Kiari interrupted them, then chided herself with the thought that she didn't care for Tariq in that way, and so it really didn't matter.

Yet for some reason, she couldn't stand being inside the Tin Sparrow any longer by herself. It felt smaller without Tariq in it, even though he was a full foot taller than she was and so the thought didn't make any sense. But she felt claustrophobic just the same.

Liora pressed the button on the door panel. When it slid open, half a dozen pairs of eyes reflected the light, adding to the glow of the felis' bodies.

Each cat's head reached Liora's waist level, and she was reminded again of Kiari's comment that they could tear a limb from a human. The thought of Kiari sent Liora stepping out into the darkness. The felis she had saved brushed up against her leg with enough strength that she had to put a hand to the door to steady herself.

"It's good to see you, too," she said aloud. The fact

that she was talking to a creature that couldn't understand her made her feel self-conscious. She dropped to one knee.

The cat's green eyes closed when she ran a hand across the soft fur of its neck. A purr rose from its chest. Another felis nudged her arm, and when she pet it, a third nuzzled her neck. Within minutes, Liora was sitting with her back against the door and all six of the cats lounging against her in various states of contentment. As soon as she switched from one to the next, the felis she left would give an unhappy harrumph and nuzzle her with the demand of being petted again.

"This may have gone too far."

Liora quieted the softly growling felises with her hands. The rumbles that emanated from their deep chests quieted, but they stuck protectively close to her.

She tipped her head at Devren. "They haven't killed me yet; I'm considering it a win."

Devren shook his head and kept his careful distance. "I've never seen felis act like that. It's like they think you're one of them."

Liora rose from the ground and the big cats dispersed. The one she had saved stayed close to her side. Devren eyed it when they drew near.

"Did you come here for a reason?"

"I didn't want you to miss the chance to eat. Once the Darvinshin brothers start in, there won't be much left," Devren told her. He hesitated then said, "Also, I want to apologize for not patching your shoulder up first. Tariq was right to be upset. I should have evaluated you beforehand."

Liora walked at his side toward Echo. "It's alright. I took care of it. I'm not your responsibility."

"You're an officer of the Kratos," Devren reminded her.

Liora conceded. "That's true, but from what I've seen, your officers can take care of themselves."

"We take care of each other," Devren replied.

Liora's hand strayed to the cat at her side. A glance over her shoulder showed the others trailing behind.

"What will happen to the felis when we leave?" she asked.

Devren followed her gaze. "I'm not sure. They've never acted like this. Some of the citizens have been talking about how one fought beside you. My sister thinks we should tame them. We've never tried before."

"What do you think should be done?"

Devren met her gaze, his dark eyes holding hers. "I think that wherever you go, you change things."

A shudder ran down Liora's spine. She glanced away. "I'm not entirely sure that's a good thing."

"That's left to be seen." Devren paused, then said, "In my opinion, it's a very good thing."

A smile quirked at the corners of Liora's mouth.

The felis left them at the edge of town. Liora and Devren continued to the tables spread above the glowing grass near the church house. Bandaged citizens were being helped to chairs while others filled platters with aromatic foods that made Liora's stomach growl.

"They welcomed the Kratos crew to the front of the line," Devren suggested.

"I prefer to wait at the back," Liora replied. "I don't mind standing for a while. The citizens deserve to eat first after the bravery they showed during the fight."

She caught Devren's look.

"What?" she asked self-consciously.

He gave her a warm smile. "Nothing. You just continue to surprise me."

Devren followed her silently to the end of the line. Talking at several of the tables they passed stopped, and Liora felt their gazes on her back. She thought she was used to being stared at from her time in Malivian's circus, but this was different. Instead of bars separating her from the crowd, she walked among them, and the fear she was used to seeing from pushing in the minds of spectators was instead caused by the blood rage and mindless killing from her Damaclan heritage.

Liora's appetite disappeared.

"I think I'll go back to the Sparrow," she told Devren.

He caught her arm. "Why are you leaving?"

Liora knew those eating closest to them could hear their words. She didn't want to say anything that would upset the citizens further.

She lowered her voice. "I don't belong here."

The expression on Devren's face said he guessed exactly why she wanted to go. His voice was firm and carried when he said, "You bled for us, Liora. If it wasn't for you, many more Echo citizens would be in that church or preparing to rest below ground. I'm grateful for your Damaclan blood and your training. You saved lives today. Stay and eat with us."

Devren met the gazes of several men at the closest table. Caught staring, they turned back to their food and pretended to ignore the pair.

Liora stayed in line, but only because leaving after Devren's words would be far more rude. Talking returned to the clearing, and she let her gaze wander through the crowd.

Liora's heart gave a little backflip when she spotted

Tariq eating at a table near Mrs. Metis. A hand touched the human's shoulder. He smiled at Kiari. The young woman set what looked like a pie near Tariq's elbow. He said something and she laughed loud enough that it carried over the commotion of the clearing. Her hand slid to the back of his neck and she began to massage his shoulders.

Tariq stilled. Liora couldn't tell if he was happy about Kiari's attention or not. Tariq glanced up and met Liora's gaze. She wanted to leave, to run, to hide, to do anything but be standing there at that moment, but it was too late.

Tariq caught Kiari's hand and said something quietly to her. She nodded and turned away. Liora couldn't see her expression to know how she felt about whatever he had told her.

"We'll fly out in the morning," Devren said, tearing Liora's attention from the pair. "The sooner we can get back to the Atlas, the better. I don't like leaving them for that long."

"I'm just glad you knew where to find us," Liora told him.

"I figured Tariq would head here." Devren gave her a questioning look. "Where did you go? When we got back to the ship on the Gaulded, you were gone. There was a certain Calypsan who was convinced you had taken his ship. Unfortunately, the video surveillance at the docks went out at just that moment, so they couldn't tell for sure."

Liora caught his smile. "Hyrin?"

Devren nodded. "He said he needed the practice. Besides, I knew if Tariq went with you, it was for a good reason."

Liora tried to ignore the slight question in his voice

when he mentioned his friend. "We had a lead on Chief Obruo. I couldn't pass up the chance to stop him."

"Did you?"

Liora shook her head. "He got away, but he shot Malivian."

"I can't say I'm sorry about that," Devren replied. "He deserved to pay for keeping you in a cage."

"Apparently he got paid for keeping me in that cage." Liora could tell Devren wanted more information, but she didn't feel like talking about it. "We've reached the food."

"Dish up whatever you'd like," a rotund woman with a kind smile invited. "We've plenty where that came from."

"Thank you, Temla," Devren replied. "You are too kind."

"It's nice to have you boys back for a visit," Temla told him. "And a fight like that reminds our people what it means to be a community." She winked at Liora, who found herself staring. "We were born fighting; we come out of these things stronger."

She handed Liora a plate and a set of utensils. Liora followed Devren down the table where men and women dished legumes in mouth-watering sauces, stewed meats, and a variety of cheeses onto their plates. A few of the citizens who served them wouldn't meet Liora's gaze, though others surprised her.

"Where'd you learn to fight like that?" Sveth asked as he ladled soup into a bowl and handed it to her.

"You could be our own private army," his friend with an arm in a sling said.

"Seriously," Sveth continued. "Maybe you're what we need to get the volts past the Scavs."

"Tariq mentioned the problems you've been having. We'll fly with you as far as the Maffei Two Galaxy," Devren told him.

Gratitude filled the faces around them.

"Really, Dev? That's great!" Sveth said. "That's only a click from Gaulded Two Zero Five. We should be fine after that."

"Thank Tariq. It was his plan," Devren replied as the men followed them to the table.

"What was my plan?" Tariq asked. He held Liora's gaze.

She looked away.

"Liora, sit with us!" Officer Shathryn said. The Kratos exterior analytical specialist scooted over to make room for her at the other end of the table.

Grateful for the chance to get away from the men for a while, Liora joined them.

"How have you been?" Officer O'Tule asked. "Captain Devren said he sent you and Tariq on a mission. We had no idea when we'd run into you again."

"There's been way too much testosterone on the Kratos with you gone," Shathryn continued. She paused and stared at Granson's backside when he walked past. "Although I'm liking the levels of testosterone here on Verdan," she said with an approving nod. "Maybe we can stay put for a while."

"We're shipping out in the morning," Devren told them.

"You take away all the fun," Shathryn replied.

"Don't mind her," O'Tule told Liora. "She's just upset the Colonel hasn't been back in contact with us."

"That's right," Shathryn said with a nod. "Cute and with stars. Can't get much better than that."

"Except for the fact that he's put our faces out to the mercenaries," Officer Straham replied. "How you can crush on him after that is beyond me."

Liora could have sworn the older officer's hair was even grayer than the last time she had seen him. The worry lines around the eyes of the late Captain Metis' second in command had definitely deepened.

"Who I like is my own business," Shathryn replied.

An older woman with long pale hair walked up to the table.

"Did I hear that you're going to escort our volts to the Gaulded?" the woman asked.

"Hello, Consul Blairia," Devren said, rising to his feet. "You heard correctly. We're happy to help out."

The consul wrapped Devren in a big hug. "I knew you boys would be back."

She motioned for Tariq to stand. He did so with a reluctant smile and she grabbed him in the hug as well.

"We've missed both you boys. I told everyone there was no way you could leave Echo for good. Now you've come back to help." She let them go and stepped back. "We sure appreciate it."

"We're happy to help," Tariq told her. "Our ship is your ship."

Consul Blairia grinned. "And our home is your home. Just see that you come back more often, you hear?"

"We hear," Devren replied. "We've already promised my mother the same thing."

The consul nodded. "Then she'll see to it that you do. Glad to hear it."

"Are introductions too much to ask?" Shathryn asked from their place further down the table.

Devren waved toward them. "Consul Blairia, meet

Officer Shathryn, Officer O'Tule, and Officer Day. The worried-looking one across from them is Officer Straham."

The consul crossed to their seats. "Pleased to meet you." She gave Officer Straham a warm smile. "And I remember you from when Devren's father used to visit. My condolences for your loss."

"Yours as well," Officer Straham said. There was a touch of red to his cheeks when he shook the consul's hand. "It's good to be remembered."

"Yours is a face I wouldn't soon forget. Handsome ages well," Consul Blairia replied. She turned away and left the officer staring after her.

"Officer Day, is it?" the consul asked.

Liora stood. "Yes, Consul. Thank you for your hospitality."

The consul looked her up and down with a no-nonsense expression. "I've heard a lot about you, Ms. Day. It seems many of our citizens are a bit afraid of your abilities."

At that moment, the felis Liora had saved padded out of the jungle and walked straight to her side. Silence fell over the entire assembly. The felis nudged Liora's hand and when she pet its head, its rumbling purr filled the air.

The consul had drawn her gun at the felis' appearance. Several of the closest humans had done so as well. Liora glanced at the head of the table. Devren's gun was out and half-raised in case he needed to use it. Tariq's weapon was still in its holster and there was a thoughtful expression on his face.

"I thought perhaps they had over exaggerated the details," Consul Blairia said, her words quiet to avoid startling the animal. "I see they were telling the truth."

She stood there for a moment as though debating what course of action to take. To Liora's relief, the consul slid the gun back in her holster.

She held out a hand toward the felis. "May I?" she asked.

There was tightness around her eyes that belied her calm demeanor. Asking to pet a creature known for killing humans was definitely beyond her comfort zone; Liora gave the consul credit for bravery.

She held out her hand for Blairia's while keeping her other on the felis' head. The cat's purr slowed when Liora drew the consul's hand over to hers. She watched the felis' movements still. The big cat's muscles tightened. Liora's free hand strayed to her knife in case she needed to defend the consul.

She pushed a feeling of calm toward the big cat as soon as Blairia's hand was on its head. The felis' purr paused for a moment, then resumed. Consul Blairia smiled and a sigh of relief was heard throughout the gathering. Citizens chuckled at each other and a few others rose to pet the cat.

Liora stepped back to let them pass. She continued to push a feeling of calm and contentment toward the animal to keep it from being overwhelmed by all of the people eager to touch the species they had grown up fearing. To her relief, the felis eventually closed its eyes and appeared to enjoy the attention as much as those from Echo were to give it.

Liora heard familiar footsteps come up behind her.

"I saw your hand by your knife," Tariq said quietly.

She glanced back at him. "I had to be sure."

"Would you have killed it?"

Liora was quiet for a moment before she said, "If I

had to."

Commotion ran through the Echo citizens. Liora followed their gazes to where several other felises peered from the jungle. A few took hesitant steps toward their comrade. Liora pushed comforting feelings toward them as well. The animals responded by coming into the clearing.

Consul Blairia reached out a hand and the first stretched its head forward to be petted. Liora couldn't help the smile that spread across her face.

Tariq watched her, his expression unreadable. "I feel you pushing at them."

Surprised, she looked at him. "You aren't supposed to. I'm directing it at the felis."

"I feel it just the same." Tariq looked unsettled. "I'm just not sure how to feel about it."

His words made Liora's chest tighten; her smile faded. "I'll try to be more careful."

"I didn't mean—"

"Tariq, come with us," Devren came up with Sveth and Granson behind him. "Since we're flying out in the morning, the guys want to strategize about the best path to the Maffei Two Galaxy."

"The Scavs seem to guess every path we plan to take," Sveth said. "It's going to take some serious flying to get past their lookouts."

Tariq gave a reluctant nod. "Count me in."

He glanced at Liora. She pretended to be occupied by petting one of the younger felis that rubbed against her leg. She couldn't decide if it was relief or regret that filled her when he finally followed the others to the Metis' house.

Chapter 10

"Let me come with you. I can fight, and I can't stand it here anymore."

The whisper brought Liora out of her fitful sleep. She was grateful to have been freed from the haunting images of the slain Coalition officers following her in her dream through Echo's jungle with ever-reaching hands. She sat up slowly and listened for what had awoken her. Her shoulder ached. She cradled her right hand in her lap to ease the pressure.

"I can be helpful," Kiari's voice pleaded near the

window. "I can shoot; you know I can. And I could help you in your medical bay. I've been careful to learn everything Mama taught me so that I can be an asset to your ship."

"It's not my ship." Tariq replied, his voice low. "It's your brother's."

"He's not going to mind...." Kiari began.

"Kiari, he's the captain. I'm not going to go against him."

"He hasn't said no," she pointed out.

"And he hasn't said yes," Tariq replied. "I don't think it's a good idea."

"Tariq..." Kiari sounded heartbroken. "I'm so tired of Echo. It's so small. I want to see the Macrocosm. I need to leave this galaxy. Please!"

"It's not a good idea."

Liora heard Tariq begin to walk away in the darkness. His quiet footsteps were becoming as familiar to her as breathing.

"But I love you."

Liora's heart slowed.

Tariq's footsteps paused. The grass shifted when he turned around.

"What did you say?" Tariq's voice was soft.

The sound of Kiari moving toward him reached Liora's ears.

"I love you, Tariq," she repeated. "I've loved you since we were young and I used to follow you and Dev on your adventures in the jungle. I always volunteered to carry your medical bag, remember? It was just so I could be close to you."

She paused and the silence pressed against Liora's ears.

When Kiari spoke again, her voice cracked slightly. "Then you left, and you were gone for years. I told myself you would come back. When one of Dad's letters mentioned that you had gotten married, I was devastated. I tried to move on, but you owned my heart, so I waited." She sniffed. "I'm sorry you lost Dannan and Lissy, I really am. I could be there for you. I wouldn't try to take Dannan's place. I would just be a comfort."

"Kiari." Tariq's voice was tight.

"Hear me out," Kiari replied. "I've waited this long. I'm not going to let you leave without me because I don't know how much longer I can wait and keep my sanity. I need you."

"Kiari, I don't—"

"Yes, you do," Kiari cut him off. "You need love in your life, Tariq. I've seen the haunted look in your eyes, and I've noticed that your hand is never far from your gun. You've seen things that have scarred you. You need sanity in your life and the assurance that somebody understands. I can be that person for you."

Sharp pain made Liora suck in a breath. She realized she had her fingers clenched into fists so tight the wound across the back of her hand was tearing open again. She forced her fingers to relax and stood. She didn't want to look out the window, but she couldn't keep herself from doing it anyway.

Tariq was kissing Kiari. Their shadows were unmistakable against the glow of the grass and the jungle trees beyond. Tariq's hands held Kiari's waist and her arms were wrapped around his neck.

Emotions surged through Liora with such abruptness she could barely breathe. She shoved them down, grabbed her knife sheath from where she had hung it on the chair near her bed, and left the room.

She needed something, anything, to break her mind away from what she had seen. The image of Tariq and Kiari kissing replayed over and over in her thoughts, tormenting her, driving her on.

There was one thing that drove all thought from the mind of a Damaclan, but Liora didn't have anything to kill. She had fought those who followed Devren to Verdan, and there were no more enemies left upon whom to vent her rage.

Liora had to settle for a weak replacement. When she stalked through the kitchen, she grabbed two rags from Mrs. Metis' basket near the stove. Liora pushed the outer door open and crossed the glowing grass.

She had no way of knowing what hour it was. The dark sky on the internally lit planet looked the same no matter what hour of day or night. All she knew was that any hope of sleeping had faded completely with the sight outside her window. The Gull would leave with or without Kiari; the decision would be made by the captain of the ship. Liora had to make sure she was in a mindset to accept whichever happened.

She wrapped the rags around her hands and tied them at her wrists. Taking extra care to make sure the bandages across her palm were snug, Liora raised her hands and glared at the side of the Calypsan's Tin Sparrow.

Her first punch left a dent in the hull. Liora ducked and jabbed, landing a second punch in the same place as the first. She ducked, spun, and backhanded the hull. Liora sucked in a breath at the jolt of pain that ran through her right shoulder. She clenched her jaw and hit the hull again, conscious not to spare her injured limb.

Liora fell into a training cadence. She ducked, spun,

and hit with the precision and strength of a lifetime of battles. It was the way she had kept herself sane in Malivian's steel cage, and it was the way she had survived Obruo's fierce upbringing. Pain wasn't an obstacle; pain was an annoyance to push past. If her hand or arm hurt, she couldn't feel it.

Relief came from the numb, repeating pattern locked into her muscle memory. She battered the side of the Tin Sparrow, and relished the impact to her knuckles, the way her body responded with a hook and an undercut before she ducked and bobbed away from her imaginary foe. She blocked with an elbow, swept behind her with a foot, and jabbed the metal hull before bouncing back to start the cadence again.

Liora lost all track of time. Sweat made her shirt stick to her back. While she didn't hit the hull with full force, she slammed it hard enough to remind her knuckles what it felt like to fight. The numbness felt good; it felt normal. The new life she had stepped into when Devren freed her from the cage on the Osprey Kirkos was confusing and filled with choices she had never had to make. Training reminded her that she was in control. Nobody would ever keep her in a cage again. She was in charge of her own destiny.

The voice in the back of her mind whispered that she was the soulless one; she was the girl who would end it all.

"Liora?"

Liora spun with her hands up, her mind still caught in the vestiges of the training cadence. She could tear apart whoever had interrupted her. She was in control.

"Whoa, girl. It's alright."

Tariq's voice broke through the red haze. Liora

dropped her hands and let the fight fade from her body.

"Are you okay?" Tariq watched her, his expression uncertain.

Liora nodded. Her heart thundered in her chest and her breath came in a rush, but for the first time since they had landed on Verdan, she felt like herself again.

"I went to your room, but you weren't there." Tariq gave the Sparrow's hull a meaningful look. "You apparently had important things going on."

"So did you," Liora replied.

She turned away from Tariq's questioning look and concentrated on removing the rags from her knuckles. Her hands shook slightly from the intense impact and her fingers had a hard time untying the knots.

"Let me help you."

He took her right hand in his, but Liora pulled her fingers free.

"I can do it myself."

Tariq crossed his arms and gave her a searching look.

"Did I do something wrong?"

Liora concentrated on untying the bandages. She gave up using her fingers and tried to work the knots free with her teeth.

"I know I left after I kissed you," Tariq said with regret in his voice. "When Kiari knocked, I couldn't think, let alone figure out what the right thing to do was. You throw me off balance, Liora. I don't know my right hand from my left when I'm with you. It's unsettling."

Silence followed his words. Liora finally had to admit that she had no chance of untying the knots and she held out a hand to him. He accepted it with a small half-smile and began to untie them with deft fingers.

"You were right to go with her." The words were

hard to say, but Liora knew that if Kiari was joining the Kratos crew, she had to accept the fact now before it created a rift in Devren's team.

Tariq's fingers stopped and he held the partially-untied bandage in both hands. His gaze slowly lifted to Liora's face.

"You think I should be with Kiari?" His tone was level.

Liora swallowed against the knot in her throat. "I think you make a good couple."

Tariq watched her for a moment before turning back to the knots. He got the one free for her left hand and unwrapped it. His movements were abrupt and rough whereas a moment before they had been almost too gentle for Liora to bear.

"I guess given your life experiences, I should trust your ability to judge who is the best fit for me," Tariq said with irritation in his voice.

He tossed the rag down and motioned for her other hand. Liora hesitated, but she wanted the rags off and couldn't get them by herself. He opened his hand wider. Liora set her right hand in his.

She fought back a wince when he prodded at the knot with fingers like steel rods. As much as training had numbed the pain, the retaliation from her arm and hand wounds were making themselves known in angry jabs. Tariq's rough treatment didn't help. He pulled at the knot hard enough that she finally yanked her hand from his grip. She held her arm and glared at him.

"Actually, I trust your lips to judge who is the best fit for you."

Tariq watched her for a moment, then his eyes widened. "You saw Kiari kiss me."

"I saw it after hearing how in love with you she is. I hope you are both very happy on the Kratos," she retorted, her tone gruff to hide any feelings that might try to sneak through. "Don't worry. I plan to leave the crew as soon as I have the chance."

Tariq stared at her. "But how…?"

"I told myself that your choice of standing outside my window for your little midnight kanoodling was sheer coincidence, but I haven't quite gotten myself convinced."

"Is that…" Tariq gestured at the Tin Sparrow's Hull. "Is that why…?"

"No," Liora replied, her chest heaving angrily. "I like to beat myself into numbness out of the sheer fun of it."

She couldn't explain when her self-control had fled. Tears burned in her eyes. When she blinked, they broke free. She turned away from him and stormed toward the jungle, ready to be anywhere but at his side.

"Liora, wait," he called.

Liora ducked under the glowing branches of the nearest tree. She heard his footsteps and pressed on faster, anxious to put as much distance between them as possible.

She stopped when she found the bog where she had rescued the felis. It surprised her how quickly she had reached it. Exhausted from training and the fury of emotions, Liora took a seat on a log near the yellow bubbling liquid. Tariq's footsteps came up behind her; she didn't turn around.

"Liora, it wasn't what it looked like."

He put a hand on her shoulder. She winced and he pulled his hand away.

"You're bleeding," he said. "You need to get patched

up."

"I already patched it up," she replied quietly.

"You probably tore the stitches hitting the ship back there. I've never seen anyone take out their frustrations like that. Let me check it."

He reached for her shoulder again. She jerked away from his touch. "Leave me alone."

He stepped around in front of her. His face showed pent-up fury.

"You are the most stubborn person I've ever known in my life. Let me check it out before you're the one I'm giving a blood transfusion to."

Liora turned her head away when he drew the edge of her Ventican shirt down to reveal her shoulder.

Tariq drew in a breath. "Just what I thought," he said, his voice quieter. "You need to get this taken care of."

"I'll deal with it."

Tariq was quiet for a moment. He crouched slowly and took her right hand in his. Without a word, he worked on loosening the knots much more gently than before. When the knot was free, he carefully unwrapped her hand. Part of the bandage showed blood, but a quick check revealed that the healing wound had held despite her intensive battering.

Tariq crumpled the rag into a ball and rose. He passed it from hand to hand as though debating what to say.

"I broke Kiari's heart."

The heaviness of his words made Liora look at him. Tariq studied the rag instead of meeting her gaze.

"I told her that after losing Dannan, I didn't have the ability to love anyone that way again."

Liora forced herself to ask, "How did she take it."

"You saw." His brow furrowed as he kept his eyes on

the rag in his hands. "She tried to convince me otherwise. She said I didn't need to love her like I did Dannan, and that if I let her come with us, I would learn to love her in other ways."

He rubbed the back of his neck with one hand and glanced at Liora. "Saying no isn't always easy." His mouth lifted wryly on one side and a touch of embarrassment brushed his cheeks with red. "Kiari can be very convincing when she puts her mind to it. She used to get into all kinds of scrapes with us when we were younger, and she never got in trouble while Dev and I were perpetually grounded."

For a moment, Liora saw a younger Tariq in his boyish smile and the way he couldn't bring himself to meet her gaze. It was endearing, as much as she tried to tell herself it wasn't.

He shook his head, his eyes on the bog as his smile disappeared. "But I told her I couldn't do it. I wouldn't draw someone on without the hope of filling that place in my heart. It's not empty. It's so full of rage and pain that the thought of letting someone else in is impossible." He threw the rag into the bog. The cloth sizzled and disappeared beneath the yellow liquid.

Liora's heart went out to him. "That couldn't have been easy."

He glanced at her. "Kiari slapped me and ran back into the house."

"She slapped you?" Liora repeated, amazed.

Tariq lifted his shoulders. "I guess that's what you do when someone bares their soul to you, right?"

Liora shook her head. "I don't think I'll ever understand girls."

Tariq chuckled. "That makes two of us." He held out

a hand to her. "Come on. Let's get you patched up before the Gull flies out. If we're quick, we can catch one of Mrs. M's famous flapjack breakfasts."

Liora gave in and put her hand in his so he could help her up. "Deal."

They walked side by side toward the house. She could see the structure through the trees when a rumbling growl stopped them in their tracks.

"That's not good," Tariq said.

Liora peered into the darkness of a tree that for some reason didn't give off the glow of the others. A form moved, and it was much bigger than she had first thought.

"I thought the felis was the biggest threat to Echo," Liora said, backing up.

"They're usually the biggest threat," Tariq modified, backing up with her, "Unless, of course, there's an ursilis around. They're rare."

"Good to know," Liora replied.

She stared at the creature that emerged from the shadows. When it shuffled forward, its black fur which had camouflaged it took on a deep green glow. Beady yellow eyes glowered in a massive head filled with teeth. Its paws left huge gouges from claws that appeared too big for even its massive body.

"Did you bring a gun?" Tariq asked, drawing his.

Liora pulled out her knife.

"This is going to be interesting," Tariq muttered.

The sound of paws in the underbrush caught Liora's ear. She slid her knife back in her sheath.

"What are you—" Tariq stopped speaking at the sight of the felis pack.

The big cats placed themselves between the ursilis

and Liora. Low growls emanated from their whiskered, fanged faces. The ursilis paused, looking from them to the humanoids as if debating whether it was worth the fight. Liora's felis hissed. The ursilis backed up. The cats followed. The ursilis swung its head from side to side. The felis swiped at its nose. The ursilis spun on its back feet and lumbered through the trees with the felis pack following close behind.

"That was amazing," Tariq said. He holstered his gun and glanced at Liora. "I guess it pays to save a felis from boiling in the bog."

Chapter 11

"Done."

Tariq pressed a bandage to Liora's shoulder and she held it in place so he could wrap it with a clean cloth to keep it there.

"That should hold unless you decide to pick on a ship again. The Calypsan would be furious if he saw you treating his Sparrow like that."

Liora fought back a smile at Tariq's teasing. "He was furious before we took the ship. I think there's got to be a better word for how he'll respond if he ever sees us again." She settled her shirt and tested the range of motion of her shoulder. Satisfied with the results, Liora rose from the small chair.

"Irate?" Tariq said, leading the way into the kitchen where the scents of batter and tarlon eggs made Liora's mouth water.

The rest of the Kratos crew already sat around the table laden with enough food to feed an army.

"Outraged," Liora shot back. "Thank you very much," she said as she accepted the plate Mrs. Metis handed her. It was already piled high with more food than she could eat in a week. "This looks delicious."

"I just want to send you guys off with full bellies," Mrs. Metis said. "I know those rations you get aboard ship aren't the freshest."

"Don't tell Jarston," Officer O'Tule said, "But you'd beat him any day at a cook-off."

"Thank you, my dear," Mrs. Metis replied with a pleased smile.

"Full of wrath," Tariq said, taking a place at the table.

Liora took the seat across from him and thought for a moment. "Fuming."

Devren gave them a curious look. "What are you two talking about?"

"About how that Calypsan is going to react if he ever sees us again," Tariq told him.

"You mean the one you stole the starship from?" Shathryn asked.

"You stole it?" Mrs. Metis repeated.

At Devren's mother's disapproving look, Tariq amended, "Not stole, exactly. We borrowed it with the intention of not returning it."

"That's stealing," she scolded.

"Semantics," Tariq said.

Devren shook his head with a grin. "Ask the Calypsan."

"Yeah," Shathryn said. "He'll be piqued when you show up."

"Pique's a good word," Tariq said.

Shathryn nodded. "I know. I use it all the time; especially when I'm talking about men. Though by the looks of that Calypsan, he was about as primeval as they get while still able to say actual words."

"I don't think those were words he was saying when we saw him last," Officer Straham said as he poured a generous helping of tarberry syrup across his flapjacks.

"We're leaving the Sparrow here," Devren told his mother. "I hope you don't mind. Returning it won't exactly leave us in the good graces of the Belanites, and we need all the help we can get right now."

"As long as you don't mind me selling it off for scraps," she replied. "I don't want some Calypsan showing up and accusing us of stealing his ship."

"He's not going to show up on Verdan," Devren pointed out.

"Just the same," Mrs. Metis replied, scooping more pulon links onto the plate in the middle of the table. "I'd feel better if it disappeared one way or another."

"Whatever you'd like," Devren gave in. He stood. "We'd better get going."

Kiari appeared at the door to the kitchen. She pointedly looked at anyone but Tariq. "Sveth's out front. He says they're ready."

"So are we," Devren replied. "Let him know we're on our way."

"Let him know yourself," Kiari shot back. She

disappeared down the hall.

Devren looked at his mother. "What did I do?"

Mrs. Metis shook her head. "I'm not sure, but she'll get over it."

"Maybe she's mad at a boy," Shathryn said. "That always puts me in a bad mood."

She and O'Tule finished washing their plates and followed Officer Straham out the door.

"She'll be fine," Mrs. Metis replied. Liora followed her gaze to Tariq. She wondered how much Mrs. Metis guessed of Kiari's feelings for her son's best friend.

Devren gave his mother a hug. "We have a few preparations to make before we fly out. I'll come back to say goodbye before we take off."

"See that you do," she replied with a motherly look of pride on her face.

Tariq and Liora were the only two left at the table. Liora helped stack the bowls, then took several plates with her to the sink in the corner.

The smile Tariq gave Mrs. Metis when he rose was sad. "Thank you for all that you've done," he said.

Liora kept her attention on the pair as she washed the plates.

Mrs. Metis put a hand on Tariq's arm. "Don't worry about Kiari. She's young. She'll find someone else."

"I didn't mean to hurt her," Tariq replied with genuine sorrow.

"I know." Mrs. Metis sighed. "Maybe this is what she needed to move on."

"I hope so," Tariq said. He gave Mrs. Metis a hug. "Thank you again for taking us in."

Mrs. Metis gave him a kind smile. "You know our home is always open."

"Maybe we can come back and visit sooner next time."

"I'd like that," she said. "I miss my boys."

Tariq grabbed the pack by his chair and followed the others out the front door.

Mrs. Metis crossed to Liora.

"You have better things to do," she said with a kind smile. "Leave the dishes to the old woman."

Liora found herself smiling back. "You're not old."

Mrs. Metis looked toward the door with longing in her expression. "I find myself wishing that I was off adventuring through the stars instead of here in Verdan."

The thought caught Liora by surprise. "I'm sure Devren wouldn't mind if you came along."

Mrs. Metis laughed. "The last thing a new captain needs is his mother aboard his ship." She shook her head. "As much as my heart may be in the stars, Verdan is my home. You're always welcome, with or without the others."

Her words warmed Liora's heart. "Thank you. That means more than you know."

"Take care of my boys," Mrs. Metis said.

"I will," Liora promised.

She was caught off-guard by Mrs. Metis' hug. Instead of feeling awkward like those from the crew, the woman's hug filled her with warmth and security.

"And take care of yourself," Mrs. Metis said, stepping back. "You have a lot to give to this Macrocosm yet, Liora Day. Have some adventures for me."

Liora smiled. "I will, Mrs. M. Thank you."

When the Gull landed on the SS Kratos, Liora stepped onto the Iron Falcon with a feeling of coming home. She used to miss her mother and few members of her clan, but for the first time in her life, she realized she had actually been homesick for the big starship with O'Tule's paintings at each intersection.

Liora entered her room and paused. Instead of the bare walls she had become accustomed to, the panels had been painted with various sunrises; on the left wall, two suns came up behind purple mountains; one the right, a sun rose from behind an ocean of water, its rays reflected in the silvery waves; on the wall across from her, the scene was of a sun caught above the ledge of a red rock canyon.

The one that held Liora's attention had been painted above the bed. She set a hand on the painting of a sun rising from a white, stark valley. There was beauty in the sandy slopes and the trickle of water down the edge of a ravine. It looked just the way she had left it after her clan had been killed.

"I hoped you would like it."

Liora turned to see O'Tule and Shathryn standing in the doorway. O'Tule gave her a hopeful smile. "You mentioned you wanted paintings."

"This looks just like Ralian," Liora replied in amazement. "How did you do that?"

O'Tule and Shathryn exchanged pleased smiles.

"We did some research into your clan," O'Tule said. "I hoped you wouldn't mind."

"It's perfect," Liora told her. "Thank you."

The intercom buzzed.

"Calling all crew members to the bridge," Officer Duncan's voice announced.

"Off to the Atlas," Shathryn told Liora. "Time to see if Hyrin's got a lead on destroying the Omne Occasus. I can't say I'd be sorry to see that thing go. It's definitely taken our lives and turned them upside-down here."

"And the sooner we get rid of it, the sooner we can talk to the colonel again, right Shath?" O'Tule asked, nudging her friend as Liora followed them up the hallway.

Shathryn threw a grin at Liora. "The colonel, and possibly the major. I've heard he's got green eyes that can see into your soul."

O'Tule shook her head. "You listen to way too much gossip."

Shathryn laughed and patted a strand of her bushy purple hair back into place. "How else am I supposed to know where to find all the hot guys?"

Devren nodded to them when they arrived. "We're taking Sveth's ship to the Maffei Two Galaxy. They've lost several cargo transports and can't afford to lose another. Also, it'll give Hyrin time to get in touch with Tramareaus."

A groan went through the bridge.

"He's not that bad," Devren said with a half-smile as though he had expected the response.

"Yes, he is," O'Tule replied.

"What did I miss?" Liora whispered to Officer Duncan.

The dark-skinned man with the bands through his ears leaned over to her. "The women seem to have a complaint about him."

"That's an understatement," Shathryn said, swiveling to face them from her seat at the monitors. "Tramareaus happens to be the most vile creature who ever lived on Titus, and that's saying a lot because I've met plenty of disgusting lifeforms, and he beats them all by a longshot."

"Isn't it a bit risky to go to Titus, given our most wanted status?" Officer Straham asked.

Devren nodded. "It is, but the only way we can destroy the Omne Occasus is to figure out what it's made out of. Hyrin's stumped, so we have to move on to the next best thing."

"I never thought I hear the words 'Tramareaus' and 'next best thing' in the same conversation," Shathryn muttered.

"I know it's not the best plan," Hyrin began.

"It's the worst by a zillion," O'Tule pointed out.

Hyrin's sideways eyelids blinked rapidly, revealing his discomfort. "If we can't figure out both forms of energy that make up the Omne Occasus, tampering with it could blow us and the closest galaxy into oblivion. I'd rather know what I'm dealing with than risk accidentally wiping billions of people off the star charts."

Silence filled the bridge.

Devren set a hand on his captain chair. "Then it's decided. We'll leave Sveth's team at Maffei Two, then pick up the Omne Occasus at the Atlas and head to Titus. Along the way, we'll hide the Kratos and disguise the Gull. It might not be the safest ship to land on Titus, but with the warrant out, it'll be harder to recognize us."

"Incoming," Hyrin announced. "It's from the Aphrodite."

Devren snorted. "Leave it to Sveth to name his Copper Crow Aphrodite. He always had an unhealthy attachment to his machines. Put it on the screen."

Sveth's face appeared on the main monitor.

"We're ready to follow you, Captain Metis."

Devren rolled his eyes. "That was my dad, Sveth."

His red eyebrows rose. "So what does your crew call you?"

"Ornery," O'Tule answered.

"Crabby," Shathryn echoed.

"A hopeless romantic with a keen attention to his duties," Officer Straham said.

Everyone looked at him.

"What?" Straham asked. He rubbed a hand across his short gray hair. "It's true."

Devren shook his head and turned back to the screen. "They call me Captain Devren. It works."

"Alright, Cap Dev," Sveth replied with a salute. "Ready when you are."

"We're going to take it fast," Devren said. "Stay on my six and radio if you see any Scavs."

"Will do, Cap. Over and out."

Devren looked at O'Tule. "Ornery?" he asked.

She shrugged. "I couldn't think of anything else."

Devren sat in the captain's seat. "Hyrin, take us out."

Liora followed their route on the star chart above Hyrin's station. They reached a transporter and Devren contacted Sveth.

"We'll go through first. As soon as it's charged, take it through. We'll be ready."

"Sounds good," Sveth answered. "Just be warned. The Scavs have a tendency to hang out on the flip side."

"Thanks for the warning," Devren replied. When the screen went dark, he rose from his seat. "Officer Shathryn, arm the cannons. Officer O'Tule, send full power to the shields." He glanced behind him. "Officer Duncan, notify the crew of the jump. Put them on full alert in case we're ambushed."

Officer Duncan's calm voice echoed the captain's words over the intercom.

Devren nodded at Hyrin. "Prepare to jump."

Hyrin maneuvered the arm of the Kratos to the link

on the transporter. The toggle came out, locking them into place. O'Tule pressed a button and red lights flashed throughout the bridge. A low warning tone sounded.

"Weapons are ready," Shathryn announced.

"Shields are at full power," O'Tule seconded.

"Captain?"

Devren nodded at Hyrin. "Let's jump."

Liora gritted her teeth against the chilling, pulling sensation, then they were across.

"Mercenaries," Shathryn called out. "I count five ships."

"They're firing on us," O'Tule announced.

"Return fire," Devren replied. "We need to protect the transporter so the Aphrodite can make it over."

"The solar sails are out," Hyrin said.

"Let me know as soon as it jumps back," Devren told him. "We need to be ready to defend Sveth's ship."

"Brace for impact," Shathryn announced.

The ship rocked as two missiles struck the starboard side.

"Answer in kind," Devren ordered. "Officer O'Tule, damage report."

"Shields are holding," O'Tule replied. "We're at ninety-five percent."

"Uh, Captain," Shathryn said, her voice hesitant. "A Falcon just appeared from behind them. Its signature says the SS Artemis."

"A Coalition ship?" Devren replied. "They must have come searching for the others when they didn't return. Things are about to get heated. Any way we can get word to the Aphrodite?"

"We won't have contact with them until they cross over," Hyrin reported.

"The Artemis is opening fire," Shathryn said.

"The Mississippi transporter jumped," Hyrin called.

"Concentrate all firepower on the Artemis. If the mercs try to sneak around the sides, answer with the cannons." Devren studied the monitor as missiles streaked toward the Iron Falcon. "They're bringing out snipers. The bullets are small enough to get through the shields. I need someone to handle them before they damage the ship."

Officer Straham rose. "I'm on it."

"Me, too," Liora echoed.

At Devren's surprised look, she said, "I'm not doing anything here. Let me give it a shot."

"Literally," Straham said. "I could use a second gunman."

Devren nodded. "Be careful. Stay behind the ship."

"Will do," Straham answered.

Liora jogged beside him to the loading deck. She followed wordlessly into the cargo bay and stepped into one of the hanging atmosphere suits.

"You know what you're in for, right?" Straham asked.

"I know if we don't find a way to stop the Artemis before the Aphrodite gets here, Verdan's lost more than just another cargo transfer," Liora replied.

Straham nodded. "Right. Let's shoot some snipers." He attached the helmet to his atmosphere suit.

Liora zipped up the front of the body-hugging, stretchy cloth. It fit over her Ventican uniform without hampering her movements. She pulled on the helmet and took a breath behind the close-fitting shield. While the sound of her breathing was loud, she could see clearly to fasten the sheath of her knife over the leg of her suit.

"Ready?" Straham asked.

She looked up to find him holding out a gun almost as long as she was tall.

"It's an energy pulse sniper rifle. Just look down the sights and pull the trigger," the older officer directed as he led the way to the cargo bay door.

"I can handle that," Liora assured him. She slung the rifle on her back like he had and fought down a rush of nerves at the unfamiliar weight.

"One last thing," Straham said. He picked up a cable with a clip on either end. He attached one end to a loop near the waist of his atmosphere suit and did the same to hers. "Just in case."

He pushed the button and a door slid up to reveal the small pressurization chamber. They stepped inside and the door slid shut behind them. Straham put a hand to the second panel. A warning beep sounded and numbers flashed on the screen. Liora followed Straham's example and grabbed the bars along each side as the room depressurized and gravity disappeared. The door between them and the vast reaches of space opened.

"Here we go," Straham said over his headset.

"Be careful," Devren told them. "They're sending out Grebes."

"What are those?" Liora asked.

"Small trajectory guidance crafts," Straham replied. "The snipers can use them to get closer to the Kratos."

"Handy," Liora acknowledge. "Do we have any of those?"

Straham glanced at her through his shield. "Nope, but I'll have Lieutenant Argyle add it to the shopping list if we ever get back in favor with the Coalition."

"I'll let him know," Devren answered with a hint of wryness in his voice.

"Thanks, Captain," Straham replied. "It's about time we upgraded our equipment."

Chapter 12

Straham edged out of the starship. Liora followed close behind. The older officer kept one hand on the ship, using the rungs and handholds placed along the Kratos' hull for just that purpose.

"Straham, Day, the snipers are firing at the secondary fuel storage," Officer O'Tule called over their headsets. "Shathryn can't get a bead on them. You're going to have to take them out."

"Will do," Straham replied. He glanced at Liora. "We're going to have to pick things up a bit."

He grabbed one of the rungs with both hands and rocketed himself upward along the side of the ship. Liora followed, her heartbeat pounding in her ears and the tether between them the only reassurance that if she missed the final handhold, she wouldn't go shooting off into the black expanse of space above them.

Straham latched onto the top rung and waited to be sure that Liora had done the same before he removed his gun. Liora followed suit. She rested the gun along the edge of the ship and looked down the sights.

It wasn't hard to follow the small bursts of light from the snipers' rifles to the men and women who fired at the Kratos. Nearly a dozen of them dotted the sides of the Artemis, while several more were occupied with holding onto the Grebes. The Grebes turned out to be small, domed thrusters barely large enough protect those who angled them toward the Kratos. As much as Liora wanted to pick them off before they drew nearer, the main threat to the Kratos were the snipers who peaked out just long enough to shoot at the fuel storage before ducking back behind the Iron Falcon's protective sides.

"One at a time," Straham said quietly. He drew in a breath, let it out slowly, then squeezed the trigger at the end of his exhale.

They didn't hear the impact or the pained yell of his target, but Liora saw the sniper's gun spin through the airless void on a trajectory toward darkness. She put her eye to the sights and followed a pulse of light to a gun on the lit hull. The sniper poked out just long enough to aim again. Liora let out her breath and squeezed the trigger. The sniper's head jerked back and he slid out of sight.

"Nice," Straham said. Satisfied that his ward wasn't about to get them both killed, he took careful aim again.

Liora followed. She picked off two more in quick succession.

"They're falling like flies," Shathryn announced.

An explosion shook the side of the Kratos.

"What's going on?" Straham called.

O'Tule sounded frazzled when she answered, "Their missiles are getting past our defenses. They're firing faster than we can shoot them down."

"Double the response," Devren ordered. "Send out pulse bombs to draw the missiles away from the ships.

"The wall of the secondary fuel storage has been compromised," Lieutenant Argyle announced. "We can't take many more hits."

"Sveth's ship is here," Hyrin told them. "They're under heavy fire from the mercs."

Liora peered over the side of the Kratos long enough to see four of the smaller ships advancing on the Aphrodite.

"What's the best case scenario?" she asked Straham.

"Best case is we get someone aboard the Artemis, use the transportation chamber to send over a bomb, blow it up, then we can concentrate the firepower from both ships on the mercs," Straham answered.

"That's a suicide mission," Devren replied, his voice tight. "I forbid it."

Liora shot one of the snipers who drew close. He grabbed his knee, letting go of the Grebe.

"We have our chance," she said.

"No," Devren told her. "Stay put. Our firepower combined with the Aphrodite can take care of it."

"They're shooting my ship full of holes!" Liora heard Sveth's voice say. He must have been shouting loud over the ship's intercom for her to hear it on the headset. "My beautiful ship is being torn to pieces!"

"Concentrate your fire on the mercs. We're targeting the Iron Falcon," Devren told him.

"They're loaded for ursilis," Sveth replied. "And five against two isn't exactly winning odds. I say let Liora and Straham go."

A blast of missiles sped toward both ships. Return fire from the Kratos and Aphrodite shot down several. One slammed into the Kratos and two hit the other ship. Liora and Straham held tight against the answering jolt.

Liora steadied her sniper rifle and shot another Coalition officer.

"Best case scenario, we survive this somehow and limp to the closest Gaulded," Shathryn said. "But we aren't going to be welcome there for repairs, and if another Coalition ship comes onto us, we're doomed. We need to survive this intact if we're going to get the Omne Occasus to Titus."

As if in answer, two more missiles cleared the Kratos defense system and impacted the hull.

"Shields are down to thirty percent," O'Tule announced.

"We've got ten," Sveth answered.

"One merc ship down," Shathryn called with a note of triumph. "Those platinum hungry sellouts deserve to sleep in the depths of space. It serves them right for picking up our warrant hoping for an easy payout."

"Brace for impact," O'Tule called.

The ship shook again.

"Twenty-five percent," she said. "Captain, we aren't going to hold together much longer."

Straham and Liora picked off the last two snipers along the Coalition starship's hull. Liora turned her attention to the two hiding behind their Grebes near the starboard side. She took a shot, but it glanced off the protective dome of the little craft. The sniper took aim at the fuel storage again. Liora glanced around quickly. Her gaze rested on the Grebe from the first sniper she had shot. With no one to steer it, the vessel drifted close to the Kratos hull.

"I have an idea," Liora told Straham. She motioned toward the Grebe.

"I'm not sure it's a good one," he answered.

Aware of the tether between them and the safety it provided, Liora knew she needed him on board before she acted.

"One of us flies the Grebe, the other acts as a pendulum. If the one who pilots can arc the other behind the snipers, we'll have a shot."

Officer Straham hesitated, but a glance back at the snipers showed that they had no other option unless they wanted to sit back and watch their ship be picked to pieces.

"I'll fly," he said.

Relieved that she wouldn't have to figure out how to steer the Grebe in such a short amount of time, Liora climbed hand over hand down the ship behind Straham. Another explosion nearly threw them from the side, but they reached the end of the Kratos without incident.

"What are you guys doing?" Hyrin asked.

Liora looked down and found that she was standing on the outside of one of the bridge's wide windows. The crew stared up at them from the inside.

"We're improvising so we can save your butts," Straham replied.

"Be careful," Devren said, his gaze worried.

The bridge and crew looked shaken by the impacts. Liora knew exactly how they felt.

The Grebe floated a ways beyond the ship.

"Hold onto something. I'm going to jump for it," Straham directed. He jumped without giving her time to respond.

Liora fumbled for a grip. Her hand slid into a groove between two of the windows. She grabbed the cord with her free hand to ensure that it didn't somehow become unattached from her atmosphere suit. Her worst fear would be for Straham to miss his mark and for her to watch him drift toward the unfathomable darkness of space without a way to bring him back.

Straham's aim was true. He grabbed onto the Grebe and jerked to a stop. The jolt nearly tore Liora's grip from the window. She held on and glanced down to see the entire crew watching them with open mouths.

"Now what?" O'Tule asked from inside.

"Now for the fun part," Liora replied.

Another volley of missiles sped toward them. The Kratos sent out defensive fire. Liora crouched at the same time that Straham got the Grebe straightened out. He gunned the engine. Liora launched herself into space.

The flash of explosions littered the space around the ships as Liora flew forward. She held onto the tether as though it was a lifeline. It felt like an eternity passed with her soaring toward the stars. For a moment, she feared the tether had slipped at Straham's end and she was the one plummeting through space; then the tether tightened and she vaulted around the Grebe toward the other side of the ship.

The snipers came into view. Liora took careful aim, squeezed the trigger once, aimed again and fired. Both snipers jerked back from their Grebes. The first floated lifelessly backwards while the second held his stomach and tried to reach the Grebe again, but it and his gun were too far away.

"The secondary fuel storage is safe," Liora reported.

Cheers replied from the Kratos.

"Now for the Artemis."

"Officer Straham, your course of action is denied," Devren replied. "Return to the Kratos."

Officer Straham pulled on the tether to slow Liora's pivot. She reached the Grebe.

"What's the plan?" she asked.

"Our shields are down," Sveth called. "We're sitting tarlons."

Straham glanced over his shoulder at the Coalition's Iron Falcon. "Captain Devren, the plan will work. We have a Grebe. If you can cover us so the Artemis doesn't notice our approach, we can get aboard and radio back. We'll be able to bring it down from the inside."

"We can circle around the starship," Hyrin replied. "If Shathryn lays down a line of fire along the starboard side, Straham and Liora could take the port side and enter through the cargo hold. With some luck, the troop might miss the Grebe entirely. What do you think, Captain?"

"Do it," Sveth called over the main intercom.

"It's the best plan we've got," Devren gave in. "But I'm adding that if you can't get into the Artemis without being seen, you fall back immediately and we pick you up."

"Will do," Straham agreed.

"Liora?"

Liora fought back a smile at Devren's questioning tone. "It's not like I take a lot of risks," she said.

"Seriously?" Devren replied. "Liora, if you don't give me your word…."

Straham nudged her.

"You've got my word. We'll be careful," she said.

"Fine. Hold onto the door latch on our starboard side. When we swing around, it'll put you under the wing portside," Devren instructed.

"And we'll trail along," Sveth said from the Aphrodite. "We'll provide cover fire and it'll get us away from these mercs before they tear us apart. Whatever happens, you two need to hurry."

Liora and Straham held the Grebe between them and pressed as close to the Kratos as they could. The enormity of what they were about to do filled Liora with adrenaline. The closer they got to the Artemis, the more she wondered if their plan was doomed to fail. A ship that big had to have a hundred eyes watching for just such an action. If that was the case, she refused to go down easily.

"Ready," Hyrin said over their earpieces. "And…now."

Straham pushed the lever on the Grebe at the same time that Shathryn fired missiles into the Artemis. The forward guns shifted, following the Kratos' flight path. The Aphrodite fell back just enough to shield the Grebe from view. Straham and Liora held onto the craft and rocketed toward the Artemis.

Straham used the thrusters to adjust their course. The gaping doors of the cargo hold stood open and Coalition officers readied a Gull in zero gravity. While the craft was generally used for space to ground transportation, it appeared they were prepared to make an exception. The missiles strapped to either side of the Gull weren't rigged to be dropped.

"They plan to fly the Gull right into one of you," Straham said over the intercom to Devren. "It's equipped to blow on contact."

"You hear that, Sveth?" Devren called. "Back off. Your ship can't handle it."

"The Kratos can't either," Sveth pointed out.

"Go starboard and watch for mercs. They're circling around. We need to keep them busy," Devren told him.

Straham and Liora drew close to the hold.

"We need to let go of the Grebe," Straham said quietly. "Hold onto the tether. We don't want the thrust to throw us off course, but I need to make an adjustment."

It took courage to let go of the Grebe's handle and rely on the tether to keep her from drifting off, but Liora did it. She watched Straham change the thrusters. He grabbed a band from his suit and wrapped it around one of the Grebe's handles. He let go of the craft and hit the right throttle. The Grebe sped away from them.

Straham and Liora drew closer to the Coalition officers. The pair's sniper rifles wouldn't be much use at the close range, and given the fact that they were drifting at the mercy of their trajectory, they would be easy targets.

"Come on," Straham whispered. "Yes!"

Liora looked up to see the Grebe enter the cargo hold on the opposite side of them. It smashed into the wall, drawing the attention of the officers who prepped the Gull. Liora landed at the edge of the hold and pulled Straham in. They worked along the wall toward the pressure door. Liora pushed the button and they both waited with bated breaths. Luckily, the commotion of the wreckage behind them held everyone's attention. The door opened and they stepped inside.

As soon as the pressure was equalized, Liora and Straham stepped into the main bay.

"We've made it inside. Where do we go from here?" Straham asked.

Hyrin's voice came over the communicators inside their helmets. "The Artemis is a newer Falcon. Its schematic is a bit different than the Kratos. Let me pull it up."

"Hurry," Straham urged. "If anyone catches onto us, we've lost the element of surprise."

"The Gull is taking off," Officer Shathryn called.

Footsteps sounded down the hallway.

"Hyrin?" Liora asked.

"Got it," Hyrin replied. "Straight, then left."

Liora and Straham took off running.

"Right, then down the hallway," Hyrin instructed.

"Shields are down to two percent," O'Tule called out.

Liora ran down the hallway with Straham right behind her. They couldn't risk anybody seeing them. If the bridge was alerted, they would lock down the transportation room. As it was, the pair could only hope that with the heat of battle, there was nobody standing guard in the chamber.

Liora rounded a corner the same time as two Coalition officers. Liora unsheathed her knife and ran between them. She slammed her blade into the first officer's back and jerked it upward, severing his renal artery. She spun around and shoved the blade through the back of the second officer's neck. They both fell to the ground without a sound.

Straham stared at her. "Glad to have you along," he

said with wide eyes.

"Let's go," Liora replied.

"Is everything alright?" Hyrin asked. "Things are falling apart here."

"How close are we?" Liora asked.

"Down the next hall, first door on the left and you're there."

The door slid aside to reveal an empty chamber.

"Thank goodness," Straham breathed. He rushed to the computer. "Hyrin, the access codes."

"Shields are down," O'Tule said.

"My poor Aphrodite," Sveth wailed over the intercom. "She's getting torn to pieces!"

"The Gull's locked on. Swing around behind the mercs," Devren instructed. "If we can shoot it, we can take a few of them with it."

"Merc missiles are locked," O'Tule said, her voice tight.

"I've lost my starboard thrusters," Sveth announced.

"Hyrin, the access codes!" Straham demanded.

"Zero, five, alpha, ocelot, seven, bravo, three, five, five, delta, lima, seven, five, zero," Hyrin replied.

Straham typed the code as quickly as Hyrin called it out. When he hit enter, the chamber buzzed to life.

"We're in," Straham told him.

"Lieutenant Argyle, you're on," Devren directed.

"Sending now," Argyle replied, his voice gruff. "You'll have to arm it, then run. You have less than two minutes before it detonates."

"Got it," Straham said.

The door slid open behind them. Two Coalition officers' eyes widened at the sight of strangers in the transportation chamber. One officer opened his mouth to call for help.

Liora threw her knife. She slammed the second officer's head against the wall as the first tried to pull the blade from his throat. Liora drove an elbow into the stomach of the officer she fought. When he doubled over, she grabbed his head in a headlock, flipped forward, and forced his body to follow. His neck gave a sickening pop as he slumped to the ground. She withdrew the knife from the first officer's throat and finished the job by driving it through his heart.

As she wiped the knife on the officer's sleeve, she found Straham watching her with a worried expression.

"I'm starting to think you're a little too good at that," the officer said.

Before Liora could respond, the chamber flashed and a block of tubes and wires appeared.

They could hear the commotion from the Kratos over their headsets.

"The Gull's locked," Shathryn said.

"The Artemis is relentless," O'Tule called out. "The Kratos is falling apart!"

"We've lost the rear thrusters," Lieutenant Argyle informed them.

"Fly closer to that merc, Sveth," Devren commanded.

"Are you insane?" Sveth shouted back.

"We have one chance at this. Let's make it count. Ready Hyrin?"

"Arming the bomb," Straham said. "Hope everyone's ready."

When nobody responded, he met Liora's gaze. "What's your call? If we arm it and can't get enough space between us and the ship, we're done for."

"And if we don't, the Kratos and Aphrodite are done

for," Liora replied. "Do it."

Straham connected two wires and pressed a button. The bomb let out a hum.

"Run," he shouted.

Liora took off out the door. Straham's footsteps followed close behind. She used Hyrin's directions backwards and led them to the cargo bay.

"Come on," Straham urged when the pressurization door took its time to open.

They darted inside. Liora's heart thundered. She watched anxiously through the door behind them, ready in case they were followed.

The second door opened to the exposed cargo hold. Two dozen officers in atmosphere suits turned to face them. Eyes widened at the sight of the strangers. Guns raised.

Liora grabbed Straham and pushed off the ground. They soared upward. As soon as they were high enough to clear the officers, she kicked off the wall. Bullets soared soundlessly through the space around them. One tugged at the sleeve of Liora's atmosphere suit. Another glanced off her shield. Officer Straham let out a cry of pain.

The explosion rocketed through the Artemis. The officers below scrambled as the floor of the hold buckled. There was no way they would get far enough away from the explosion in time. Liora searched for options. Fire burst outward and disappeared. The silent destruction of the Artemis was unnerving. A huge steel beam soared toward the pair.

"Hold onto the tether," Liora shouted.

She pushed away from Straham. The motion rocketed her to the beam. It slammed into Liora hard enough to steal her breath. She felt the tether tighten, then Straham was next to her. She looked down in time to see the Artemis break in half. She held tight to the beam that carried them away.

Chapter 13

"Glad to see them go," Hyrin said.

"The Aphrodite is limping, but least they made it," Devren replied. "Good job everyone."

Officer Straham and Liora exchanged a glance. The officer's arm was in a sling, but he had refused to stay in the medical bay despite Tariq's recommendations. Everyone was anxious to see the Aphrodite reach Gaulded Two Zero Five. Instead of leaving them at the Maffei Two Galaxy, Devren had chosen to escort them all the way given the condition of their ship.

Tariq waited on the bridge as well. "You said you hid the Diamond Albatross somewhere nobody would find it, yet it's close by," he told Devren. "I want to see the answer to your riddle."

"The answer isn't far," Devren replied evasively.

Smiles were exchanged by members of the crew. Relief that they had survived the Coalition encounter coupled with something else.

"The Atlas is in sight," Shathryn said a few minutes later.

Liora scanned the monitors, but she couldn't see a ship anywhere.

"You mean by that star?" Tariq asked.

"Something like that," Devren replied.

Liora heard a few chuckles at his response. She looked closer. Something seemed strange about the star. It should have been far larger considering the distance the monitor said was between the star and the Kratos; in fact, there was no way they could be that close to a real star.

"The star is the ship," she said, staring out the window.

Tariq glanced at her, then back at the screen. His eyes widened.

"How on Titus did you do that?"

"It's the same reason the Atlas was lost for so long," Devren replied. "It has a cloaking mechanism that reflects all surrounding light and gives off the same signature as a distant star. Stone said he thought his equipment was malfunctioning; they almost ran into it when they realized it was a ship."

Tariq leaned closer to the window. "That's incredible," he breathed."

"Stone, requesting permission to land," Hyrin said.

157

Stone's face appeared on the monitor. He was older than most of the Kratos crew, and his long dark hair had a white streak that ran from his forehead back. It gave him a grizzled, warrior's appearance. "Permission granted, Officer Hyrin. Welcome back. By our count, the rest of the Coalition and mercs followed your trail. That should give us some time to strategize."

"We know what the next course of action needs to be if we're going to get rid of the Omne Occasus," Devren told him. "I hope you don't mind if we borrow the Star Chaser."

The rebel's eyebrows lifted with interest. "Only if I come along."

"Deal," Devren replied.

Liora had trouble wrapping her mind around how big the SS Atlas was. The Diamond Albatross was the biggest ship ever built by the Coalition. Lost under mysterious circumstances and found by Stone years later and without the crew who had vanished as well, the Atlas loomed far above them as though the Kratos was a mere speck and the Albatross a whale in the vast ocean of space.

The huge doors of the cargo hold opened. Hyrin steered the Iron Falcon inside and landed the ship carefully next to Stone's Copper Crow. The doors closed and lighting flickered on, illuminating so much floor space sixty ships the size of the Kratos could have fit with ease.

Stone and several of his rebel comrades waited until the chamber pressurized, then entered the cargo hold. The Revolutionary leader gave the Kratos a critical look.

"You've had a bit of trouble," he commented.

"Our fair share," Devren replied, stepping down the loading ramp. "My crew will be up all night making repairs. Apparently the Coalition's upgraded our warrant from alive to preferably dead. They seemed to have no qualms about filling us full of holes."

"Welcome to the rebels," Stone told him.

"We're not rebels," Shathryn reminded him. She fluffed her purple hair so that it stood high above her head when she followed Devren down the ramp.

Liora and O'Tule walked down after them. O'Tule shot Liora a wide-eyed glance that said they were walking into trouble.

"That's right," Stone corrected himself with a wry smile. "You are Coalition officers just taking a hiatus from your duties by fleeing with the very galaxy imploder you were supposed to bring back to them."

Shathryn rolled her eyes at Stone. "We can't risk it getting into the wrong hands."

"Doesn't it worry you that the Coalition you give your allegiance to is the same one you're calling the wrong hands?" Stone shot back.

"Now you're twisting my words," Shathryn said. Her fingers were balled into fists.

Liora leaned against the Kratos' hull, convinced she was about to see the start of a very brutal war.

Stone raised his hands, cutting off Shathryn's argument before it began. "I'm not trying to get you upset, beautiful Shathryn. Please calm yourself. I'm merely pointing out that I would much rather have you on our side than against us. Perhaps this business with the Omne Occasus has happened for a greater reason than just the possible destruction of an entire galaxy at the hands of the Coalition or rebels."

Shathryn eyed him carefully. "Are you saying it happened to bring us together?"

Stone raised a shoulder and gave her a teasing smile. "Perhaps." He glanced behind her to Devren. "So you want my ship?"

Devren nodded. "We know a specialist on Titus that can analyze the Omne Occasus so we can figure out how to destroy it."

"And since landing the Kratos on Titus would be signing your own death warrant, you figure we can sneak the Omne Occasus to Titus on the Star Chaser," Stone concluded.

"Exactly," Devren said. "Do you have any problems with that?"

"None," Stone replied with a chuckle. "Except for the fact that my death warrants are even older than yours. I'm not sure landing with a bunch of rebels is your best idea, either."

Devren stared at him. "You have warrants out? That means...."

Stone nodded. "That I was once a Coalition officer like yourself. Sometimes, Captain, things aren't always what they seem."

Stone put his arm around Shathryn's shoulder and he walked with her across the wide cargo floor.

"Come on, Straham," O'Tule said, motioning toward the older officer. "Let's go explore. Maybe we can figure out where everyone disappeared to."

"Are we sure we want to know?" Straham asked, but he walked with her out the door.

Tariq wandered down the ramp to join Devren. "Don't worry," he told his friend. "You're just getting a glimpse of what our future might look like if we don't resolve this issue with the Coalition."

"Thanks," Devren replied dryly. "That's helpful."

"Just trying my best," Tariq said. He put his hands in his pockets and walked backwards in front of Devren. "Would being rebels be that bad?"

"Are you serious right now?" Devren asked, following his friend toward the door.

"I'm not sure," Tariq replied. "Things are changing. Not having an alliance has made me rethink a few facts. It seems we might not be fighting for what we thought we were."

Devren lowered his voice even though Liora was the only other person within earshot. "That's traitor talk. You need to button that up."

"Think about it," Tariq said.

"I don't need to think about it," Devren replied. He stormed out the door.

Tariq shook his head. He turned and glanced back at Liora. "What do you think?"

Surprised that the human was asking for her opinion, Liora thought for a moment. "I guess the path that makes sense is to join whichever side fights for what you believe in."

Tariq opened a hand as if conceding to her. "Yes, but what if neither is right?"

"Then maybe it's the fight that's wrong."

Tariq watched her for a moment. When he nodded, it was with a thoughtful expression. "You might have something there, Liora Day."

She turned back to the Kratos.

"Want to check out the Atlas?" Tariq offered.

Liora glanced back at him. "No, thank you. I've spent a lifetime on starships. I'd rather lose myself in a book."

"*The Count of Monte Cristo*?" he asked.

Liora nodded.

"Enjoy," Tariq told her. "Keep it as long as you want."

Liora walked back up the ramp to the Kratos. As much as the others were eager to explore the Coalition's lost Albatross, she longed for her quiet room and the book Tariq had lent to her what seemed like ages ago. She couldn't imagine anything that sounded better than stealing away into someone else's life upon a distant planet on the other end of the Macrocosm.

***

"I'm counting on the fact that these tags haven't been removed from the system," Hyrin told them.

"Are these from Verdan?" Tariq asked, taking one of the plastic cards the officer held out.

"Yes," Hyrin replied. "I thought they might come in handy."

"You get points for being resourceful," Devren told him. "Good job thinking ahead."

"Does it bother anyone else that we're using tags from the people we killed?" Shathryn asked. "I mean, what if they have ghosts attached to them or something." She lowered her voice and said dramatically, "They could be haunted."

Stone held up the one Hyrin had given him. "Don't worry, my dear. I'll protect you from the dead. My hope is that they have more important things to do than stalk pieces of plastic."

"What sort of things?" Shathryn asked, her gaze on the rebel.

"Wooing the one they didn't make time for while alive," he answered with a wink.

"Well, aren't you adorable," Shathryn said. She linked her arm through Stone's and his smile widened.

O'Tule took her card. "All I know is that the less time we spend with Tramareaus, the better. Is there a chance that he's not here?" No one could mistake the hope in her voice.

"He's here," Hyrin replied. "He answered my blink. He knows we're coming, but not why."

Liora walked behind Devren and Tariq. The two pushed the Omne Occasus hidden inside a cargo box on casters. She kept her hand near her knife in case anyone questioned their intentions, but given the rush of every member of mortalkind imaginable through the hallways and winding passages of Titus, she needn't have worried.

"I've never seen a place so full of people," she whispered to Tariq.

It was true. Regardless of all the circus shows on the thousands of planets Liora had been a part of, and the crowds those drew from all over the Macrocosm, she had never seen so many people in one place at the same time. Hordes of Gauls carried giant boxes containing who knows what through hallways so wide a dozen banta oxen could walk side by side and not scrape horns. Venticans, Belanites, and Talastans rushed past on their own business. The four-armed Arachnians kept to themselves while huge groups of Salamandons conversed as they walked.

Coalition officers hurried past without giving the small group from the Star Chaser a second glance. Liora felt for the first time how one could be surrounded by a thousand people, yet be completely alone. They could be at the center of attention, or ignored; there was no way of knowing. It set her on edge.

"We don't have far to go," Tariq reassured her. "The plan is to meet Hyrin in the Gladarian as soon as he's located Tramareaus."

"Ugh," Shathryn and O'Tule said at the same time.

Devren glanced back at them. "Do you have to do that every time someone says his name?"

"Yes," Shathryn replied. A shoulder bumped into hers. She continued on as if it didn't bother her. "He's loathsome, Captain. I would be happy to never see him again in my life. If it were up to me, I would change his name to Disgustingmareaus, and warn every girl in the Macrocosm to stay clear of him."

"Me, too," O'Tule echoed.

"Remind me not to get on your bad side," Stone said from behind the group.

Shathryn threw him a wink. "I don't think that's possible."

"I don't know what their problem is," Officer Straham said from his place next to the Omne Occasus. "Tramareaus seemed nice the last time we met."

It was apparently the completely wrong thing to say. Both girls huffed and whispered annoyed remarked back and forth for the next several minutes.

"Remind me to keep my mouth shut next time," Straham finally said.

"That usually works best for me," Tariq replied.

Stone chuckled. "With women, always know that perception is truth. If they feel that way about a man's character, it is true about him. You would be best not to contradict their opinion."

O'Tule set a hand on Shathryn's arm. "I knew I liked him for a reason.

They walked with the rushing crowd down the huge hall. Other hallways branched off with signs in several languages that told of armories, spacecraft parts, sundries, water storage, and atmosphere cleansers. Though huge chunks of the crowd wandered off down these halls, it didn't appear to make even a dent in the amount of people rushing forward. Liora kept a hand on the box to keep from getting separated from her crew.

The booming voice of an announcer sent a familiar chill down her spine.

"Coming up next, watch the faceoff between

Arachnians and the wielder of Zamarian steel. Lay your bets before the bell tolls. The strongest steel in the Macrocosm against sixteen limbs. It's a battle you can go an entire lifetime and never see again."

The thought of seeing people once more being shown off as creatures in cages doing tricks for the masses made Liora's stomach turn over. Even though she was away from the circus, it was hard to think of those still trapped within the greedy clutches of callers and owners looking to pad their pockets with as many bars as they could wring from an eager crowd.

Liora reluctantly followed the others into a long, low-ceilinged corridor. The sound of fighting ricocheted off the walls above the chaos of thousands of people bartering, betting, and swapping yarns about their travels.

Devren led the way to a table near the bars of a fence. The men carefully positioned the box beneath the table so it was out of the way of the crowd. Glancing down, Liora saw that they were at the edge of the fighting ring. Two stories below, four men and two women fought in a huge circle where purple moss covered the floor. Every type of mortalkind imaginable yelled at the humanoids as they battled inside the arena. A Ventican got stabbed in the stomach. He fell immediately to the ground, his body motionless.

"Don't worry," Devren told Liora, his smile warm. "Killing is not allowed in the Coalition's headquarters. They would lose far too many officers that way. Their weapons are dulled but tipped with a powerful sleep aid. Last one standing wins."

The thought that Devren was trying to protect her from seeing death was humorous to Liora. She cracked a smile. A glance to the left showed that Tariq was watching her with an amused expression of his own.

"It's barbaric," Officer Straham commented.

"It's amazing," Stone replied. "There's nothing quite like the rush that comes from being cheered or booed by thousands of spectators, your comrades at your back and the chance to win hundreds of platinum bars."

Shathryn stared at him. "You've been down there?"

Stone nodded. "A few times." At her wide-eyed look, he shrugged. "What can I say? I'm a warrior at heart."

She put her arm through his and leaned her head against his shoulder. "The more I learn about you, the less I want to leave your side."

Stone's cheek twitched as if the touch of her purple hair tickled his skin. "I'm not sorry to hear that," he told her.

Liora leaned closer to the fence. Men and women all around the circle leaned over yelling and throwing things from the second floor to the ground as they goaded the fighters on. A glance up revealed so many other levels that it made Liora dizzy to look at them all.

"Heads up," Tariq said. He grabbed Liora's shoulder and pulled her back just as a black boot fell past them to the arena floor.

One of the gladiators grabbed the boot and threw it at a female Crustacite. She caught it in her clawed hand and chucked it back hard enough to knock him off his feet.

"Maybe they don't need the sleeping aid," Officer Straham noted.

Liora and Tariq watched two other humanoids fall. The two left standing waved at the crowd and bowed. Members of the audience threw taffala petals and cherook feathers. The white and purple objects floated down in a gentle rainstorm.

"Gaveria and Talan from Hoarth have taken the match," the announcer proclaimed. "Collect your winnings. Betting is now closed for the Zamarian against the Arachnians. Warriors, take your positions."

Devren pushed his transmitter button.

"Hyrin says they're on the way," he informed them. "All we have to do is lay low so we don't attract the attention of any officers who might recognize us."

"Liora Day."

The voice boomed from the arena.

Liora's heart slowed. She looked behind her at the Gladarian's floor. The Zamarian armed for battle glared up at her. He looked vaguely familiar. Liora searched her memory.

"Liora, who is that?" Tariq asked.

"They're coming," Officer Straham said with panic in his voice. "We're drawing attention."

"They're going to find us out," O'Tule whispered with an edge of hysteria.

"You killed my mother," the Zamarian shouted.

The realization of who called her name hit Liora hard. She stared down at the Zamarian whose mother had shown her kindness and given her the Ventican clothing on Gaulded Zero Twenty-one, the Gaulded Chief Obruo had blown up in his search for her.

Liora put a hand on the top bar.

"What are you doing?" Tariq asked.

She could feel the gazes of the advancing Coalition officers. If the Zamarian continued to shout, they would be all over the group. There would be no chance of hiding the Omne Occasus.

Liora vaulted over the railing.

Chapter 14

Purple chalky powder rose from the moss-covered floor of the Gladarian arena when Liora's landed with her knees bent and hands at the ready in case the Zamarian attacked.

"Zran," Liora said.

Blue streaks marked the Zamarian's face and ran down his hands in the marking of his people. He gripped the katana he held so tightly his knuckles turned white.

"I've searched the Macrocosm for you, Liora," he growled.

"This is unprecedented," the announcer's voice echoed through the Gladarian. "We've never had a contestant join a fight from the stands. Betting will reopen for the next three minutes."

"I heard about what Obruo did to the Gaulded," Liora began.

"To our home," Zran shot back.

"To your home," Liora conceded. "I'm so sorry."

"There's an exciting update to our match," the announcer said with awe in his voice. "If I'm not mistaken, our new contestant is a Damaclan! We've never had a member of that most violent of races in our ring. The betting odds have been increased. Give us a moment to balance the match."

Zran took a step forward. Liora kept her gaze on the center of his chest in case he decided to attack without warning.

"My mother was killed because of you. She trusted you," Zran spat.

"You were right to warn her about me," Liora replied. "But I didn't kill her. I am truly sorry for her death."

Zran's eyes narrowed. "It's too late now. She always took pity on the oppressed. Look where that got her."

"It wasn't her fault Obruo set the bomb," Liora pointed out.

"It was yours," Zran shot back. "You deserve to pay for her death."

"Due to the addition of another opponent, we've added a surprise," the announcer called. "Noble audience, my finely feathered, furred, scaled, or skinned friends, prepare for our four Arachnian warriors along with the addition of something we were waiting to save for the finale, but has been called upon for this fine occasion.

Welcome the maned chenowik from the planet Supmut!"

A rumble of surprise came from the audience. Liora glanced up to see men and women pressed against the railings on every level of the Gladarian. She met Tariq's gaze.

Though she couldn't hear his voice above the commotion of the crowd, she clearly read "Get out of there," on his lips when he said it.

The wide doors at the opposite end of the arena opened.

"You had to jump down here, didn't you?" Zran demanded.

Liora glared at him. "You called me out. I had no choice."

"Oh, the poor Damaclan," Zran shot back. "What's going to happen to her?"

The four Arachnians with their customary swords in each of their four hands stalked across the moss. Those who had bet for them cheered and yelled the names of their favorite warriors.

"Why are you here?" Liora asked.

"What else is there?" Zran replied, his voice thick with hatred. "You took everything from me."

"Obruo took everything from you just like he's trying to do to me," Liora told him. "I didn't even know he was still alive when I left the Gaulded."

The announcer's voice echoed through the arena, "Just a reminder to the audience, while the Arachnians' weapons are tipped with our special knockout aid, nobody has control over the chenowik. It is one of the deadliest creatures this side of the Holmberg Two Galaxy."

Liora and Zran both shifted their gaze to the last

open door. The Arachnians moved carefully along the arena wall away from the dark hole. A form moved inside. A clack of claws sounded and the creature stepped out.

Audience members gasped and moved back from the rails. Liora took an inadvertent step back and saw Zran do the same. He muttered something in a language she didn't recognize and raised his katana. He glanced at her.

"Are you planning to fight, or are you going to run away again?"

Liora drew the knife from her sheath.

Zran rolled his eyes. "Great. I feel much safer now."

Liora narrowed her gaze. "There's a reason Obruo blew up an entire Gaulded trying to kill me."

Zran's mouth shut. He blew out a breath from his nose and took another step back when the chenowik cleared the door.

The creature towered above the Arachnians. Captured from Supmut, the chenowik had the ability to swim or walk on its four clawed, finned feet. The animal dripped with a slimy green ooze that made the moss hiss when the beast lumbered forward. The same slime hung from each corner of its toothy mouth. Long, skinny fangs protruded in all directions. Its sides were huge and covered in sweeping spikes. Liora couldn't tell if they were hard or flexible. She didn't want to get close enough to find out.

"I never thought I'd depend on a Damaclan in battle," Zran muttered. He glanced at her. "This means nothing. You die as soon as this is over if that beast doesn't kill you first."

"Good luck with that," Liora replied flatly.

Liora and Zran paced slowly backwards. The chenowik's attention was on the Arachnians. They kept together and barely gave Liora and Zran a glance.

Zran was silent for a moment, then said, "Do we go after the Arachnians or the beast first?"

Surprised by his question, Liora glanced at him. "I thought you've done this before."

He gestured toward the chenowik. "Not *this* before. I'm pretty sure no humanoid has done this before. This is insane."

Liora nodded. "I agree." At his incredulous look, she said, "The Arachnians are our greater concern. If they knock us out, we'll be prey to the chenowik. Keep them between us and the creature, eliminate them first, then turn our attention to the walking balloon fish."

At Zran's incredulous snort, Liora realized Tariq's sarcasm might have worked into her speech.

She made her way to the wall. "Keep behind me. I'll handle them."

"The only thing I have left is my pride," Zran replied. "I can fight for myself, thank you very much."

He pushed past her with his katana raised. Liora gritted her teeth and followed.

Zran didn't flinch when three of the Arachnians turned at their approach. The Zamarian pulled a second blade from the sheath on his back and attacked.

There were so many blades flashing in the bright arena lights that it was hard to keep track of who swung what. The Arachnians had Zran backed against the wall before Liora could reach them. The chenowik quickened its pace and the drool from its multi-fanged mouth increased in anticipation of the feast.

As fast as the Zamarian was, he had no chance of blocking so many blades. Liora knew her odds of besting the chenowik would increase with him at her side. She had to help him before the Arachnians knocked him out with their treated blades.

Liora had no qualms about killing Arachnians who attacked her, but the rules of the game were supposed to save their lives. The placement of the chenowik blurred those rules, but she decided to stick to them.

Liora let out a yell to catch their attention. It worked almost better than she hoped. Two of the Arachnians who had attacked Zran bore down on her with blades flashing. Liora blocked one after the other, grateful for the reflexes of a Damaclan that allowed her to track the swords.

A scream echoed across the arena. Shouts from the audience followed. Liora glanced over to see the chenowik bite down on one of the Arachnians near Zran. A blade stuck through the beast's gaping top lip, but it didn't appear to notice. The thin fangs tore the Arachnian apart. His arms flailed weakly, then stopped moving altogether. The chenowik put one clawed fin foot on the humanoid and dug into the Aranchian's chest with relish.

Liora didn't have to best the Arachnians at swordplay, she only had to find an opening and let the treated blades do the work. She ducked, blocked, and found her opening. Her knife darted out. The point caught the left Arachnian's arm just below her wrist. She let out a shriek and dropped her sword. Liora ducked under the other Arachnian's slice and scooped up the treated weapon. She stabbed the first Arachnian in the shoulder, spun and blocked two other jabs, and sunk the blade into the second Arachnian's thigh. Both warriors dropped to the ground.

Liora grabbed up another blade and strode toward Zran. The chenowik gave a satisfied slurp and ambled toward the Zamarian and his attacker. Zran blocked and stabbed. His eyes darted toward the creature's advance and the Arachnian's blade almost took him in the throat.

The cheers and calls of the crowd were deafening. The fact that they had enjoyed the Arachnian's death at the claws of the chenowik bothered Liora. She couldn't say why it did, but it angered her. Rage pulsed at the edges of her thoughts. She glared from the Arachnian to the chenowik.

The chenowik's eyes rolled from the fierce battle between the two warriors to the Arachnians who lay still where Liora had left them. Choosing the lesser danger, the huge beast shuffled forward. Liora was torn. She could rescue Zran from the Arachnian and turn her back to the others for the chenowik to eat, or rescue the four-armed humanoids who would no doubt have left her to die.

Liora made a split-second decision. Zran appeared to be holding his own. If Liora didn't stop the creature, it wouldn't matter if Zran won his battle or not; they would both be eaten. Besides, she might be a killer, but she wasn't about to watch a creature devour two helpless Arachnians she was responsible for sending to the ground.

Liora picked up another treated sword and advanced toward the creature. The roar from the crowd increased. A dozen different languages rained down on her. She twirled the swords to get a feel for their weight. The chenowik's eyes locked on her. Its spikes bristled. Liora had a feeling there wasn't much flexibility to them. Given the amount of spikes and fangs around its face and body, she would have to be very careful to aim her swords where they would actually hurt the creature.

Liora ran forward. She faked to the left, then lunged

to the right and slammed a sword through a small break between the chenowik's spikes. She had forgotten that the blades had been dulled for the arena battle. The sword bounced off the chenowik's thick skin, jarring Liora's arm and sending her to the ground.

The chenowik pounced. Its claws scrabbled against her sides and its weight pressed down on her with suffocating slime. The crowd's shouts came dully to her ears. Liora lost her grip on the other sword. She struggled to reach her knife. The blade slipped from the sheath. She grabbed it and thrust upward.

The chenowik let out a strangled cry and stumbled backward; the knife tore through its soft, unprotected underbelly. Its retreat opened the wound further. Entrails bulged out. Liora rolled clear and rose to her feet. She knew not to let the creature gain its bearings. It let out angry, guttural cries and continued to retreat when she advanced toward it.

It opened its mouth in a growl of protest. Strands of flesh from its recent Arachnian meal hung from its long fangs. Liora looked for another opening. Footsteps sounded behind her, then Zran was at her side.

"How do we flip it?" he asked.

Liora glanced around them. There was nothing in the arena that would help their fight. The chenowik leaned heavily to the side and trailed blood with its retreat.

"We have to take out its legs on the right side," Liora told Zran.

"I've got the back," he replied.

He jogged around wide enough to keep the creature's attention on Liora. She moved warily to the left. The chenowik chomped its teeth and followed. It was daunting to look up into the huge, gaping mouth. Liora saw a severed hand caught between its spikey back teeth.

The creature let out a bellow. As soon as it turned to attack Zran, Liora darted beneath its spikes and stabbed deep into its front right foot. The chenowik's leg collapsed and it rolled faster than she could escape. Liora ducked and felt the spikes press against her back. Amazingly, the Ventican cloth of the outfit Zran's mother had given her kept the spikes from piercing through. The chenowik rolled onto its back completely and Liora was free.

The cheers from the arena rose so loud the ground shook as she leaped on top of the chenowik and stabbed her knife deep into its belly. She ripped downward and opened its stomach. The chenowik let out a gurgle; its head rolled back and slime poured from its mouth.

Liora jumped down. She spotted Zran on his knees a few feet behind the creature. He clutched his arm and blood colored his chest. She reached his side and held out a hand. Zran gave her a searching look.

"It doesn't bring your mother back, but I'm alive because of her," she said quietly. "There are very few people who will show kindness to a Damaclan. I wish she had listened when you warned her away from me."

Zran surprised her by grabbing her hand and letting her help him to his feet.

"If she had listened to me and turned you away, she wouldn't have been my mother," he replied.

She ducked under his arm and helped him toward the door that opened at the end of the arena. Purple cherook feathers and white taffala petals fell like rain into the arena. All manner of mortalkind cheered from the stands for the two warriors. The sound was deafening. Liora couldn't decide how she felt about being applauded for killing the chenowik. It reminded her too much of her clan's approval when she killed Vogun and gained her status as a clan member.

Men in gray suits rushed out with stretchers to collect the fallen Arachnians. She wondered how they would remove the slain chenowik with its belly torn open.

Her unspoken question was answered when three Kelnians walked by with devourers on chains. The six-legged, scaled creatures scurried forward as fast as their handlers would let them. The scent of blood brought screeches of excitement from the small devourers. The Kelnians, known as the erasers of the Macrocosm, appeared nonchalant about taking their pets to eat the chenowik. Liora knew the snout-toothed creatures would have the chenowik eaten in a matter of minutes. They would return nearly quadruple their size and sleep contentedly for the next month in the artificial lairs made by their handlers.

"If that was you or I, they would have no qualms about eating us as well," Zran pointed out with a disgusted expression. "You'd expect humanoids to have an ounce of moral decency, but you know what they say; never trust a Kelnian with your family."

"Unless that family's Obruo," Liora replied. She regretted the words as soon as they left her mouth.

Zran stared at her. "Obruo's your family?" His voice lowered with realization, "And he tried to blow you up? You're right. Maybe I'd take the Kelnians."

Men in stripped suits and with strange skullcap hats came up to them when they walked through the door.

"Congratulations," the one with the black skullcap said. "You've won!"

"Nobody thought you would beat the maned

178

chenowik," a second told them with a grin as he shut the door behind them.

"Of course not," another said.

"Nobody ever beats a chenowik," one echoed from the back.

"So who would have thought you would take the bowl," the first said.

"The bowl?" Zran repeated.

"The stakes, the winnings, the bowl," the man in the black skullcap explained. "You two took the cake, the total, the entire profits, and since you won without the Arachnians, you don't have to split it with anyone. Congratulations!"

The man shoved a heavy canvas bag into Liora's hands. They went through another hearty round of congratulations, then disappeared back up the wide, highly-lit hallway.

Zran's eyebrows pulled together. "What just happened?"

"I'm not sure," Liora replied.

She set the pack on the ground and unzipped it. The amount of bars inside made both of them stare.

"Are those iridium?" Zran asked.

Liora hefted one. "Looks like it."

Zran whistled. "We're rich."

Liora shook her head. "You're rich. I don't need it. Besides, I owe you."

"You saved my life from that chenowik," Zran pointed out. "You don't owe me."

"Just the same, it's yours." She gestured to his arm. "But you need to get that taken care of."

A small door Liora hadn't noticed in the side of the hallway opened and two little pink-skinned women in starched white jumpsuits came out. Each woman wore a hat bearing the red H that marked the healthcare field.

"At your service, madam and monsieur," they said at the same time.

"I'm fine," Liora told them. "He needs the help."

"Throwing me to the chenowiks?" Zran asked.

Liora smiled at the reference. "We beat that one already. They can't be that bad."

Zran eyed the two women who waited motionlessly by their door. "I'm not so sure about that."

"Where will you go after this?" Liora asked.

Zran didn't meet her gaze. "I'm not so sure about that, either."

The way he stood there holding his bleeding arm with a lost expression on his face made Liora's heart go out to him.

"Come find me after they patch you up. My crew has some business here, but we'll be taking off as soon as we can. Find the Star Chaser at the loading docks, but be quiet about it."

Zran eyed her. "Am I sure this is something I want to get in the middle of?"

Liora shrugged with a tip of her head toward the pack she held. "Either way, I've got your winnings. Find the ship and you can decide from there."

Zran gave in. "Fair enough."

Liora left him in the hands of the two women. She crossed the hallway to the wide door at the end. Cheers ran through the crowd again as another group of warriors were selected for battle. Their shouts and jeers echoed along the hall. Anxious to be away from it all, Liora pushed the button beside the door. It slid open.

"What on earth were you thinking?" Tariq said the

moment she appeared. He grabbed her shoulders and pushed her against the wall. "Are you crazy? What made you thinking jumping into the arena pit in the Gladarian was smart? Or did you think at all?"

The battle rage from fighting the chenowik still simmered beneath the surface of Liora's self-control. Tariq's anger set it free.

Liora slid her hand over the top of his arms, grabbed his right wrist, and twisted while she pushed down to break his hold. Maintaining her grip on his wrist, she ducked under his arm, punched him twice in the right kidney, ducked back the other way, and used her momentum to throw him over her back to the ground. She put a foot on his chest and glared down at him.

"You forget yourself," she snarled.

Tariq stared up at her.

Liora fought back the urge to knock him out with a punch to the jaw for good measure. She took a steeling breath and turned away. Scooping up the canvas bag she had dropped, Liora stormed up the hallway in the only direction it led.

Chapter 15

Tramareaus was completely the opposite of what Liora was expecting. When she entered the room Tariq silently led her to, the Artidus man with dark skin gave her a graceful bow. His third arm swept the top hat from his head and when he smiled up at her, Liora found herself captivated by his seemingly bottomless dark eyes.

"My lady," he said with a lilting accent. "You must be Liora Day. I've heard a great deal about you."

Unsettled, Liora glanced at Devren and Hyrin. Both were busy studying the exposed Omne Occasus. Hyrin was saying something quietly Liora couldn't hear. Shathryn and O'Tule stood in the opposite corner. Shathryn's arms were crossed over her chest and she appeared to be in a deep discussion with her friend. Stone waited a few feet away as though concerned by the direction of their discussion.

"As you can see, we've come to a bit of difficulty," Tramareaus continued, "Come this way and allow me to explain."

Liora walked with him to the Omne Occasus. Devren glanced up and his face filled with relief.

"Liora, thank goodness. What were you thinking when you jumped off that rail?"

Liora let out a breath. "Tariq already lectured me. I get it. What else did you want me to do? If I had waited a few seconds longer, every officer in the Gladarian would have been at your table to investigate why there was a Damaclan in the crowd. The Omne Occasus would have been uncovered, and your entire crew would be in holding right now. I had to act."

"Our table."

Liora studied Devren. "What?"

"You said your table. It was our table. You are a part of us, Liora. And we have a right to worry when one of our own jumps over a railing to brawl with who-knows-what in the arena. It was foolhardy."

Devren's softer tone broke through Liora's defensive attitude. "It was," she admitted.

"If I can be so bold as to interrupt," Tramareaus said, "I'll continue the breakdown of our situation."

"Please continue," Hyrin replied.

The Talastan's eyes blinked sideways rapidly, telling of his nervousness. Liora steeled herself for whatever

Tramareaus would say.

The Artidus gave her a charming smile and clasped his hands behind his back. "As I was saying, this bomb is made out of two kinds of energy that I have heard of but never seen before." He pointed at the red orb inside the transparent box. "Using several different spectroscopic instruments, I've been able to measure the intensity and frequency of the energy these orbs are giving off. According to my research, the red orb is an energy called Feren. It's a hot energy that requires extreme amounts of liquid to annihilate it. This blue orb is Bilar. It's a cold energy annihilated only by a very concentrated sum of volts in amounts I can only begin to imagine."

Tramareaus frowned and ran his free hand down his face to smooth his goatee.

"Each orb by itself is highly unstable. If the vial was to break and the orbs to touch, an explosion the size of this galaxy would most definitely wipe out anything within. Great care needs to be taken in destroying the orbs individually. As I was telling your captain, I am unsure who designed this weapon and what type of metal they are using. It is something I've never seen before." He paused, then said in a softer voice, "And I hope to never see it again." He looked at Devren. "You were right to hide this."

"I keep telling myself that," Devren replied. He held out a hand. "Thank you for your help. We'll do what we need to."

Tramareaus shook it. "Good luck." He walked with them to the door and held it open when Hyrin and Stone pushed the crate out.

The girls barely glanced at him when they walked by. Tariq followed, then Liora.

Tramareaus gave her another sweeping bow. "My lady, it was a pleasure to make your acquaintance. Good luck on this and all endeavors throughout the Macrocosm. Take care of the Kratos crew."

"I will," she said. She stepped into the hallway with an unexplainable smile on her face.

Devren gave her a questioning look.

"I don't see why everyone thinks he's that bad," she said with an embarrassed shrug.

Shathryn and O'Tule spun in unison to face her.

"Oh, just you wait," Shathryn said. "He might seem charming now, but he's like that with all the women. He'll capture your heart, then leave it to bleed out on the floor while he woos some yellow-haired Talastan from Gaulded Two Zero Seven." She turned back around and stormed up the hall, her booted footsteps echoing.

O'Tule patted Liora's arm sympathetically. "It was a hard week," she whispered to Liora. "She got over him when she met a handsome Ventican, but she's the queen at holding a grudge."

"Good to know," Liora replied.

They reached a main hall and fell in with the rushing crowd. Everyone huddled close to the Omne Occasus disguised in the crate. Knowing the volatility of the energy inside set Liora on edge. The others' expressions showed that they felt the same way.

"He's got to be here," a woman called. Her frantic voice carried over the crowd. "Harriman Trun. His keycard was used. He has to be around here somewhere." Her voice cracked. "I told them he was still alive. He just has to be."

Hyrin's eyes widened and he looked back at Tariq. "Hide your card, now!"

Tariq slid the keycard into his pocket.

"I have to use it to get out to the docks," he said. "It'll trigger her again."

"Why is it triggering her at all?" O'Tule asked.

"She must be the officer's wife," Hyrin said, his voice level.

The realization that she was looking for an officer who was killed on Verdan struck Liora hard. The woman stood on a raised vent on the side of the wide hallway. Her eyes scanned the crowd with frantic intensity.

"Where are you, Harri?" the woman asked. Tears streamed down her face and she clutched a uniform shirt to her chest.

"If she contacts the authorities, they might put an alert out for the rest of the officers killed on Verdan," Hyrin said. "We've got to get off Titus, now!"

"We'll split up," Devren suggested. "Stone, Shathryn, go with Tariq. Give us five minutes to reach the docks and get the Star Chaser fired up, then hurry through. We'll be ready to leave the second you show up."

"Sounds good," Tariq replied. "Except there's one flaw to your plan."

Devren looked at him. "What?"

Tariq motioned past his friend. "Them."

A glance forward showed at least two dozen armed officers standing before the gates to the loading docks. They asked for keycards and checked the humanoids before allowing them to pass through.

"What's this about?" a Terrarian with huge glasses asked.

"Standard inspection," an officer in red replied. He held out a hand. "Keycard."

When the Terrarian handed it over, the officer

scanned the keycard. A hologram face surfaced on the officer's reader. He looked from it to the Terrarian.

"Go on through," he said with a nod.

The Terrarian accepted the keycard and walked between the gates.

"We aren't getting out that way," Devren said.

"Isn't it the only way out?" O'Tule asked.

"Yes," Hyrin replied.

"I'll draw them away."

Everyone looked at Tariq.

"Do I want to know how?" Devren asked.

Tariq shook his head. "Plausible deniability."

He took off through the crowd in the opposite direction. At Devren's orders, everyone moved to the wall to wait for whatever opportunity Tariq was about to give them.

"I hate it when he does that," Devren muttered.

"He's brave," Stone noted.

"He's alright," Shathryn replied, her arm looped through the rebel leader's.

"Where is he going?" Liora asked Devren.

"If I know Tariq, he's going to trigger the keycard somewhere at the other end of the complex. Hopefully it'll send all the officers on a search and we'll be able to sneak through," Devren replied.

"Then how does Tariq get back?" Liora asked.

"That's my job," Hyrin answered. "Get me to my computers and I can crash the command center. Without them, we're sitting tarlons." The Talastan shook his head. "I hate being away from my computers."

Sirens sounded and lights flashed above the gates. The officers' monitors beeped at the same time.

"Yes, sir," they responded almost in unison. The

group took off through the crowd, leaving only one officer next to the gate to man the station.

"My turn," Shathryn said.

She strode forward and Devren motioned for the others to inch behind. Shathryn reached the officer and gave him a big smile.

"Well, aren't you cute?" she asked.

The gilled Salamandon blushed noticeably. "I don't know if I'd say that."

"Of course you should," she continued. She leaned against him and took off his hat. "Although it's too bad you have to wear this to shade your beautiful eyes."

"They're orange," the Salamandon said. "I thought they creeped people out." His gills opened and closed quickly on either side of his neck.

"They don't creep me out," she replied. "Is there any chance I could steal a few minutes of your time?"

"W-what did you have in mind?" the Salamandon officer asked.

Shathryn motioned behind her for the crew to sneak though. The officer glanced back, but she turned his face to her again.

"Something like this," she said.

Shathryn planted a big kiss on the Salamandon's lips as Devren and the Kratos crew hurried through the gates. Stone's expression was confused when O'Tule pulled him past.

"Don't worry," O'Tule whispered. "She's acting. Shathryn loves to act."

The crew reached the Star Chaser and carried the Omne Occasus inside. Each of them double-checked the ties that kept the crate from sliding in the cargo hold. After the conversation with Tramareaus, it felt as though they loaded their own doom back onto the ship.

"He's heading for the gate," Hyrin was saying when Liora reached the Copper Crow's small bridge.

"Will it work?" Devren asked, watching the screen intently.

"It'll still say Harriman Trun, but it should show Tariq's picture. With any luck, he'll be on board before they put two and two together," Hyrin replied.

O'Tule leaned over his shoulder. "Is that the picture they'll see?"

"Yes."

"He looks mad," she noted.

Liora smothered a smile at the image on Hyrin's screen. Tariq had his arms cross and glared as if he wished he was anywhere else than having his picture taken.

"I remember that," Devren commented with a grin. "That was the day my father told him he was promoted."

"He didn't like that?" Liora asked.

Devren shook his head. "Our chief medical officer got the boot when we found him shooting up with the meds instead of using them to treat the crew. With the promotion, Tariq was the youngest chief medic in the history of the Coalition. It was a lot of pressure."

"Not as much as he'll get if he's caught going through the gate," Hyrin said.

Everyone watched the monitor in silence. Over the camera Hyrin had tapped, they saw an exhausted looking Tariq approach the gate. Someone else was with him. Liora realized with surprise that it was Zran, bandaged and looking as grim as Tariq as if he knew the risk they faced.

Fortunately, the Salamandon officer appeared frazzled

after his encounter with Shathryn. His hat was skewed, and her red lipstick still colored the side of his long, thin mouth.

"He tasted like fish," Shathryn said. She winked at Stone. "You're a much better kisser."

"I'm glad to hear it," he told her.

"I'm not," O'Tule replied. "Gross."

Tariq and Zran wordlessly handed the Salamandon their cards. He scanned them with his wrist monitor and barely glanced at the hologram faces that appeared. He waved them through.

Tariq and Zran were halfway across the docks when the alarm sounded. Both men took off running. The Salamandon answered his monitor. His eyes widened and he ran through the gate after them.

Chapter 16

"I can't believe we pulled that off," Tariq said.

"That was a close one," Zran agreed. "I didn't figure I'd fall in with rebels when I left Titus."

"We aren't really rebels," O'Tule pointed at.

At Zran's questioning look, Liora explained, "There's still hope that the Coalition might pardon the crew once we get things resolved."

"Are you sure?" Zran's question hung in the air.

"We're not rebels," Shathryn echoed, but without her usual bite when someone mentioned it. She was too busy

191

gazing longingly in the direction of the Star Chaser that followed on their starboard side.

They were back in the Kratos. The crew sat in the mess hall preparing to eat Jarston's most recent invention.

O'Tule eyed the red soup with uncertainty. "How do I know this soup is safe to eat?" she asked loudly to change the subject.

"Of course it's safe," the cook called from the kitchen. "It's not like you can be poisoned by steamed manikoma in nukmuk sauce."

"Are you sure?" Shathryn asked.

"There's one way to find out," Zran said. "I'm hungry enough to risk poisoning at this point."

O'Tule laughed, then covered her mouth as if surprised such a sound had come out of it.

Zran smiled at her and took a bite of his soup. Everyone watched him with careful scrutiny.

"As much as I want to dramatically fall off this chair and fake dying, I can't do it," Zran admitted. "This soup is way too good."

"I like him," Jarston called out. "He can stay."

"You say that about anyone who likes your cooking," O'Tule replied.

"Exactly," Jarston said, poking his head from the kitchen window. "If they like my cooking, they must have good taste. We need more people with good taste aboard this starship."

Zran chuckled. "I can't argue with his logic."

Liora lifted a spoonful of the soup. She had yet to try anything from Jarston that wasn't amazing, so she wasn't surprised when the savory herbs and spices from distant planets filled her mouth with a refreshing, filling flavor.

"Where were you off to after Titus?" she asked Zran.

"Or were you planning to fight in the Gladarian for the rest of your life?"

"I'm really not sure," Zran replied frankly. "After I lost my mother, I sort of lost my path, too."

"That's horrible; we were devastated to hear about Obruo blowing up the Gaulded," O'Tule said. "All those poor people. How did you escape?"

Zran's gaze found the floor. "I had been trying to get my mother to leave for a long time, but she felt having a home on the Gaulded gave her the opportunity to help those in need."

Liora's heart gave a remorseful beat.

"I couldn't take it anymore," Zran continued. "I told her I was going to Titus to earn enough to buy us an apartment on a homestead ship." His grip on his spoon tightened. "I had just landed when I heard about Gaulded Zero Twenty-one being blown up by a Damaclan."

Everyone's eyes went to Liora. Hyrin and Devren entered the room, ending further conversation.

"We're on course for the water planet of Gliese," Devren told them. "It's one of the largest ocean planets on record. Hopefully there's enough water to absorb the energy from the red orb."

Hyrin took a seat next to Liora. "Exactly," he said. "Tramareaus," he ignored the sounds of disgust from O'Tule and Shathryn, "Said we need extreme amounts of liquid to destroy the hot Feren energy. I can't think of more liquid than a water planet."

"Will it destroy the planet?" O'Tule asked.

"We're not sure," Hyrin replied with less certainty.

"Better than an entire galaxy," Shathryn said.

"Unless you live on that planet," Zran pointed out quietly.

Liora felt the ship shudder. Everyone looked at each other.

The intercom buzzed. "Captain, we're under attack!" Duncan called out.

"On our way," Devren replied.

The crew jumped up and ran from the mess hall toward the bridge. Another explosion hit, knocking them against the wall.

"Why is this beginning to feel familiar?" Tariq asked before he ducked into the medical wing.

"Don't get used to it," Devren shouted after him.

"Then shoot back," Tariq called over his shoulder.

They reached the bridge just behind Hyrin. The technical specialist pressed a button and the screen revealed four Coalition starships bearing down on them.

"They appeared out of nowhere," Officer Straham said. "We had no warning. They began firing without even trying to contact us."

"They must have followed the Star Chaser without us knowing," Devren said. "We led them right to the Kratos."

"We have to get to the Kansas transporter," Shathryn reported, her voice tight. "It's our only chance."

Four missiles lit up the screen.

"Those are the new high impact heat signature tracers," Hyrin told Devren. "They're not messing around here."

"O'Tule, full power to the shields. We can't outmaneuver those."

"Already done, Captain," O'Tule replied.

"Duncan, tell the crew to brace for impact," Devren ordered.

Duncan's voice spoke over the intercom. Liora could

imagine Lieutenant Argyle's engine crew rushing for safety. Shathryn pushed a button and the warning sirens sounded.

"Hyrin, answer in kind."

Hyrin pushed several buttons on his screen and two missiles fired. Two others left from the Star Chaser just visible on their starboard side.

Everyone watched the missiles in silence. With no way to avoid them, the impending explosion filled the air with tension. O'Tule grabbed Shathryn's hand. Shathryn's gaze stayed on the window where the blunt nose of the Star Chaser could be seen.

"Four, three, two," Hyrin called out.

The impact struck them to the front and the right side, rocking the starship hard. Crew members were thrown to the ground. Sirens went off and the lights darkened on the bridge.

"Emergency lighting," Devren called out. He stood shakily. Blood dripped down the side of his face from a gash on his brow.

Hyrin held his bleeding lip where it had struck the monitor. Liora helped Duncan up. The older officer climbed shakily back to his seat.

"Shathryn?" O'Tule said.

Shathryn lay motionless on the ground.

"Shath?" O'Tule repeated more urgently.

"Call Tariq," Devren commanded. "Officer Straham, take over Shathryn's duties. I need to know the status of our ship. Hyrin, report."

Hyrin typed frantically on his keyboard, but the monitors didn't respond.

"Electronics have been damaged," Hyrin said. "I can't give us a visual."

"Switch the screen to real view," Devren said.

Hyrin pushed several buttons, but the front screen stayed blank.

"Incoming," O'Tule said from where she knelt on the floor with Shathryn's head pillowed in her lap. "Liora, can you get that?"

Liora hurried to O'Tule's seat. She pressed the alert O'Tule indicated. A fuzzy transmission of Stone's face appeared on the small screen above O'Tule's station.

"Are you guys alright?" he asked, his voice cracking.

Unsure what to say, Liora looked back at Devren.

"We're hit hard," Devren replied. "We've lost our monitors. We're blind here."

"We're not much better off," Stone said. "But our monitors work. I'll send you a patch. Hold on."

Liora selected the incoming transmission. The monitor showed what was in front of them from a side viewpoint. The four Coalition ships were much closer. More missiles sped toward the Kratos.

"Hold on," Devren called out.

The impact of the missiles on the monitor showed pieces of the hull tearing away. Explosions shot out, then vanished in space's void. A panel of metal drifted off. Steam vented along with a stream of liquid.

Inside the Kratos, the warning sirens stopped entirely. The emergency lighting flickered, revealing crew members jammed against the wall and beneath monitors. The scent of electrical smoke filled the air.

"Report," Devren croaked from the floor to the left of his chair.

Liora and Hyrin pulled back to their seats. The door to the bridge slid open. Tariq appeared looking in the same shape as the bridge crew. He held his left side and limped in.

"Who needs help first?" he asked.

"Shathryn," O'Tule and Duncan said immediately.

Tariq met Liora's gaze. She saw the pain he contained. He gave a nod as if relieved to see her up. When he knelt beside Shathryn, she heard the catch in his breath.

"They're sending up a curvator," Hyrin said; astonishment and horror colored his voice.

"Shields are down completely," Liora reported from her flickering monitor.

"Are they planning to blow up the Omne Occasus with the Kratos?" Devren asked. "That would destroy us all."

"Maybe they don't believe we have it," Hyrin replied. "Brace yourselves." There were tears in the Talastan's eyes and when he blinked, they slid down his cheeks.

"Get out of there," Stone demanded. His image and voice flickered off and on. "Or we're all done for!"

Lieutenant Argyle's voice came over the intercom. "Thrusters are down. We're losing hydraulic fluid faster than I can fill it."

"Give us anything you can," Devren replied.

"We're sitting tarlons," Argyle told the captain.

"We can't move," Devren reported to Stone. He paused, then said, "Thank you for the support you've shown. You've been a true friend. Get to the transporter before the curvator hits the Kratos."

Stone's eyes narrowed. "You're not getting out of this that easy. You disable the Omne Occasus and save this galaxy. That's an order, Captain."

His monitor went blank.

"The curvator is on its descent," Hyrin said, his voice

thick with emotion. "Crew, brace for impact."

O'Tule reached up and grabbed Liora's hand. She and Tariq hunched over Shathryn to shield her from the blast. Devren pulled up to his captain chair and sat, his gaze on the screen above Hyrin's station. Hyrin gripped the arms of his chair so hard his yellow hands turned white.

"This is it," he said. A tear splashed onto his keyboard.

Movement out the window caught Liora's gaze.

"The Star Chaser," she said.

Shathryn's eyes flickered open.

Devren rose to his feet.

The Star Chaser gunned its engines a moment before the small red dot that was the curvator reached the Kratos' position on the screen. The belly of the Star Chaser showed in the window, then it was above them.

"No!" Shathryn shrieked.

The percussion of the curvator striking the Star Chaser shoved the Kratos away from the Coalition ships. Several of the monitors flickered back on. The emergency sirens sounded again.

"Hyrin, aim for the transporter," Devren called out. His face was pale against the red blood on his brow.

Shathryn's sobs filled the air as Hyrin used the reverse thrusters to maneuver the ship. The Coalition fleet tore through the remains of the Star Chaser. Debris floated past the monitor.

Hyrin flew with shaking hands. Liora watched the screen as the Kansas transporter drew near. Hyrin didn't wait for it to couple. He maneuvered the arm and readied the toggle.

"Four more missiles are heading our way," Liora reported quietly. "Five seconds to impact."

Hyrin gently nudged the arm into the link. With the monitors flickering on and off, he had to perform the procedure manually. The scrape of the metal shook the Kratos.

"Three seconds," Liora said. Her heart raced as she watched the small red dots draw closer. Her monitor beeped quietly; the sound was barely noticeable within the call of the sirens.

Hyrin adjusted the toggle. It caught inside the link.

"Now, Hyrin," Devren shouted.

Hyrin hit the button.

"Two, one," Liora said.

She braced. Tariq's hand grabbed her shoulder. Instead of the pain of another explosion, the pulling sensation and rush of cold through her body stole her breath.

Liora opened her eyes to see the vast expanse of empty space in front of them where the Coalition ships and the wreckage of the Star Chaser had been.

"Stone," Shathryn called out. She curled in a fetal position and her body shook with sobs.

"Destroy the transporter," Devren ordered quietly.

Hyrin wiped his cheeks. "Captain, that's a death sentence if we're caught," he said.

"It'll be a death sentence if they come through before we can get out of here," Devren replied. "We need time to repair the Kratos, get to Gliese, destroy the orb, and leave without the Coalition being the wiser. Do it. That's an order."

Hyrin maneuvered the ship away from the transporter whose sails were unfurling to recharge from the starlight.

"Let's get you to the med wing," Tariq said gently to Shathryn.

She shook her head.

"You hit your head hard," the medical officer urged. "I need to check for a concussion."

Shathryn refused to move. O'Tule climbed to her feet with a worried expression.

"Shoot down the sails first," Devren told Hyrin, his focus on the monitor. "We can't risk it returning before we can destroy it."

Liora rose and O'Tule took her seat.

"Thank you," O'Tule said quietly, her gaze on her friend. "I couldn't leave her."

Tariq slipped his hands beneath Shathryn to carry her.

Liora was about to return to her own seat when Tariq gasped and dropped back to his knees on the floor. His jaw clenched tight and a sheen of sweat showed on his forehead.

"Tariq?" Liora asked.

"I got thrown on the way here," Tariq replied tightly. "I'm fine." He tried to rise back to his feet, but pain washed his face pale. "I don't have time for this," he said through gritted teeth.

Liora set a hand on his arm. Before he could protest, she pulled at his pain. She heard his breath catch in his throat at the sudden absence. Answering pain filled her ribs with such sharp agony she knew he had broken several of them.

"I can help," she said. She reached toward Shathryn with her free hand. The pain was unbearable.

"I've got her," Tariq replied.

With the pain momentarily gone, he lifted Shathryn in his arms. Keeping a hand on his shoulder, Liora followed them out of the bridge.

It took all of her strength to reach the medical wing.

Sweat beaded on her forehead and hot and cold rushed through her limbs. Liora kept a hand on Tariq's shoulder as he settled Shathryn onto a bed and gave her a sedative to slow her frantic sobs. She finally fell into a deep sleep.

"You can let go now," Tariq said.

Liora focused on him through the haze of pain.

Tariq watched her, his eyebrows pulled together and light blue gaze unreadable.

"Liora, you don't have to do that anymore."

She nodded. "I'll pull away gently. Sending it all back at once could shock your system." She forced a smile. "We don't need you unconscious as well."

"No, we don't," he said. He led her to a chair and helped her sit, his touch gentle.

Each movement hurt her ribs.

"Go ahead."

"More of the crew will be on their way," she said, her voice tight. "You'll need to be able to tend to them."

He crouched so they were eye level and gave her a smile that she had never seen before. It turned up one side of his mouth even though his brow was creased and his lips pressed together. It looked as though he couldn't decide whether to kiss her or scold her.

He reached up and brushed a strand of hair from Liora's cheek.

"Liora, I can handle it," he assured her gently.

Liora nodded, unable to think clearly past the fire that trailed his fingertips along with the pain in her side. She closed her eyes and focused on her ribs. Slowly, steadily, she eased the pull and let the pain return to Tariq. She heard his teeth grit together, but continued to let go of her hold on the pain.

She opened her eyes slowly. Tariq held his side and

forced a smile despite the pain that made his face white.

"There," he said, his voice raspy. "No big deal." He paused, then said, "Except I might need help up."

Liora rose and ducked under his arm. She eased him to a standing position.

"We should wrap those ribs," she suggested.

Tariq nodded. "Let's do that."

She helped him over to the supply closet and pulled out a wrap bandage. She glanced back to see Tariq trying to get his shirt off. Bruises that were nearly black colored his left side. When he tried to lift his left arm, a gasp escaped his lips and he lowered it again.

Liora slid her fingers beneath the hem of his shirt and lifted it carefully.

"You hit a wall?" she asked to distract him from the pain.

"The corner jumped out at me during one of those explosions," Tariq replied; his voice caught as she eased the shirt over his head. "I thought you were in charge of keeping that from happening."

"What?" Liora asked, caught off guard.

He lowered his arms and smiled at her. "Wall security, remember?"

The memory of their conversation shortly after Liora had been given a position aboard the starship surfaced. She couldn't help the smile that touched her face.

"I guess it is my fault, then."

Tariq nodded, his expression solemn. "Got to keep those walls in line."

She shook her head and couldn't get her smile to leave. "Ridiculous."

She put the bandage against Tariq's bare chest and wrapped outward toward his bruised ribs.

His breath caught at the touch of her hand on his skin. "I can do that," he said, his words quiet.

"I've got it," she replied as softly. "It's hard to keep a steady pressure if you wrap ribs by yourself."

He took in a sharp breath as she stepped around behind him keeping a firm hold on the bandages.

"I hate that you know that from experience."

Liora slowed what she was doing. She looked up and found him watching her in the mirror next to the supply cabinet. She was suddenly very aware of her palm on his side. His skin felt hot to the touch and she didn't think he had a fever. She pulled carefully, easing some of the pain he felt.

He turned to face her. The movement caused the bandage to fall away. He didn't appear to notice.

"Liora, you don't need to do that."

"Do what?" she asked, pretending not to know what he was talking about.

He caught her arms in his hands.

"Liora."

She looked up at him. The expression in his light blue eyes made her heart beat so loud she wondered if he could hear it.

"You don't have to take my pain," he said.

"I don't feel it," she fibbed.

His eyes narrowed. He shook his head. "Don't lie to me. I see it in your eyes. These ribs hurt, but they hurt a lot more a minute ago. I can't let you do that." His voice lowered and he said, "I won't let you carry my pain for me."

"Somebody should," she whispered.

As if he couldn't help himself, Tariq leaned down and cupped her face in both of his hands. He kissed her gently on the lips.

Liora closed her eyes. His taste filled her with warmth. She felt surrounded by him, his scent, his strong hands, and the way the pain disappeared even though she still pulled it from him.

When he stepped back, she fought to get her bearings. He looked at her as though he felt the same way.

The intercom buzzed. "Tariq?"

Tariq cleared his throat. "Uh, yes, Lieutenant?"

"I have three bleeding boys and another out after hitting his head on the output shaft coupling. I'm sending them all your way," Lieutenant Argyle said.

"I'll be ready," Tariq replied. He looked at Liora. "Back to work."

"I'll stay," she replied, answering his wry smile with one of her own. "You might need me."

Chapter 17

A half hour later found Liora stitching the minor wounds of one of the engine crew while Tariq stapled a gash down another crew member's calf. They were the last two Lieutenant Argyle had sent over. The others had been bandaged and returned back to work a little worse for wear. Liora found if she concentrated hard enough, she could keep Tariq's pain to a manageable level without needing to touch him.

"It threw us around like rag dolls," Officer Unman said, keeping his attention away from the wound Liora stitched along the pad of his hand. "I was in the middle of tightening a cuff when bam, I was thrown across the room into the water recycling unit with the screw driver stuck in my hand."

Liora tied off the thread. "Lucky the screw driver didn't stab you in the eye."

Officer Unman laughed. "I know, right?" He opened and closed his hand. "Hey, that's pretty good. I didn't know you worked in the medical wing."

She glanced at Tariq and found him watching her. His smile deepened and he turned back to bandaging the wound he had finished stapling.

Liora put gauze to the gash and wrapped it in a cotton bandage. "I just stared," she told Officer Unman.

The intercom buzzed.

"Brace for impact."

Tariq swore under his breath. Liora pulled the officer off the chair to the floor. They braced against the wall. Tariq leaned over Shathryn to keep her safely on the bed. An explosion shook the Kratos.

"Not again," Tariq said, jumping to his feet.

The intercom buzzed again. "Prepare for boarding."

A chill ran through Liora. She and Tariq exchanged a glance.

"Stay here," Tariq ordered the officers. "Keep the door shut."

Tariq hit the door lock when he ran by and it slid shut behind them. They took off up the hall.

"What's going on?" Tariq demanded the second they reached the bridge.

Devren's face was white. The bandage Tariq had wrapped around his brow showed blood.

"Damaclans," he said.

206

Hyrin pointed at the monitor.

It was the one word Liora had never wanted to hear. She followed Hyrin's finger to the screen in front of him. By the markings, the ship was Damaclan for sure.

"They know the state of the ship. If they fire again, we're done for," Devren said. "Our only hope is to invite them onboard and give them whatever it is they want."

"What if they want the Omne Occasus?" Tariq asked.

Devren shook his head. "By the way they're talking, I don't think they know what we have. Hopefully they're just pillaging."

"I never thought I'd hear that as a good thing," O'Tule said quietly from her station.

Devren watched the ship pull closer. "I had Straham hide it in the cargo hold behind the Gull. Our best hope is that they'll overlook it."

"That's placing a lot of weight on hope," Tariq told him.

Devren said what they were all thinking. "Hope is the only thing we've got right now."

Liora wanted to be anywhere but on the bridge of a ship in the process of being taken over by Damaclans. The thought that they would be entering the Kratos at any moment made her stomach tighten. She ducked back out the door.

"Liora," Tariq called.

"I can't be here," she replied.

Liora didn't stop until she reached the walkway before the engine room. The thought of coming face to face with Damaclans again was almost more than she could bear. She paced from one end of the walkway to the other. Memories of her childhood swarmed her thoughts.

She saw Obruo beating her with the mastery staff in an effort to break her so she wouldn't complete the Damaclan training. The faces of the impassive Damaclan elders leered down at her. They didn't want her to be one of them. She was a half-blood, inferior even though the law demanded that she be raised according to her Damaclan heritage. The Damaclan children her age laughed at her torture. They enjoyed that she was Obruo's target.

She had promised herself when her clan died that she would avoid Damaclans for the rest of her life. The race was small considering the greatness of the Macrocosm. Up to that point, except for Obruo, it had been doable. Now an entire Damaclan ship was next to the Kratos. She pictured a dozen of them landing in the holding bay.

Damaclans were dangerous. Devren had no choice but to hope the Damaclans were only pillaging for their own gains. The Kratos had little to give after everything they had been through. Her crew, the crew she had fought and bled beside, were at the Damaclans' mercy.

Liora's hands clenched into fists. If there was one she knew, it was that Damaclans had no mercy.

She rushed back up the walkway, past the cargo bay, the medical wing, and the living quarters, then up the hall to the bridge. She slammed her hand on the panel and the door slid open in time for her to see a Damaclan lift Devren by his neck into the air.

The human struggled to break free. Everyone's weapons were on the floor and half a dozen Damaclans kept the other crew members from going to their captain's defense. Tariq was pinned to the ground. A Damaclan had an arm around his throat and a knee in his back while he waited for his chief to give the kill order.

"Put him down," Liora commanded.

All eyes shifted to her.

The Damaclan who held Devren took in the markings along Liora's neck.

"I didn't think I'd find a member of Obruo's clan on the wreckage of a Coalition ship in the middle of the Phoenix Dwarf Galaxy," the Damaclan said, his voice deep.

His hold on Devren's throat tightened. Devren clawed at his hands, but the huge Damaclan didn't appear to notice.

"Let him go," Liora said.

"Obruo's not here," the Damaclan replied. "And even if he was, I don't have to answer to the blood of the—"

Liora pulled the sleeve back from her right arm and held it up. The Damaclan stared at her for a moment. He slowly lowered Devren to the ground and stepped back. Devren fell to his knees gasping for breath.

"Let them up," Liora said. "All of them."

At the chief's nod, the other Damaclans let their captives go.

Tariq rose quickly to his feet. He grabbed up his gun and aimed it at the chief.

"Tariq, don't," Liora said.

Tariq looked at her, his eyes wide and chest heaving.

"He was going to kill Devren," Tariq said. "I should shoot him through the eye for that. What's going on here?"

The Damaclans kept silent, their full attention on Liora. She took a stealing breath and said, "What is your clan?"

"Clan Incendo," the chief replied.

Liora nodded. "Chief Incendo, have your clan repair

the Kratos using parts from your ship. You will be our escort to the planet of Gliese and guard our ship when we land. After that, your services will no longer be needed."

The chief withdrew his knife. The hilt of the burnished bone blade had been carved into a black hunting cat that resembled the felises of Verdan. Tariq's finger tightened on the trigger. Liora stepped carefully to the side to shield the chief with her body.

"Liora," Tariq growled.

"My blade is yours," the chief vowed.

Liora accepted the weapon. She put the blade to her finger, drawing a small amount of blood. Everyone watched in silence as she rubbed her finger along the hilt, coating the black cat. She handed the weapon back to the chief.

"Your blade is accepted," Liora said.

The chief left the bridge. The rest of the Damaclans followed.

"What was that?" Tariq demanded. He winced in pain as he helped Devren to his feet.

"Y-you're the one," Hyrin said with wide eyes.

"What are you talking about?" Tariq asked. He looked from Liora to Hyrin with impatience.

"Royal blood is religion to Damaclans," Hyrin explained without taking his eyes off Liora. "Last time I checked, their queen lived on the planet Ralian."

The name gripped Liora's heart in a tight fist. She nodded.

"What happened to Tenieva?" Hyrin asked, his voice tempered with compassion.

"My mother died," Liora said. She refused to let impact of what she said affect her.

Hyrin let out a low whistle. "Our Liora is the

Damaclan queen."

Liora clenched her jaw at his words. It was something she had refused her entire life. Before she had completed her training, they had a queen. After, when the clan realized she would survive to take up the role, they treated her with the respect she had longed for her entire life. Yet gaining it had felt bland and empty. It should have been her birthright, but they had refused to believe she was one of them until she proved it by killing Vogun. The day after she received the tattoo marking her royalty, they had all been killed.

"It doesn't matter," she said shortly. "They'll help us get to Gliese, then they'll be gone."

She left the bridge and headed straight to her room. When she put her hand to the panel, the door slid open and the paintings O'Tule had crafted along the walls caught her gaze. She stared at the one above the bed. The sun rose above the white, stark valley. The sandy slopes reflected the sun rays. Water trickled in a small waterfall down the edge of the ravine that fed their valley.

It was the same view she had seen after the clan had been killed by the nameless ones. She had walked from the valley, the lone survivor, the haunted one. She was royalty to no one, a cast off not good enough to die beside her mother.

She knelt on the bed and put her hand on the painting. No matter what she told herself, it was the home of her birth. Her heart ached when she looked at the sandy valley.

The door slid open and Tariq stepped inside. His head tipped slightly to the side when he saw her kneeling on the bed.

"I thought the bed was too soft."

Liora withdrew her hand from the painting. "It is."

Tariq motioned to the edge. "May I sit down?"

She nodded.

He sat, then stood again with a hand on his side. "I think I'll stand."

"Are your ribs bothering you?" she asked.

"The pain killers are kicking in. I should survive." He gave her a smile. "And so will Shathryn and the engine crew, thanks to your help."

"I'm not sure Officer Unman was thrilled about an untrained assistant doing his stitches."

Tariq leaned against the wall and crossed his arms. "Actually, he seemed just fine about letting the gorgeous, mysterious Damaclan tend to his wound. He has no idea how completely stubborn you can be."

"Oh, I'm stubborn?" Liora replied with a half-laugh. "You're the one who tried to carry Shathryn to the medical wing with broken ribs. How far do you think you would have gotten?"

"Without you?" Tariq asked. At her nod, he rubbed the light shadow of scruff on his jaw thoughtfully. "To the bridge door."

That brought another laugh from Liora.

Tariq's smile softened. "That's what I've been waiting to hear."

Liora moved to the floor and pulled the blanket she used for sleeping over her legs more for comfort than warmth.

"You carry way too much, Liora. You don't have to hold it all inside," Tariq said gently.

Liora shook her head. "Some things don't need to be spoken about."

Tariq raised an eyebrow. "Like the fact that you're the

Damaclan queen? Hyrin's been filling us in a bit more on what that means. Apparently, you're like a goddess to them, which is why they dropped everything to help us. Maybe that was something you could have shared?"

Liora fought back a smile at the teasing sarcasm in his tone when he said the last few words. "It wasn't important," she replied. "My goal was to never seen a Damaclan again after leaving Ralian."

Tariq's smile faded. "Obruo changed that."

Liora nodded and lowered her gaze to the floor. "Yes, he did. He changed everything."

"He's still out there somewhere," Tariq told her. "We'll find him."

She glanced up at him. "I just worry about how many more people he'll hurt before we do."

Tariq let out a slow breath and gave a nod. "We'll have to watch our step. If we keep our visits to Gaulded and planets to a minimum, he won't have many places to go."

Liora's heart skipped a beat. "Tariq, what about Verdan?"

"What about it?" Tariq asked, though his voice was reflective as though her words made him think.

"Tariq, Obruo could trace us there easily, especially with the slain Coalition officers. He obviously has the ear of many who can get him that kind of information, or else he wouldn't have known I was at Gaulded Zero Twenty-one before he blew it up."

Tariq shook his head. "Verdan is a hard planet to get into. He wouldn't make it through the lightning unless he could prove citizenship or had express permission from either the Kristo Belanite family that owns the Gaulded or from a Coalition colonel. And we're not there anymore."

"That didn't matter on the Gaulded," Liora pointed out.

She could tell the thought of Mrs. Metis and the citizens of Echo being in danger at Obruo's hands bothered him.

Tariq ran a hand through his hair to push the black strands from his eyes.

"Verdan is a protected planet by both the Gaulded and the Coalition because of the volts we put out. Obruo crossed lines when he blew up a Gaulded. I don't know how many more risks he can take before he loses all of his allies," Tariq said. "But just the same, after Gliese, we'll head to Verdan and make sure everything's alright."

"Okay," Liora replied. His words eased the tightness she felt. If they were protected, Obruo would have a difficult time getting inside the lightning field to reach the planet. But there had been other places.

"You're thinking about the other stops we've made, aren't you?" Tariq asked, watching her face.

She nodded. "Tariq, everywhere we've been is in danger. The Gauldeds, the people I've spoken to. Obruo won't stop."

"Neither will we," Tariq reassured her. "First, we have to concentrate on destroying the Omne Occasus. After that, I promise you, we'll find Obruo and make him pay for what he's done to us."

Liora expected to feel reassured by Tariq's words, but instead, she felt only fear for Tariq. What if Obruo found a way to kill the human? He almost had during the circus on planet Luptos. If they were ever in a situation like that again, she didn't know what she would do.

That was the truth of it. She had never expected to

care about anyone so much. She held feelings for Devren that confused her, emotions drawn from his kindness and the way he always looked out for her; but with Tariq, it was different. Tariq felt like the feather that floated just out of reach, like a feral animal that wanted to be loved, but couldn't quite draw near enough to be touched.

When Tariq looked at her as he did just then, as though her thoughts mattered more to him than anything else in the Macrocosm, she almost believed that perhaps he could give his heart to her.

Yet there it was again, the way his gaze dropped to the floor and something akin to guilt showed in his eyes. She knew he missed his wife, the woman Obruo had ripped from his life so violently. She didn't know how to fix it, or if he wanted her to.

But the thought of Obruo getting his merciless hands on the human scared Liora more than anything. Obruo knew how to make people suffer; he relished in it. If there was anything Liora had learned growing up in Obruo's household, it was that the Damaclan leader knew how to bide his time and wait patiently for the perfect moment that would inflict the most pain.

The thought sent a tremor down Liora's spine.

"Are you alright?" Tariq asked.

She met his gaze, so concerned yet so cautious as though he fought an inner battle he didn't know how to win.

Liora nodded. "I'm fine. Thank you for checking on me."

Tariq knew her words for the dismissal they were. "You're welcome," he replied. "You should get some rest." He made his way to the door and put his palm on the reader. When it opened, he looked at her. "I keep meaning to reprogram this so it only opens for you."

She shook her head. "I don't mind."

He nodded and ducked out the door. It slid shut behind him. She glanced up at O'Tule's painting one more time, then pulled her pillow down and curled up on the floor.

Chapter 18

"Welcome to Gliese," Hyrin said.

"It's not what I expected for a water world," O'Tule replied.

She glanced at Shathryn as if hoping for a response, but the exterior analytic specialist had barely said anything since Tariq cleared her from the medical wing. Tear tracks showed on the woman's face, but she didn't cry when the others were around.

"It's not water like we're used to," Hyrin explained. "It has all different phases. We can expect steam, high-pressure ice, and darkness. The water vapor and clouds that make up the atmosphere absorb any starlight, so with water fathoms deep, there's going to be a type of darkness unlike anything we've experienced before."

"Sounds like fun," Tariq said dryly.

Devren glanced at him. "Your type of adventure, right?"

"Any kind of adventure is my type," Tariq replied.

Devren grinned. "That's what I thought." He glanced around at his crew. "Officer Straham, you and Shathryn maintain orbit with the Damaclan ship."

The officer didn't look pleased about the order. "I'm not sure I'm comfortable having Damaclans as bodyguards." He gave Liora an apologetic look. "No offense."

"None taken," she replied. "Damaclans have earned our reputation."

"Just the same, they won't go against Liora's orders," Devren told him. "You're safe up here and they'll protect the ship in case the Coalition finds some inconceivable way to get here."

"Yes, Captain," Officer Straham replied.

Shathryn merely nodded, her gaze blank.

"What do you want me to do?" Zran asked. He looked like one of the crew now that he was dressed in a Kratos uniform. The black and blue set off the blue streaks that marked the Zamarian's arms and face.

Devren glanced at Liora. She nodded, indicating that he could be trusted.

"We're not sure what's going to happen when we get down there. If anything goes wrong, I need a crew up here ready to act," Devren replied. "Things could get dangerous."

"Count me in," Zran said, holding out his hand.

Devren shook it. "I appreciate that."

He led the way down the hallway. They were almost to the cargo hold when the intercom buzzed.

"Captain, there's a starship approaching. It looks Damaclan," Duncan announced.

Devren looked at Liora. "You don't think your friends brought some backup, do you?"

Damaclans wouldn't betray her, unless....

Liora took off running up the hallway. She burst onto the bridge.

"Pull up the ship," she demanded.

Officer Straham fumbled for the right button. When he hit it, Liora's heart skipped a beat. Painted on the side of the craft was the same symbol as the tattoo beneath her left ear, a blade in the center of the Eye of the Tessari dragon.

"Obruo," she said.

Tariq and Devren ran into the room in time to hear what she said.

"We're in trouble," Tariq stated.

"We need to get the Omne Occasus out of here," Devren replied.

He looked back over his shoulder at the others. "Hyrin, can you separate the Feren orb from the Omne Occasus?"

"I can," Hyrin replied. "But it'll make the imploder unstable. I was hoping we could wait until we reached Gliese's atmosphere."

"We have to do it now," Devren told him. "Stabilize the Omne Occasus the best you can and disguise it in the crate. Put the orb in the Gull. Tariq, help him. We need to leave, now." Devren turned to Officer Straham. "As soon as we're gone, take off. We'll call for pickup when we've cleared Gliese."

"We might not be able to contact them until we're through the atmosphere," Hyrin called over his shoulder as they ran down the hallway.

"We'll cross that bridge when we come to it," Devren replied. He put a hand on Officer Straham's shoulder. "For now, circle behind the planet. If you are followed or attacked, head for the transporter."

"The Gull wasn't mean to support life for more than a few hours," Officer Straham said with a worried expression. "If you get stuck...."

"So don't you and Duncan head off to party at Callisto and forget about us," Devren told him.

Duncan shook his head in the corner. The bands woven through his ears shook. Liora couldn't remember ever seeing him look frazzled in all the attacks they had been through, but even his gaze was tight when he looked at the Damaclan ship on the screen.

"Let's go," Devren commanded.

Tariq and Hyrin reached the Gull at the same time. Hyrin's face was pale and he held the black box in his hands carefully as though a viper would jump out and bite him if he jarred it the wrong way.

"I don't feel comfortable about this," he said, buckling into a seat.

Devren took the controls. "Everything about this mission has turned on its head," he said. "Our only goal is to get rid of this mess as fast as we can and get on with our lives."

"If there's anything left of them," Tariq replied, sliding onto the passenger seat.

"Thanks for that," Devren said dryly. He pushed the

intercom button. "Open the cargo hold."

"The second Damaclan ship is waiting for you," Officer Straham said.

"Thanks for the warning," Devren told him.

Devren hit the thrusters before the door slid open completely. The sides of the Gull scraped metal before it shot clear of the Kratos.

"Impatient, are we?" Tariq asked.

"I'm drawing fire away from the Kratos. The last thing we need is for Obruo to get a missile inside with the rest of Omne Occasus in there."

A monitor beeped.

"Missiles left side," Tariq announced.

Devren jerked the starship to the right and put it in a dive toward Gliese.

"If we can reach the planet, maybe we'll be able to lose Obruo in the water," Hyrin said.

Several missiles sped past the ship.

"He's not fooling around," Tariq pointed out. "He'll try to stop you before you reach the surface."

"There won't be a surface," Hyrin replied. At their questioning looks, he explained, "Water planets aren't made up of one form of water. There are many forms I've never even seen before. My guess is that the atmosphere will flow right into the water, which surrounds the water core."

"Either way," Tariq interrupted Hyrin before he could go into more detail. "Obruo's out for blood. We need a way to fight back that doesn't endanger the orb."

A missile struck the Gull.

Tariq muttered a curse. "He's damaged the missile compartment. I can't fire back."

Devren spun the ship to the right, dodging another

strike. The hazy cloud of Gliese loomed in front of them. Devren hit the thrusters and the Gull darted into the misty atmosphere.

"The computer's gone haywire," Hyrin reported from his seat behind Devren's. "The atmosphere's interfering with the read."

"We're flying blind," Devren replied.

Hyrin nodded. "That's another way of putting it."

The clouds darkened and the Gull's navigation lights turned on. A missile clipped the back of the ship. Devren pulled to the left, but Obruo stayed close behind.

"Turn off the lights," Liora told them. "His computers should be malfunctioning as well. If we go dark, he'll have no way of tracking us."

Hyrin nodded. "She's right. The atmosphere blocks out any light from the nearby stars. In a few seconds, we won't be able to see our hands in front of our faces."

"Do it," Devren said.

Tariq switched off the external lights, then those in the cabin. Hyrin was right. Without the ship's lights, they were left in complete darkness.

"I'm angling slightly left," Devren said quietly. "That way if he follows our trajectory, it'll throw him off."

Liora felt the slight change in direction. Without the ability to see, her other senses strained. From her seat behind Tariq's chair, she caught a slight hum.

"What's that?" she asked. It felt right to talk softly with the darkness pressing in on all sides.

"What?" Hyrin whispered back.

"That humming sound," she replied.

"I hear it now," Tariq said. "It seems to be coming from the right."

Gray showed through the window beside Tariq.

Everyone squinted, trying to make it out. The gray brightened and became a glowing orb nearly the size of the ship.

"What on earth?" Hyrin gasped.

The orb drew near. Liora looked past the light to its source and her stomach twisted.

A creature with clear fangs and milky white eyes drifted closer. Its mouth opened slowly, revealing translucent fangs nearly as long as the ship was tall. Fin-like appendages waved in the liquid, keeping the creature in place.

Liora could barely wrap her mind around how big the creature was. Their ship would be a mere morsel to such a beast. It was the first time in her life that she felt like prey instead of a predator.

"Uh, Devren," Liora said.

Tariq glanced at her, then past the orb to where she was looking.

"Dev, get us out of here!" he demanded.

"What—" Devren's eyes widened. He slammed his palm on the controls and they shot forward. The rear camera showed the orb fading back into the watery darkness.

"I don't like this place," Hyrin said.

"More lights," Tariq told them.

Wary, everyone peered at the glow in front of the ship. It drew nearer and widened in ripples of green and pink that billowed deeper. Strange hollows and curved spikes surrounded it.

"Is that alive?" Hyrin asked with a hint of fear in his voice.

Devren steered the Gull carefully closer. To their surprise, the ship's nose bumped into the object far sooner than it looked like they would. Everyone was jerked forward in their seats.

"Ice," Hyrin said.

"I've never seen ice look like that," Devren replied.

"It's the pressure," Hyrin explained. "The deeper we go, the more pressure the water is under. With the temperature changes, the water that turns to ice floats, but it wouldn't be as cold as the ice we're used to."

"So we should go for a swim?" Tariq suggested.

Hyrin stared at him with wide eyes. "You would drown. There's no telling what phase of water you would encounter, and with the high-pressure…."

"I'm joking," Tariq told him. "I don't want to go out there."

Everyone watched another strange ice sculpture flow past. It looked like a demon beast trying to claw out of the dark depths. There was no way of telling what made it glow, but the green and pink hues gave it a haunting appearance Liora saw again when she closed her eyes.

"Creepy."

She opened her eyes at Tariq's voice. The glowing ice had drifted past, yet other shapes showed the deeper they got. Creatures nearly four times the size of the Gull floated effortlessly in the darkness. Huge tendrils hung down from the domed heads that glowed dimly in the darkness.

"Jellyfish."

The others looked at Liora.

"Malivian had a display of Earthling jellyfish. They glowed like that when he put lights in the aquarium," she explained. "They were much smaller than these, but they always seemed harmless to me."

As if to contradict her, another jellyfish floated past.

In its tendrils it held another of the creatures with the glowing orb, only this one's face was half-eaten. Its jaw hung sideways and the translucent teeth glowed with the faint orange color of the jellyfish.

"Deeper," Tariq said.

Devren did as his friend suggested.

"How much further in do we need to be?" Liora asked Hyrin. "And what is your plan for destroying the orb?"

"According to Tramareaus." Hyrin paused. He cracked a smile and said, "I'm so used to groans of dismay when I say his name that I almost expect them now." At Liora's impatient look, he continued, "The orb needs to be exposed to as much water as possible. The waterproof box I put it in has a latch lock which will be easy to open out there."

"Your plan is to go into the water and open the box?" Liora replied.

Even Devren gave Hyrin an incredulous look.

"What?" Hyrin asked. "I figured it would be easy. Suit up, go out there, open it…" His voice died away as though he realized what he was saying.

Heading out into the freezing dark water filled with mysterious and abnormally large, toothy and tentacled creatures didn't exactly make the best plan.

"I'll do it," Tariq said.

"I will," Liora told him.

The ship shook and a siren sounded. The lighting flickered on and off.

"What's going on?" Tariq asked.

"I'm not sure," Devren said.

"Obruo will see us." Liora watched the rear camera, convinced the Damaclan leader would show up at any moment.

The ship shuddered again. Another alarm began to beep.

"Everyone get suits on," Devren commanded. "If we lose pressure down here, we're done for."

Tariq handed him an atmosphere suit and pulled on his own. Liora assisted Hyrin with suiting up. The Talastan's hands shook as he fumbled with the zipper. Liora helped him get it fastened.

"Thanks," he said. His voice sounded muted inside the close-fitting helmet. "I'm more at home on the Kratos. I don't know why Captain Devren insists on bringing me along on these things."

"Because you're the only one who knows anything about the orb," Devren pointed out over their headsets. "What is that?"

Everyone pressed to the front of the ship. Liora's hand touched the window. Whatever had shaken the ship held them tight. Huge, triangular suction cups stuck to the glass. They were being pulled forward despite Devren's attempts to free them.

"Uh, Dev," Tariq said. He pointed.

A huge, gaping maw opened in the dark depths. Other tentacles wrapped around the ship. A tongue wriggled in the beak-like mouth that could easily swallow a ship much larger than the Gull.

The ship's lights flashed. The creature let out a bellow that was more sound vibration than sound itself. The sides of the ship reverberated.

Something impacted the side of the ship so hard it knocked one of the tentacles free.

"Obruo!" Tariq shouted.

The rear camera showed the Damaclan ship appear

out of the darkness. Other missiles sped through the water toward the Gull.

"Captain," Hyrin said, his voice tight.

"I know," Devren replied. He moved the thrusters to shake the ship from side to side, trying to rock it free.

"I have an idea," Liora said. "Give me the orb."

"No good idea starts like that," Tariq pointed out.

Liora glared at him. "We can't fire our missiles. Between Obruo and this beast, we're as good as dead." She pointed at the water outside the window. "If Obruo doesn't kill us, that creature is going to." She looked at Hyrin. "The orb will react to contact with liquid, right?"

"In theory," Hyrin replied.

Liora refrained from pointing out that it wasn't the most helpful answer.

"If I can get the beast to let us go and we disable Obruo's ship, we can release the orb and escape Gliese while leaving Obruo to his fate," she replied.

"And how to you plan to get the beast to let go?" Tariq asked.

Liora pointed to the orb. "I'll feed it that."

Tariq shook his head. "You're insane."

She shrugged. "Your job is to disable Obruo's ship, so perhaps you're the insane one."

He gave her an incredulous look. "Why did I even come on this obviously doomed mission?"

"Your insatiable thirst for adventure?" she replied, holding out a welding torch from the ship's tool closet. She took another for herself and hooked it behind her belt.

"How do you know me so well?" Tariq replied dryly, though there was a hint of worry in his amused gaze. "What's this for?"

"Propulsion," she replied.

"Of course."

She looked at Hyrin. "Quick answer needed, where can Tariq do the most damage to Obruo's ship in the least amount of time?"

"An Iridium Osprey like the one Obruo is flying has only two weaknesses; its finicky heat sensors and the external exhaust system. The flaps have a tendency to close, which overheats the engine and causes an imbalance in the internal engine temperature. That slows the engine and taxes the motors. They'll shut down to avoid locking up. If you can get the flaps to stay closed, Obruo will lose power quickly." Hyrin looked pleased with himself.

"That was the quick answer," Devren said from the pilot seat. "Better go before he tells you the long one."

"It'll be that easy, huh?" Tariq replied with a hint of sarcasm.

Hyrin nodded. "Easy for you." He handed Tariq a roll of repair tape.

"What does that mean?" Tariq asked.

Hyrin shrugged. "I would probably mess it up, but you're cool under pressure." The Talastan's sideways eyelids blinked quickly. "Good luck."

"Thanks," Tariq replied.

His sarcasm was completely lost on Hyrin. The Talastan merely nodded and took the seat next to Devren.

Tariq glanced at Liora. "And good luck feeding that beast. Just make sure it doesn't get greedy and eat you as well."

"I'm not worried about that," Liora replied. But a glance outside the closest window showed them drawing closer to the gaping mouth. "Let's get this over with," she said.

Chapter 19

"It's going to flood when we open the door," Hyrin announced. "Everyone check your oxygen levels. The door opens in five, four, three...."

When he pushed the button, the door slid open and thick water rushed inside with such force that it shoved them against the far wall. Tariq grabbed Liora's hand and pulled her forward. The sight of the dark water with apparently limitless depths below them was unnerving. Liora gripped the orb box tightly. If she lost it, they would all be doomed.

Tariq turned on his blowtorch. When he squeezed the handle, the small flame's force pushed him toward Obruo's ship.

"Be careful," Liora said over her headset. "Hide your torch if you can. If he sees it, it'll make you a target."

"Got it," Tariq replied, his voice tight. "You be careful, too."

"I will," Liora promised.

She checked that her torch was secure and inched her way around the ship. The sight of the gigantic creature looming out of the depths with nothing between her and its sweeping tentacles sent chills through Liora. The tentacle wrapped around the ship was thicker than she was tall, and if it succeeded in pulling the Gull to its beak mouth, it wouldn't even have to swallow for the ship to be lost inside.

Liora steeled her nerves and pushed away from the ship. The water felt thicker than anything she had ever swam in before. It took a huge effort to control her movements and keep herself upright. She struggled to detach the torch from her belt, but when she had it gripped firmly in one hand and the orb box tucked tightly beneath her other arm, she squeezed the handle.

The torch flared and propelled her forward.

"Liora, look out," Devren called over his headset from the Gull.

Liora glanced toward Obruo's ship. A missile flew straight in her direction. She squeezed the torch handle harder and shot through the water. The missile sped past barely millimeters from clipping her.

"Too close," Devren said. "He saw your torch."

"What about Tariq?" Liora asked.

She didn't have time to look over her shoulder and

check on the human. Her ears popped painfully with the pressure of the water.

"Obruo doesn't seem to have noticed me yet," Tariq replied. "I'm hoping to keep it that way."

"He's sending more missiles at the Gull," Devren told them. "I'm going to angle the ship sideways in the hopes that I can get one of the missiles to clip the tentacles."

"Good luck," Liora told him.

The open mouth loomed in front of her. Its beak was wide in anticipation of the meal it pulled slowly toward it. Another missile sped past barely an arm's length from Liora. It slammed into the side of the creature's huge face. The creature blinked one large reflective eye, but didn't show any other outward appearance of being struck.

They had only one hope of getting free from both the creature and Obruo. Liora was nearly to the mouth. She tried to hook the torch back behind her belt, but it slipped from her hand. She made a grab for it, but it fell between her fingers. It vanished into the darkness below her feet, and with it, her only chance of escaping the orb after she opened it to the water.

"Vents are closed," Tariq announced. "The doors are opening. I think Obruo knows what I've done." He paused, then said, "Damaclans with Grebes. This'll be fun."

"Get out of there," Devren commanded.

"I'm trying," Tariq replied.

"The Gull's thrusters are failing," Hyrin said. "If we don't get out of here now, we're not going anywhere ever again."

"Liora?"

She was their only hope of getting free. Liora put a

hand on the side of the creature's mouth to keep from being sucked inside. The beak vibrated beneath her gloved hand. Her fingers shook as she opened the box. Upon contact with the water, the red orb pulsed, then changed to black. Liora shoved it inside the creature's mouth and pushed away from the beak. The orb drifted into the huge black void that made up the creature's throat. The beak closed with a click that vibrated through the water.

Time slowed. Liora could hear the chaos inside the Gull as another missile hit it. Tariq shouted something. Shots were fired. Liora couldn't help any of them. Her eyes were locked on the creature that kept the Gull from leaving. Its reflective eyes closed, then opened wider than before. Its tentacles stopped moving.

"It let us go," Devren called out. "Get back here!"

The creature's head seemed to shrink. Liora wondered if she was seeing things. She closed her eyes and opened them again to see the beak being sucked inward as though something was trying to turn the colossal beast's head inside out. Its eyes disappeared and its head followed. Its tentacles writhed and were sucked in as well.

Liora felt herself pulled forward toward the black hole in the water. Panic filled her. She tried to swim free, but the force was too strong and the water too thick.

"Liora!" Devren yelled.

"Get out of here," she replied. "You can't risk the Gull."

"You're worth more than a Gull," Tariq said.

His hand slipped beneath her arms and she was jerked backwards. A glance showed that Tariq held onto one of the Grebes from Obruo's ship. He angled them toward the Gull. Hyrin stood at the open door waving them inside.

"Obruo," Liora began.

"He's having engine problems," Tariq replied.

She caught his smile.

"Good job."

Tariq was about to reply when his gaze moved past her and his eyes widened. She looked back to where the creature had been. In its place, a black hole loomed bigger and bigger. It pulled water and ice floes inside. The gently glowing structures vanished as soon as they reached the void.

Tariq waited until the last minute to let go of the Grebe. He and Liora sped inside the Gull, bowling Hyrin over.

"Get us out of here!" Tariq shouted.

Liora reached the door panel. Her last glimpse as the door slid shut was of Obruo's ship getting sucked toward the black hole. The Damaclan's gaze locked on hers through the window. She was sure whatever he shouted wasn't pleasant. Her only regret was that it would be the last thing the other Damaclans heard before they died.

The door shut completely and the Gull surged forward. The venting system cleared the water from the hatch, leaving Tariq, Liora, and Hyrin tangled on the floor as the Gull shot into the atmosphere.

Tariq began to laugh; Hyrin joined him. Relief filled Liora and soon she was laughing so hard she had to pull off her shield to keep from passing out.

"That really was an adventure," Tariq said, gasping for air.

"I'm just glad the tape worked," Hyrin told him. "I've never tried it under water."

Liora and Tariq stared at him. Tariq started laughing again.

"So will the orb destroy the planet?" Devren asked.

"I hope not," Hyrin replied. He pushed to his feet.

The others followed him to the window. Through the cloudy haze below, they could see the black hole deep in the water. Obruo's ship hesitated on the edge.

"Come on," Tariq muttered.

Liora's hands gripped the bar beneath the window. She stared intently at the ship, willing it to disappear into the black void so she would never have to worry about Obruo lurking in the shadows of her life again.

"It's close," Devren said from the pilot seat.

"Not close enough," Tariq replied.

"It's shrinking."

Liora's words quieted everyone. Instead of the hole growing and enveloping the ship, it was retracting slowly in the water.

"No," Tariq growled.

His hand gripped Liora's shoulder as he peered out the window. The hole shrunk in front of their eyes until it was half the size it had been, then a quarter.

"I can barely see it," Hyrin said.

A moment later, it disappeared from view. Obruo's ship hung motionless in the water. Liora willed it to vanish like the orb had, but it stubbornly refused.

Devren steered the Gull through the cloudy atmosphere. Hyrin took the seat next to him. Liora slid down to sit on the floor, exhausted by her struggle in the water. Tariq joined her. A sound of surprise escaped her when Tariq rested his head on her shoulder.

He chuckled. "I figure I deserve a break after going through with your suicidal plan."

Liora fought back a smile. "I suppose you do."

She hesitated, then rested her head against his.

He made a little approving grunt.

"I could get used to this," he said.

A smile spread across her face.

"The Kratos is gone."

Everyone sat up at Devren's statement. A glance out the window showed empty space before them. Devren pushed the communicator.

"Officer Straham, we're ready for pickup."

Silence met the captain's words.

Hyrin tried again. "Gull to Kratos, please respond."

There was no reply.

"What's that?"

Liora followed Hyrin's gaze to a piece of metal that flashed in the ship's navigation lights.

Devren steered their craft closer. The metal rotated slowly. Liora's heart slowed when it turned to show them half of a crest on the side. It was part of the Damaclan's ship. The only way the piece would be floating free was if the side of the ship had been torn into.

"We're in trouble," Hyrin breathed.

"Let's keep our heads," Devren told him. "Chart us a course to Verdan."

"Why Verdan?" Hyrin asked in surprise.

"We have a tendency to find our crew members there. If the Kratos is in trouble and Officer Straham was forced to run, I'm hoping he'll think of it. I know Shathryn and O'Tule will."

"Good call," Tariq said. "Will the life support sustain us long enough to get there?"

"Not a chance," Hyrin replied.

"Maybe we can make it to the transporter and radio

from there," Liora suggested.

Hyrin ran some calculations. "I put us about two clicks short."

"Are there any class F or above planets between here and there?" Devren asked.

"Not that I can pick up on this system," Hyrin replied. "The Gull is a space to ground craft. It's not equipped for this."

"How long do you think we have before Obruo catches up?" Tariq asked him.

A smile crossed Hyrin's face. "That's the beauty of messing with the ventilation system. If he gets them untaped, which I'm sure he has, the exhaust that should have been blowing out of the vents from the engine is not, and so water will flood in, swamping the engine. He'll be forced to shut down the entire thing, drain the engine, and then start it up again. It'll be a while."

"But when he gets here...," Devren said.

"We'll be target practice," Liora finished.

Devren sat back in his chair. "Send out the distress beacon."

"Any ship within the same system could pick it up," Hyrin contended. "We might get stuck between a Coalition ship and Obruo. That's one place I don't want to be."

"We don't have any way of knowing what happened to the Kratos," Devren countered. "As it is, our only option is to wait for Obruo to come out of Gliese even angrier than he was when he went in with the intent to kill us. Personally, I don't want to be here when he surfaces."

"Good point," Hyrin replied. He punched in a distress code, then hit the button. The monitor flashed as the code was sent to anyone within range.

"Now we wait," Liora commented.

"Wishing you had stayed on the Kratos instead of joining this little mission?" Tariq asked. "Or is it your insatiable thirst for adventure?"

Liora shook her head. "I just like to see what happens next."

"What happens next is we wait," Hyrin replied. "We wait and we hope someone answers our distress call who isn't Obruo armed and ready to blow us into little bits."

"I like that you're an optimist," Devren told him.

Hyrin crossed his arms and sat back in his seat, his gaze on the monitor. "I'm a realist, Captain." A beep sounded. "But I'm not a realistic ready to die. That's an answer beacon!"

"So soon?" Liora said in surprise.

"Someone must have been working out here," Hyrin replied excitedly.

"Or looking for us," Tariq reminded them.

"Either way, we've caught their attention. Let's just hope we haven't traded one set of missiles for another," Devren said.

Chapter 20

The appearance of the Golden Condor was one nobody expected. The biggest make of ship besides the Atlas Albatross, Golden Condors were generally owned by many businesses working in similar fields. They went from system to system either mining, manufacturing, or selling goods in the form of an entire shopping complex. The fact that one would answer the distress call of a single ground ship shocked the crew on the Gull.

"Is this a good idea?" Hyrin asked. He stared up at the ship that loomed far above them.

"It might be the best case scenario," Devren replied. "Generally merchant ships don't care about the Coalition, mercenaries, or death contracts no matter how high the reward."

"I hope you're right," Hyrin replied.

Devren steered them carefully through the docking bay that looked as though it could comfortably fit fifty ships the size of the Kratos at the same time instead of one puny Gull. Cargo carriers and older mining units took up half of the floor space inside the cargo hold. As soon as they were clear, the hatch slid shut. Devren carefully landed the Gull away from the other crafts.

"Personnel approaching. They're armed," Hyrin reported.

"Take it slow," Devren told them. "We're at their mercy. They could easy turn us over to the Coalition."

"Or scrap our ship and sell us as slaves on Pion Seven," Tariq pointed out.

"On that note," Liora said. She put her hand to the door panel.

The panel slid aside to reveal twelve guards armed with pulse rifles. The guns weren't aimed at them, but the guards held the weapons at ready. Two humans waited beside the guards, a young man who looked a year or two older than Tariq, and an older woman with the stripes of a captain on the sleeves of her uniform. The woman stepped forward the moment Devren's foot touched the floor.

"Welcome to the SS Eos," the older woman with long blonde hair said. "I am Captain Hart. We received your distress signal and you happened to be not far from our destination, so we swung by."

Devren shook her hand. "I am Devren Metis, captain

of the Kratos. This is Tariq, the Kratos chief medic, Hyrin, our technical specialist, and Liora, a member of my security team."

Liora noticed that Devren refrained from introducing any of them as officer. They still wore their atmosphere suits even though they had left the helmets aboard the Gull after the hold pressurized, so the Coalition sigils were covered. She hoped they could remain anonymous.

Captain Hart nodded at each of them in turn. "Welcome aboard."

Devren concluded with, "Something happened to our ship and we missed our pickup. We appreciate the assistance."

"You'd be dead within hours floating around out here," the dark-haired young man behind her said. He stepped to the side of the captain and held out his hand. "My name is Brandis. My family owns this ship."

Hyrin whistled from his place next to Devren. "Your family owns a Golden Condor? Something this size is usually shared by several companies."

Brandis nodded. "My family owns five Condors; the Eos is one of the older models. We run merchant services from system to system."

"Our next stop is Mirach's Ghost Galaxy," Captain Hart said. There was a hint of tightness to her voice when she continued, "We're also running late."

Brandis gave the Kratos crew a warm smile. "My apologies. We are indeed behind schedule. We must be off. My crew will show you to the available quarters." His head tipped slightly to one side when he asked, "Where are you trying to go?"

"Verdan," Devren answered smoothly. "I have family there and I'm hoping the ship we were supposed to catch will be in contact."

"Verdan is in the Cas One Galaxy," Captain Hart said. "It's several clicks out of the way even after the next stop. We couldn't break there without delaying—"

Brandis held up a hand and the captain fell silent. "We will stop in the Cas One Galaxy after Mirach's Ghost. I apologize that we cannot do so earlier, but we have prior commitments."

"I understand," Devren replied. "We are grateful for your assistance and hope we don't put you too far out of your way."

The captain's cloudy expression said otherwise, but she didn't argue with Brandis. Instead, she motioned to one of the armed guards. "Please escort Captain Metis and his crew to the quarters on twenty-seven beta. See that they have a change of clothes and a chance at the showers before dinner."

"Thank you," Devren told her.

She nodded curtly and turned away.

Brandis watched her go. "Don't worry about Captain Hart. She hates it when we're behind schedule. I'll have a word with her."

"No need," Devren told him. "We appreciate your hospitality. You've gone above and beyond."

"Such is our family motto," Brandis replied. He motioned toward the guard who had sheathed her gun and waited silently for them. "Please go with Insa. She will see that your needs are met and you make it to dinner."

He left and several of the guards fell in behind him. Liora and Tariq exchanged a glance.

"That was weird," Tariq whispered.

"This whole situation's weird," Liora replied. "It feels

like too much of a coincidence."

"There's one way to find out," Tariq told her. He motioned toward Insa who led them through the far door.

Liora nodded. She raised her voice. "Excuse me?"

Insa glanced back at her. "Yes?"

"It was very nice to be picked up," she said, trying to sound casual. "Did you happen to be in the area?"

Insa shook her head and pushed a button for the elevator. "We had just left the Milky Way Galaxy. I'm not sure what brought us here."

They stepped silently into the elevator. Devren gave Liora a curious look. Liora lifted her shoulders in reply.

Hyrin cleared his throat. "How does a ship this size get from the Milky Way to Gliese so quickly?"

"It felt like we hit one transporter and then another. I don't remember us traveling so fast before," Insa answered.

She escorted them to a long, empty hallway.

"These rooms are yours." She nodded to Liora. "Miss, yours is the first on the right. Clothes will already have been put on your beds and you'll have a chance to relax a bit. Dinner is at eighteen hundred."

"Thank you," Devren said.

They watched her go.

"This is getting stranger," Tariq commented.

"What?" Devren replied with a hint of sarcasm. "You don't accept that a Golden Condor with an obviously tight delivery schedule went clicks out of its way to scoop up an obsolete Gull with four unknowns aboard?"

Tariq shook his head. "Not one bit."

Devren crossed his arms in front of his chest. "The way I see it, whatever this Brandis guy says, goes. The question is, why rescue us?"

"Maybe he has information about the Kratos?" Hyrin put in.

"Maybe things will clear up at dinner," Liora replied. "I could use some real rest." She gave them a look over. "And you boys need a shower. We all smell like Gliese's fish water."

Tariq snorted with humor and Devren cracked a smile.

Liora put a hand to the panel and her door slid open.

"You could call Liora our sanitation expert," Hyrin suggested.

"Security officer works just fine with me," Liora replied, stepping into her room. The door slid shut behind her.

"If I said that, Liora would kill me," she heard Tariq say on the other side of the door. "You're lucky you're a Talastan. Nobody hits a Talastan."

She smiled and looked around the room.

The quarters were far bigger than her room on the Kratos. Given the ship's size, it shouldn't have been a surprise, but they were strangers and didn't bring anything of use to the Golden Condor. It followed that they should be given the smallest accommodations possible; yet the quarters she stood in would have housed an entire family aboard a homestead ship. A bedroom branched away to the right of the living room she stood in, and the bedroom had its own private washroom complete with a shower.

A change of clothes waited on the bed. They were new and clean, but Liora preferred her Ventican outfit. It had saved her life enough times that giving it up now would be foolhardy.

Liora washed her clothes in the shower, then hung them up to dry while she let the warm water fall over her shoulders. She used the taffala scented shampoo to wash her hair. The ends were getting longer than she liked.

She thought of asking Shathryn to cut it again, and a pang of worry went through her at the thought that they had no idea what had happened to the Kratos or its crew. Hopefully answers would be available on Verdan. According to Tramareaus, there was only a short window of time in which they could get rid of the other orb from the Omne Occasus. Given what had happened on Gliese, she had some idea of what would happen if they failed to do so before it activated.

A knock sounded on the door just as Liora pulled on her dry clothes. She strapped the knife to her thigh before she answered. Tariq stood there with wet hair and an embarrassed expression. He looked different without his uniform. The civilian clothes from the Eos made him appear more relaxed. He held something out. She realized it was the bandages for his ribs.

"Could you assist me with this?" he asked.

"Of course," Liora replied. She motioned for him to come inside. The door slid shut behind them.

When she turned around, Tariq's shirt was in his hand. His left side was nearly black with bruises. Liora touched his skin gently with her fingertips and he winced before gritting his teeth. Touching his skin sent warmth up Liora's arms. It took an effort to push the sensation aside.

Liora let out a slow breath and picked up the bandages. She held them in place with one hand and pulled them steadily tighter with the other.

She heard Tariq's breath catch.

"I'm sorry," she said, her voice soft.

"It doesn't hurt," he replied.

"You're a liar."

She looked up at him with a smile. Her smile faded at the intense emotions in his eyes. His light blue gaze burned as he stared down at her.

"Tariq," she said, her voice barely a whisper.

He covered her mouth with his. His fingers closed around her arms and he pulled her closer. The bandage for his ribs fell forgotten to the floor. Her fingers brushed the bare skin of his back. Tingles ran all over her body. She pressed against him, returning his kiss with an intensity that surprised her. She had never wanted anything in her life more than she wanted to be held in his arms forever.

When he finally stepped back, they stared at each other, flush and out of breath.

"I interrupted your chance to rest," he said with a half-smile.

"And I haven't even wrapped your ribs," she replied. She picked up the bandages. She felt almost embarrassed to look at him. She glanced out of the corner of her eye and found him watching her.

"I really did just come over for that," he said, sounding sheepish. "I don't know why all of my intentions go out the window when I see you."

She met his gaze. "All of your intentions?"

A roguish grin swept across his face. "Well, most of them."

She wrapped his ribs with gentle fingers, careful to keep the pressure even so it would give him support.

When she was done, he took a testing breath.

"Much better," he said with a sigh of relief.

He crossed to her bedroom and came back with an armful of blankets that he began to spread on the living room floor.

"What are you doing?" she asked.

He glanced back at her. "Making you a bed that you'll actually sleep in."

His actions touched her. She had spent so many years in a cage that beds were impossible to lay in for long without feeling so soft they were claustrophobic. He spread the blankets out with care and folded one end down before setting the pillow on top.

"Your bed, miss," he said with a grand sweeping gesture. "Allow me to tuck you in as a thank you for taking care of my ribs."

He waited as though expecting her to lay down.

"Are you serious?" she asked.

He gave her a straight look that was belied by the hint of amusement in the depths of his blue eyes. "I'm always serious, Liora."

She gave in, feeling foolish as she settled on her back on the bed he had made.

"This may be the best floor bed I've ever slept in," she admitted with a half-smile as he lowered the blanket on top of her.

"It was made with all the expertise I possess," he replied.

It was a strange moment, him standing above her, his expression torn as though he wasn't quite sure what his next action would be.

There was something in his face that held her heart, a wistfulness as if he wished they could just forget everything for a moment.

She wanted him to stay, even if it was just to talk until

dinner time. The heaviness of her eyelids and the exhaustion that had filled her body since swimming beneath Gliese's dense water made it difficult to keep her thoughts clear.

"Get some sleep, Liora," Tariq told her. "You look exhausted."

"You do, too," she said, noting the shadows beneath his eyes and the way he looked as though he, too, could barely keep his eyelids open.

He reached for the door panel.

"Stay." The word slipped out before she could stop it.

Tariq looked down at her, his gaze shielded as though he didn't dare let how he felt show. "You want me to stay?"

Liora tried to sound casual despite the way her heart pounded in her chest. "I have a perfectly good floor bed here. Why head all the way back to your room when there's room here for both of us?"

The barest hint of a smile touched Tariq's mouth. "My room is across from yours."

"Oh," Liora replied. She felt a brush of heat color her cheeks.

Instead of leaving, Tariq knelt slowly on the edge of the blanket. Liora moved to one side of the pillow so that there was room for him. He settled there without a word. For a moment, they lay side by side. Liora scolded her heart, telling herself that being so near to him was no reason for it to try to pound out of her chest.

Tariq lifted his arm. It felt so natural to duck beneath it and rest her head on his chest. She could hear his heart beating beneath her ear. A smile touched her lips at the realization that it was pounding just as hard as hers.

"I've never trusted anyone enough to be this close to

them," she admitted softly.

"I don't know if I'll be able to sleep with you so near," he replied, his voice husky.

His fingers touched her hair, softly drawing the strands behind her ear. She set a hand on his bare chest, feeling the way each breath made her head gently rise and fall.

"I'm falling for you, Liora."

His words made her heart slow.

He continued, his voice tired but with the sound of a smile. "I haven't felt this way in such a long time that I barely remember what it is."

"Is it good?" she asked.

"Far better than I ever remembered," he replied. His voice dropped off with a slight outlet of breath.

Liora glanced up and found his eyes closed. She set her head back on his chest with a smile and closed hers as well.

Chapter 21

The dream felt vaguely familiar. Liora walked down the hallway with a feeling of coming home. She smiled at the pictures on the walls, photographs of the smiling couple with the sweet little baby girl. Beneath one of the picture frames, a streak of red caught her attention. It was out of place, bold amid the pale grays of the dream. It was wrong.

Liora reached her fingers out and touched the blood, but something was different. They weren't her fingers. There were scars she didn't have, and they were thicker.

The palms were bigger and there was a ring around one of the fingers.

Liora moved on, following the streak of red. She reached a living room with black and white couches. Across one lay a purple handmade blanket that looked familiar, yet foreign, as if she knew what it felt like to lay cuddled beneath it, and then as though she had never touched the blanket before.

A cry of terror brought Liora's head up. A woman cowered in one corner. A man with tattoos down the left side of his neck advanced toward her. Liora couldn't move or make a sound. The dark blade of the bone knife in his hand buried deep in the woman's stomach. He yanked the blade upward. It cut easily through the flesh, opening the woman from her belly to her neck. He pulled his blade clear and she collapsed to the floor.

A little girl sobbed in the opposite corner. Liora fought to move, to defend her, to do anything she could to stop the Damaclan who brought terror to the familiar house. Her muscles locked, fighting in protest against whatever held her. The blood that dripped from the Damaclan's blade as he advanced toward the girl splashed with agonizing clarity on the white carpet.

The Damaclan's grip tightened. A smile spread across his face. He reached for the girl. She shrieked and tried to escape, but he was faster. He caught her by one arm and lifted her easily. The little girl cried. Liora shouted. The Damaclan's head jerked up. He turned to look at her, and suddenly Liora was staring at herself, a twisted smile on her face and the Damaclan markings down her neck. Her smile deepened and she drove the knife into the little girl's chest.

"Liora, time for dinner."

Liora's eyes flew open at the knock on the door. Her heart raced and her breath caught in her throat. She kept seeing her own face, the glee in her eyes and the mocking smile as she killed Tariq's little Lissy.

"Liora?"

She rolled to her knees and stared at Tariq. He looked up at her, his eyes wide and his own chest heaving.

"I-I had a nightmare," he said quietly. He sat up and rubbed his eyes as if he was having trouble clearing what he had seen from his mind.

"Me, too," Liora said.

A knock sounded on the door again.

"Liora, we're heading to the cafeteria. I think Tariq is already there," Devren called.

"I-I'll meet you there," Liora replied.

"Alright," Devren said. "I'll save you a seat."

"Thank you," Liora answered.

She turned her gaze back to Tariq. He watched her with a furrowed brow, the blanket gripped so tightly in his hands that his knuckles showed white.

"Liora, I dreamed…." His voice faded away.

"I know." It was hard to admit, harder still to see the pain fill his gaze.

"You dreamed my dream," he said.

Liora nodded. "I don't know why. I-I didn't mean to."

Tariq shook his head. "I don't know why I saw that. It felt so real."

"I didn't kill her," Liora said. She didn't know how to erase the agony from his gaze. It was as if he had experienced losing his wife all over again, and this time from Liora's hand.

"I know," he replied, but he lowered his gaze to the

floor as if he couldn't meet her eyes.

Liora had hurt him again, even if there had been nothing she could do to prevent it. Just being near her had caused him more pain. She rose.

"I'm going to go," she said.

Tariq caught her hand as she turned away.

"Liora."

He said her name so gently it made her eyes fill with tears. She refused to let them fall. As much as she wanted to stay, she couldn't face him. The sensations that came with killing his family had been all too real. Her hand remembered the weight of the knife she had held and the simple effort it had taken to plunge it into Dannan's body and then Lissy's. She rubbed her palms on her pants, but the feeling refused to go away.

She took a calming breath and forced a composed expression to chase the regret from her face.

"I'm going to head to the cafeteria before Devren comes back looking for us."

"Good idea," Tariq replied. He watched her, his eyes cloudy.

Liora crossed to the door. She put her palm to the reader and it slid open. She glanced back once to see Tariq still standing where he had been. His eyes lingered on the bed at their feet, but his gaze was distant as though he saw something else instead.

When she reached the cafeteria, Liora was still caught thinking about the dream. Someone called her name and she jerked back to the present.

The room she stood in could have fit the entire Kratos. The ceiling arched high above, ending in a dome of windows that showed the stars beyond. Rows upon rows of tables before her were filled with all manner of mortalkind. The scents of so many varieties of foods filled her nose, and the strange spices made her want to sneeze.

"Liora, over here."

She spotted Devren and the others near the wall at the far end. Devren pointed to the spot next to him where there was already a tray laden with food. Relieved that she wouldn't have to brave the long line of people still waiting to be served, Liora made her way to the others.

"Have you seen Tariq?" Devren asked when she sat down. "I knocked on his door, but he didn't answer. I assumed we would find him here." He waved a hand. "But good luck spotting anyone in this chaos."

"I haven't seen him." She hoped Devren didn't hear the way her voice fell flat at the lie. She wasn't prepared to face the inevitable questions that would ensue if she mentioned that they had fallen to sleep together in her room.

"I'm sure he'll be here soon," Hyrin said. "Tariq's never been one to turn down a good meal." He leaned closer to Liora and whispered conspiratorially, "Jarston mentioned that Tariq raids the Kratos kitchen at night if he can't sleep. He often leaves a slice of pie out for our chief medical officer just in case."

The thought brought a small smile to Liora's lips. "That's nice of him."

"There he is," Hyrin said.

"Tariq, over here," Devren called.

Liora pretended to be fully immersed in the food in front of her. She didn't glance up until Tariq took the seat across the table from her. He met her gaze, then looked away as if he couldn't quite bear to see her. She turned her attention back to her food, but the reds stood out with too much contrast to the rest and she couldn't make herself take a bite.

"And when I hit it, guts squished out everywhere," Hyrin was telling Devren.

Liora gave him a searching look.

"Uh, the bug in my room," Hyrin said. His eyes blinked rapidly as if her expression disconcerted him. "It was massive."

"I'm sure you handled it with ease," Tariq replied. "Don't you think, Liora?"

He gave her a smile, but she still saw the mixed emotions buried beneath his calm demeanor where less than an hour before there had only been something warm and enveloping.

She hadn't murdered Dannan and Lissy, as much as it felt like she had. But if she wasn't the one responsible for their lifeless bodies spilling blood on the white carpet of Tariq's homestead apartment, why did she feel so guilty? She had killed many people, so why did the two she had nothing to do with haunt her more than any of them?

Liora stood with her tray.

"Going already?" Devren asked.

"I'm not really hungry," she said, though the rumble in her stomach argued otherwise.

Devren nodded, concern bright in his eyes. "Perhaps you need some more rest. You look pale."

She forced a smile. "I am still a bit worn out. I think sleep will help."

She walked away from the table without looking at anyone else.

She thought she heard Tariq speak her name, but it could have been just her imagination. The noise of the crowd, the sound of utensils on trays, and the calls of strangers in a multitude of tongues became a muted roar she welcomed to drive the confusion from her mind.

She had dumped the uneaten portion of her food into the chute designated in several languages for that purpose and set her tray on a stack near the door when someone spoke next to her.

"It's Liora, right?"

She glanced over and found Brandis watching her.

He smiled. "I don't think we've been properly introduced."

She shoved her disconcerting thoughts away and focused. "It was kind of you to rescue our crew. We're in your debt."

Brandis shook his head. "Nonsense. We happened to be in the area."

Liora thought of Insa's comment about how quickly the Eos had rushed from the Milky Way Galaxy to the Gull.

"What a fortunate coincidence," she replied.

Brandis nodded. "Most fortunate." He indicated the tray she had just set down. "Did you get enough to eat? I hope you found the food to your liking. Our chefs try to offer a variety of options to meet the diversity of palates aboard the Eos."

"The food was fine," she said. "Thank you for asking."

Brandis paused as if searching for something else to say. She wondered why he took the time to talk to her when he obviously had so much that demanded his attention aboard the massive starship.

As if in answer to her unspoken thought, he said, "Allow me to give you a tour of the Eos. It, like the rest of our merchant fleet, offers a vast array of sights unlike anything else in the Macrocosm."

"A tour, huh?"

The voice set Liora on edge. She met the glare of a Gaul who leaned against the nearest wall with his thick arms crossed. He watched her with narrow eyes in the same way that a predator watches a pest.

"Yes, Knox. Do you have a problem with that?" Brandis replied. He showed no sign of being bothered by the Gaul's angry tone.

"I think the less this *Damaclan* sees of the Eos, the better," Knox replied; his face twisted in distaste at the word Damaclan.

"Liora and the rest of her crew are guests aboard the Eos," Brandis replied calmly. "I ask that you show her respect."

"For what?" Knox demanded. The sounds of talking in the cafeteria fell away. "For being a murderous cutthroat? For thriving on bloodshed and fear?" He leaned closer to Liora. "Want my respect, little Damaclan? Curl up and die. Perhaps I can respect the way the rotting of your body leaves the Macrocosm a little safer."

Liora felt as much as saw Tariq and Devren come up beside them. Both humans looked angry enough to take on the Gaul themselves.

"Knox," Brandis said with warning in his voice. "Apologize or face the consequences."

"I'll never apologize to a race that is far inferior in both intellect and diplomacy," the Gaul replied. He bent so that his big ox nose was right in front of Liora's face. "You Damaclans gave up any chance at respect when you chose violence instead of amity and slaughter instead of peace."

"And what facet of peace are you showing right now?" Liora replied.

The Gaul's eyes narrowed and he snorted in anger. Liora swore she saw the ghost of a smile brush Brandis' face, but she kept her gaze on the Gaul.

"How dare you question me?" he growled. He grabbed her with a meaty hand.

The moment he touched her, Liora reacted. She caught his hand in an iron grip, ducked beneath it and spun, locking his arm behind his back. She punched his kidney twice, then drove the ball of her foot into the back of his knee. He hit the ground hard. Keeping ahold of his hand, she rolled over his back and used her momentum to throw him over her. He landed on his back on the tiled floor. She grabbed a fork from Tariq's tray, knelt on his arms, and pressed the tines against his shaggy throat.

"You attacked me, Gaul," she said, her voice deep with anger. "I didn't say a word, I didn't hurt a soul aboard your ship, yet you laid into me with hatred and prejudice before you even knew my name." She glared down at him. "You say mine is a race of lower intellect? Perhaps you should reevaluate your superiority before you accost someone with the ability to cut your throat with a fork and not think twice about it."

Liora realized there wasn't a single sound in the entire cafeteria. It shouldn't be possible that so many individuals could hold completely still. Knowing what she would find, she raised her gaze to see that every person watched in silence. Some stood above the others on the chairs and benches to get a better view. Fear, awe, and confusion showed on the faces around the tables.

Liora was tired of being a show. She reminded herself that she had chosen to act. She should have just walked away, but she couldn't pass up the chance to teach the huge Gaul a lesson, especially when he laid a hand on her.

Liora breathed out slowly through her nose. She may have just single-handedly eliminated the welcome the Kratos crew had found aboard the Eos. Attacking a member of the starship that had rescued them didn't exactly fall under the friendly relations section of the crew's public affairs handbook.

Yet she vaguely recalled Brandis' smile. If it wasn't a figment of her imagination, it may be the one thing to alleviate the situation before they were sent packing.

Liora looked up at Brandis. The human watched her with raised eyebrows and a half-smile on his face as though she had just exceeded his expectations. That fact that he wasn't upset gave her hope.

Liora rose slowly to her feet, careful to keep an eye on the Gaul in case he tried to retaliate. There were a few ways she knew she could handle the situation that might allow the tension to diffuse; taking a page from Tariq's book, she went with sarcastic humor.

"I apologize for my reaction," she said loudly enough that it would carry through the cafeteria. "I get a bit cranky when I haven't had enough sleep."

Brandis chuckled and the sound of laughter rolled through the crowd.

She set the fork back on Tariq's tray. "I'd recommend washing that," she said.

More laughter met her words.

She looked at Brandis. "What were you saying about a tour?"

"Ah, yes, the tour," Brandis replied. He gave a sweep of his arm toward the cafeteria's double doors. "Right this way."

Devren and Tariq followed, with Hyrin hurrying to catch up. Everyone gave the Gaul on the ground a wide berth.

As soon as the cafeteria doors slid shut, Brandis let out a low whistle.

"That was impressive."

"I'm sorry," Liora began, but she paused when Brandis held up a hand.

"No need to apologize. If a member of my crew accosts a guest aboard the Eos, the guest should feel secure enough to defend him or herself." He paused, then said, "In your case, I'll admit that I wanted it to happen."

Liora stared at him. "You what?"

Tariq crossed his arms and glared at Brandis. "Did you set Liora up?"

Brandis held up both hands. "No, no; nothing like that." He gave Liora an assessing look. "Though the rumors of a female Damaclan wreaking havoc around the Macrocosm has preceded you. I'll admit that I was curious about the accuracy of the stories."

"So you did smile," Liora said.

"What are you talking about?" Devren asked.

"I did," Brandis acknowledged. "Knox gets a bit full of himself. He'll undergo disciplinary action for attempting to bully one of my guests, though I'm hoping he learned something from his encounter with you."

"That goes far beyond bullying," Hyrin pointed out.

Brandis nodded. "I figured Liora could handle herself."

The way he said her name with such familiarity bothered Liora. She watched him as he led the way through the ship, holding true to his promise to give them a tour. When the others were staring at the vast manufacturing system that made up the production floor, Liora caught Brandis studying her with a thoughtful expression.

He showed them through the massive water recycling chambers and the adjoining greenhouses that took up the entire belly of the ship and stretched so far the end wasn't visible from the door.

"We even grow our own flowers," Brandis said. He opened the door and motioned for Liora to step through into a smaller room. "While some of them are edible, we enjoy the rest for their aesthetic appeal. It's much easier to feel at ease aboard a merchant ship when the comforts of home are available."

Liora gazed at the variety of flowers that filled the room in every color she could imagine. She breathed deeply of the delicate scent that laced the air, sure she had never smelled something so beautiful in her entire life.

"Go ahead and look around," Brandis urged.

Liora wandered through the aisles. She had heard about roses but never seen their beauty. Her hand strayed to one with purple petals. She pulled back at the last moment, reminding herself that to touch one would be rude given the courtesy Brandis had already shown them.

"Take it," Brandis said from the next row.

"I couldn't," Liora replied.

He leaned over and cut the rose with a knife she hadn't noticed was strapped at his wrist beneath his shirtsleeve. Perhaps Brandis didn't leave as many things to chance as she assumed.

He held the rose out. "It's yours."

Liora accepted it, careful not to touch the thorns that lined the stem.

"It's beautiful," she said.

"I didn't know Damaclans appreciated beauty," Brandis replied.

At her questioning look, he appeared self-conscious for the first time. "Pardon my rudeness. I didn't mean to imply that Damaclans are without the ability to enjoy beauty; the race has just never struck me as, well, one to appreciate the appeal of flowers."

Liora took pity on his fumbling. "No offense taken. I'm only half-Damaclan. Where beauty might be seen as a weakness in my clan, I find the reminder of my humanity to be reassuring."

Brandis gave her a curious look. "Do you regret the tattoos?"

Liora glanced to the right and found Tariq watching them with an unreadable expression on his face. He was too far away to hear what they were talking about, but it was obvious he didn't know how to feel about Brandis.

Liora shook her head, grateful to have some space from him after the dream. "I can't deny my heritage. It might make me a target, but it's also a warning as much as the stripes of a swarthan. One can't detain me by accident."

"So you weren't surprised by Knox's attack."

"Not at all," Liora replied. "It tends to happen in large crowds. Damaclans aren't exactly anyone's favorite race. We leave blood and carnage in our wake. We deserve what we get."

"You mean *they* deserve what *they* get," Brandis replied. "You're not really one of them."

"Ask Knox about that," Liora replied.

Brandis' wristband beeped.

"Excuse me a moment," he said. He pushed a button on the band. "Yes, Captain Hart?"

"We've reached NGC Four Zero Four," Captain Hart replied. "The homestead ships are waiting."

"Send out the welcome beacon," Brandis told her. "Let's open shop."

He gave Liora a smile. "Come see the controlled chaos of system to system peddling."

Chapter 22

Liora stared at the hundreds of ships lined up to dock at the Golden Condor's port.

"How can they handle so many people?" she asked no one in particular.

Despite her concerns, it appeared the Eos was well-equipped for such an influx. Their view on the walkway above the market hall showed the organization of hundreds of vendors arranged by product and craft. The staff of the Eos escorted the members of each ship through with marked efficiency, and when the homestead,

Coalition, and rebel ships left, the individuals carried their purchased wares with pleased expressions.

"Impressive," Hyrin remarked.

"It seems Brandis' family has vending down to an art form," Devren replied.

"Let's see it firsthand," Tariq suggested.

"Are you volunteering to go down there?" Devren asked.

Tariq appeared bothered by his friend's surprised tone. "I have been known to mingle at times."

"By choice?"

Tariq's jaw clenched before he said, "When it suits me." He motioned to Liora. "What do you say? You might find something more appealing than a flower full of thorns."

Liora followed Tariq down the stairs and the others fell in behind them. The control they had seen above appeared to dissipate the moment they reached the floor. The crowds rushed past intent on filling the lists they each scanned through on their armbands. There was no hawking like Liora was used to at the circus. Instead, signs bearing prices were held by silent vendors who merely exchanged bars and thanked purchasers with calm, low voices. There was no haggling, and nobody appeared surprised at the amounts being charged.

"A sack of stano leaf for four copper bars?" Officer Hyrin said. "Captain Devren, we should be shopping here instead of the Gauldeds."

Devren nodded. "I was thinking the same thing. The prices are reasonable considering the goods have been flown across the Macrocosm."

Liora's eye was caught by a vendor selling jewelry. Usually, she thought of such things as frillery and useless, but the vendor also had weapons worked with such craftsmanship they appeared too delicate to be serviceable.

She selected a blade with a purple stone in the middle of the silver worked hilt.

"May I?" she asked the vendor.

At his welcoming nod, she slid the knife from its sheath. A closer examination revealed that a sunburst was crafted along the blade, its rays augmented by two different shades of metal. The handle fit her fingers like it had been made for her; she twirled it experimentally.

"It suits you," Tariq said.

She felt embarrassed to be caught browsing when they were supposed to be analyzing the sales floor.

"Don't put it back," Tariq told her when she reached for the sheath. He spoke to the vendor. "How much?"

"One platinum bar," the vendor replied. "The blade is Zamarian crafted and the silver of the handle has been enriched with Zamarian steel for strength. The stone is Marathyst from Corian. This weapon has been crafted with both beauty and serviceability in mind."

The price startled Liora. One platinum bar was worth two iridium bars or two hundred copper coins. It was far more than she had ever owned in her lifetime. She smiled and sheathed the knife again.

"Thank you for letting me look," she said.

"Anytime," the vendor replied with a gracious nod.

"We'll take it."

Liora stared at Tariq. "You're going to buy it?" She offered it to him with a startled expression. "Do you carry that much?"

Tariq gestured to Hyrin. "He carries it."

"He has a credit with the Kratos," Hyrin told her.

"Tariq never spends his money. Never." His tone told of his amazement that the man was actually purchasing something.

"I'm buying it for you," Tariq said. He nodded to the vendor. The man took the blade and began to wrap it.

Liora shook her head. "You can't buy this for me."

"I can," Tariq replied. "And I am."

Liora backed up. "That's ridiculous. You could buy a starship for that price."

Tariq quirked a smile. "You could invest in a starship, but I've never seen one for that low of a cost. It would probably implode with pressure inconsistencies the moment it cleared the hold."

"You're changing the subject," Liora pointed out.

"You're being difficult," Tariq said. "You want the knife, I have the money. It should be as easy as that."

"But you shouldn't spend that much on me," Liora replied. "You shouldn't spend any money on me."

Tariq watched her with a thoughtful expression as if her reaction charmed him. "Why not?"

Liora stepped back into the crowd and the table was lost from view. She took a few steps and was suddenly aware of the flowing throng. She felt like a rock in a stream the way the people flooded around her. Some acted as though she wasn't there; others noticed the tattoos down her neck and gave her a wide berth. Those invariably looked back as if to make sure she didn't follow them like some death bearer intent on killing anything foolish enough to make eye contact. The room felt too small for the amount of people rushing through it. Tariq's comment about a ship imploding felt very real.

Devren appeared at her side, his smile comforting.

"What do you think of all this?" he asked.

"Overwhelming," Liora replied.

Devren gave her a closer look. "Are you alright?"

Liora walked with him through the crowd, grateful to be away from the others for a moment.

"I'm not sure," she said. At Devren's questioning look, she said, "Tariq tried to buy a knife."

"He should," Devren replied. "He never spends money on anything."

"That's what Hyrin said." Liora paused, then continued, "He wanted to buy it for a platinum bar."

Devren's eyes widened. "That must be some knife."

"He wanted to give it to me."

Devren stopped. The crowd flowed around them. This time, at least with Devren there, Liora felt a little less like everyone was waiting for her to attack them.

"Tariq wanted to buy you a knife for a platinum bar?" Devren repeated.

Liora nodded.

Devren stared at her. His brow creased. "He's never bought anything for anyone other than drinks at taverns for the crew. It's not like him to put himself out there like that."

Liora nodded again.

Devren blew out a breath. "He cares about you, Liora." He watched her closely as if her reaction to his words meant everything to him.

She didn't want to hurt him. Devren had been nicer to her than anyone she could ever remember. He had freed her from Malivian's circus. He had sworn her in as a member of the Kratos crew, giving her both a purpose and a home. He had been sweet, understanding, and patient, and now he watched her with the expression of one who just realized his best friend was in love with the girl he had perhaps considered giving his heart to.

Liora owed it to him to be completely honest. "I care about him, too."

A smile spread across Devren's face. He looked as though he was so happy he could barely contain it.

"That's wonderful!" he said with a laugh. "That's amazing! Tariq needs somebody; he's been so alone. He keeps inside of himself so much I always worry about him. Losing Dannan and Lissy almost killed him."

Devren's expression changed. His smile faded and his gaze clouded.

"But you're a Damaclan."

Liora looked away from him. They were the words she had fought against since she first came aboard the Kratos. Tariq's hatred of the Damaclan race was perfectly understandable, and the dream she had just shared with him echoed that taboo. Her tattoos marked her as the thing that had destroyed his life. How would he ever be able to see past it long enough for them to work out?

"I can't fight that," Liora said.

Devren touched her arm. "Liora, if he's fallen for you, he's already fighting it. That means something."

"You think so?" Liora studied Devren's face, hoping for something she didn't dare believe.

He smiled at her. "I think so."

"It's like fighting through a zanderbin stampede to get over here," Tariq said, reaching them. He paused on seeing them so close together. Tariq looked from Devren to Liora. "Devren, we need to—"

"Devren?" a woman repeated the name. "As in Devren Metis, Captain of the SS Kratos?"

The three of them turned to find several older women watching them.

"Uh, yes, ma'am," Devren replied. "Pleased to meet you, miss…."

"Rebea Maylis. I am Stone Maylis' sister." She paused, then corrected herself. "I was Stone's sister."

The Kratos crew members exchanged glances.

"I know this isn't the most opportune time," Rebea continued, "But could we please have a moment with you? There are some unanswered questions about my brother's death that continue to haunt me."

Devren looked around. It was obvious running into Stone's sister was the last thing he had expected. He gave her a gracious smile. "Of course. Please bring your family to our quarters. It's quieter there."

Two other women and several children followed them through the long hallways of the Eos. Liora glanced at Devren and Tariq. Both men looked apprehensive about what the conversation might hold in store. Given all they had been through with Stone, the next few minutes weren't going to be easy.

"Thank you for seeing us," Rebea said when they were seated in Devren's living room. "I apologize for accosting you like this, but given the circumstances, it would be a lost opportunity if we let you go. This is my sister Nessa and my aunt Ciril."

Devren's eyes followed the children who wandered around the room pointing at things and whispering to each other.

"Are any of these children Stone's?" he asked quietly. His expression said he feared the answer.

Rebea gave him a kind smile. "No. Stone was unmarried. His heart lay in the cause of the Revolution instead of in family."

Liora thought with a pang of regret about Stone and

Shathryn's attachment to each other.

"The reason we're here is because we know Stone died in a confrontation with the Coalition," Rebea continued. "We've lost many of our men and women in such a way. The only difference is that he mentioned you before we received word of his death."

Her sister took up the story. "The night before Stone's ship was destroyed, he sent us a transmission saying that he had found a cause greater than the Revolution. It was something we had never heard from him before. We found out later that he had left the majority of those who flew with him at a Gaulded for fear of the danger they would face." Nessa paused and tears showed in her eyes when she said, "Those he left spoke of Captain Devren Metis and his, well, your fight to save the Macrocosm from something even more dangerous than this war."

Silence filled the room. Tariq and Devren appeared touched by Nessa's words and at a loss as to how to reply. Nobody knew Stone had left ship members behind.

Liora knew the loss she saw in the eyes of Stone's family. Having been the one that was usually the cause of somebody else's heartache, she had never addressed others after a death. She steeled her nerves and chose what she would want to hear given the same situation.

"Rebea, Nessa, and Ciril, Stone left a great impression on the crew of the SS Kratos. He was brave, selfless, and willing to put his life on the line to help those who looked to him for protection."

Liora pushed comfort toward them, hoping it would help when she searched for words. "I don't know how much he told you about our mission, but Stone and our captain stumbled upon a danger far bigger than any of us were prepared to face. In our effort to destroy the danger, it forced the SS Kratos to run from the Coalition. Stone joined us. He was our only ally and friend, and in the end, he sacrificed his life, crew, and ship to save us from a Coalition attack and give us the chance we needed to escape."

Liora gave them a small smile. "Thanks to your brother's sacrifice, we were able to destroy part of the danger and we are on route to eliminate the rest of it."

Devren took up where she left off. "Stone taught us a great deal about trust regardless of title or reason. He opened my eyes to possibilities beyond this war, and what it means to truly serve the greater cause." He gave them a grateful smile. "He will always be a mentor to me."

All three women had tears in their eyes. The children had fallen silent when Liora spoke, and they looked from their family to the Kratos crew members.

Liora hadn't often been around children, but she swore she saw Stone in their faces. She hoped what she said helped them. They were young, but perhaps they would remember what it meant to fight for something bigger than themselves; it was a lesson she was still learning.

"Stone always said he would die for the cause," Rebea told them. She wiped the tears from her cheeks. "When those on the Gaulded returned to our homestead ship and told us what had happened, they said he was excited for the chance to fight back. Your account of what happened helps with that." She smiled at Liora. "My brother was a kind, caring man. I'm glad to know he died fighting for others."

Everyone stood. Hugs were exchanged, and when the women and children left, silence filled the room behind them.

Devren squeezed his closed eyes with one hand. "That was harder than I thought it would be." He looked at Liora. "Thank you for what you said."

Liora let out a breath. "I feel like it was far short of what Stone deserved."

Tariq shook his head. "It was eloquent and comforting. You told them the truth, and what they needed to hear." He gave her a searching look. "I thought you weren't a big people person."

"I'm not," Liora replied. "I'm usually horrible when it comes to situations like that." She paused, then said, "But I thought about what Stone would want them to know. I hope it helped."

"I think it helped more than you know," Devren told her.

"And the pushing helped," Tariq said.

"You felt that?"

Tariq nodded, his gaze holding her. "I can always feel it when you do that."

Devren glanced from Liora to Tariq, then cleared his throat. "I, uh, forgot about something I needed to buy. I'm going to find Hyrin on the merchant level."

He left without another word.

Tariq watched the closed door from his seat on the couch for a moment. "He knows there's something between us."

"He asked me," Liora replied. When Tariq looked at her, she dropped her gaze to the floor. "He found me after you tried to buy the knife. He said you don't normally purchase things for other people." She fell silent, then continued with, "He said he was glad you found someone you cared about"

"What did you tell him?"

She looked up at Tariq's curious tone. He watched her, his light blue eyes searching her face. She held his gaze and forced out the words despite how hard they were to say, "I told him I cared about you, but I didn't know if we could get past my Damaclan heritage."

Tariq pulled something from behind his belt. When he unwrapped the package, the knife sat in his hand. He turned it over, studying the craftsmanship.

"Liora, do you know why I paid so much for this knife?"

She shook her head.

Tariq ran his fingers over the purple stone in the hilt. "Because I have never seen you want anything." He glanced at her. "You fight for everyone else, you do whatever you need to, but you never ask for anything in return." He held the knife out to her. "You deserve this."

A lump formed in Liora's throat. She took the blade, but didn't know what to say.

Tariq leaned his elbows on his knees and linked his hands over his head. When he broke the silence again, his voice was thick.

"Liora, loving me won't be easy. I'm damaged, maybe broken; I don't know." He looked at her. "All I know is that while a Damaclan…" He paused as if it was hard to say. He took a breath and continued, "A Damaclan destroyed my life with the edge of a blade. Maybe another Damaclan can heal it the same way."

Tears spilled free. He drove his palms into his eyes and a sob tore from his chest.

Liora knelt in front of him and touched his knee. He leaned his head against her. She held him, her chin on top of his head and her arms around him.

"I've got you," she told him quietly. "It's okay."

She hesitated a moment, then shoved her fears away and pushed toward him. She sent comfort, reassurance, and pushed the flicker of love that had grown inside of her to the point that it scared her with how much she cared about him.

Tariq's breath caught in his throat. His shoulders stilled. After a moment, he raised his head and looked at her. He shook his head, his eyes on hers.

"How?" he asked. He swallowed, and said, "How can you love me so much after all you know about me? What is there left to love?"

Tears filled Liora's eyes. "I could ask you the same thing," she said.

Tariq chuckled and wiped his cheeks; when she smiled in return, her tears spilled free.

"We are both so damaged." Tariq wiped her tears away gently with the pads of his thumbs. "Love sometimes seems scarier than anything else in life. Maybe it's the next battle; one that we can fight together."

"I would like that," she said, smiling at him with more tears threatening to run over.

"I would, too," Tariq replied.

He kissed her, then pulled back and looked at her. The vulnerability in his eyes made Liora's heart skip sideways in her chest.

"I would, too," Tariq repeated. He closed his eyes and kissed her again.

Chapter 23

"Captain Devren?"

"Yes, Captain Hart?" Devren answered the page from the intercom.

"We have reached the Cas One Galaxy. Verdan is in sight."

A smile spread across Devren's face. "Thank you, Captain Hart. We'll head to the Gull."

Devren turned to his crew. "Let's hope the others have left word with Mother. It would be nice to get back to the Kratos."

"I miss home," Hyrin replied. "I hope Straham's been good to my baby."

When they reached the Gull, Liora was surprised to see Brandis waiting for them.

"I've always wanted to see the famed lightning planet," Brandis said with an easy smile. "Care if I fly with you? I can have a ground craft pick me up if you plan to stay."

"We owe you much more than that for your hospitality," Devren replied. "You're welcome to come with us."

They climbed onto the Gull. A thrill of excitement went through Liora.

As if he felt it, Tariq gave her a questioning look. "Are you alright?"

She nodded. "Just anxious to be back on the Kratos. I think it's the first time I've actually been homesick for somewhere before."

Tariq smiled at her. "It's a good sign when you miss the ship you live on."

Hyrin pushed a button on the console. "This is Hyrin of the Starship Kratos requesting permission to enter Verdan."

Silence answered his call. He pushed the button again.

"This is Hyrin of the SS Kratos. Please clear a path for us to land on Verdan."

"The SS Kratos?" a voice replied. "Are Devren and Tariq with you?"

Hyrin glanced back at them. Confusion showed in his gaze.

"We are," Devren answered.

The man paused, then said, "Dev, we've had some problems. You need to get to Echo right away."

Devren stood. "What happened, Josen?"

"Just, uh, just get down there. We'll clear a path."

The lightning pulled apart and Hyrin steered the Gull through. Everyone stared intently out the window at the dark ground below.

"Where are the lights?" Tariq asked quietly.

Liora stared at the darkness. The glow of the plants and warm windows that normal heralded Echo was gone.

Hyrin landed in a dark field. Tariq slammed a fist on the door panel. The moment it slid open, he and Devren took off running.

Liora followed close behind them. The knife Tariq had given her was strapped to her side. Her hand strayed to the one on her thigh to ensure that it was buckled in place. She didn't know what they would find, but she planned to be ready for it.

She reached the open door of the Metis house. The looming darkness said more than words. Devren appeared in the doorway; the glowing torch he held illuminated his pale face.

"They're gone. The table's turned over and a window's broken. They didn't go easily," he said, his chest heaving.

Tariq appeared around the corner. "There are track marks out back. Whoever took them landed over the garden."

"I'm going to town. Someone must know what happened," Devren said.

The three of them hurried along the path to Echo. Liora glanced back and saw Brandis following them at a slower pace. He seemed to realize something was wrong, but he didn't question them.

Devren and Tariq slowed. A glance ahead showed the

reason why.

Echo had been leveled to the ground. Each building stood in ruin. Fragments and shrapnel showed the type of weaponry that had been used. The houses had been burned along with the church and tavern. The horn on the post in the middle of town that heralded the static producing thunder had been crushed and broken. Even the livestock lay slain in their pens.

After a few minutes of searching, they found a pile of bodies behind the church house. Several felis carcasses lay torn and mutilated with them. The sight gripped Liora's heart in a fist.

"They're over a week old," Devren said with tears in his eyes.

Tariq shrugged out of his overshirt and spread it across Consul Blairia's still face.

"Who could do this?" Brandis asked.

"Obruo," Tariq and Liora answered at the same time.

Liora's eyes were locked on the message scrawled across the side of the partially-burned church house in blood. Devren followed her gaze.

"I have your family."

Below the words was a rough drawing of a blade in the Eye of Tessari. It was the same emblem the tattoo Liora bore beneath her left ear.

"I'll kill him," Devren growled. Tears showed in his eyes and his hands curled into fists. "He'll pay for this."

"Yes, he will," Tariq replied. He put a hand on his best friend's shoulder. "We will find him and we'll find Mrs. M and Kiari, I promise."

Devren stared at him. "We fought Obruo on Gliese less than a week ago."

The realization of what he was saying struck Liora

hard. "Mrs. Metis and Kiari were on the ship."

Devren slumped against the side of the church. "We almost killed them."

"We had no way of knowing," Liora replied. She knelt in front of Devren. "You can't take that on yourself. They're still out there. We're going to find them. You can't give up hope."

"How do we find the Kratos?" Devren asked. He looked at Tariq. "How do we fight back when we don't even have a ship?"

Tariq shook his head. The shock of finding the town destroyed showed in his stormy eyes.

"I need a drink," he said.

He held out a hand to Devren. When Devren took it, Tariq pulled his friend to his feet.

Liora followed them into the wrecked remains of the tavern. Only two walls remained. The tables where they had spent nights being entertained by Tariq and Devren's friends lay in ashes. The thought of Sveth and Granson's bodies among those behind the church made her heart tighten even further. They deserved to be avenged.

Brandis spoke from behind her. "It's a shame what happened here."

Liora couldn't stand it any longer. She grabbed him by the throat and pinned him to the mantel above the empty fireplace.

"What is wrong with you? Why are you following me?" she demanded.

"Because I know your father," he replied, his voice tight through her grip on his throat.

"Obruo isn't my father," she growled.

"I know, because I know who your real father is."

Liora stared at him.

"You might want to let him down," Tariq suggested quietly.

Liora lowered Brandis to the ground. She dropped her hands. "Why do you know that?" she demanded.

Brandis looked at her, his gaze unflinching. "Because I'm his son."

She stared at him, willing the words to sink in.

Brandis watched Liora steadily, her fingermarks bright on his throat. "The Days own the biggest merchant fleet in the Macrocosm. If you want to find Obruo and make him pay for what he's done, you have every weapon available at your disposal."

"Why are you saying this?" Liora asked. Her thoughts whirled with what he was telling her.

"Because you are a Day, Liora, and it's time to come home."

DAYLIGHT

About the Author

Cheree Alsop has published over 30 books, including two series through Stonehouse Ink. She is the mother of a beautiful, talented daughter and amazing twin sons who fill every day with joy and laughter. She is married to her best friend, Michael, the light of her life and her soulmate who shares her dreams and inspires her by reading the first drafts and giving much appreciated critiques. Cheree works as a fulltime author and mother, which is more play than work! She enjoys reading, traveling to tropical beaches, spending time with her wonderful children, and going on family adventures while planning her next book.

Cheree and Michael live in Utah where they rock out, enjoy the outdoors, plan great quests, and never stop dreaming.

You can find Cheree's other books at
www.chereealsop.com

Find *Girl from the Stars Book 3- Day's End* wherever books are sold.

If you enjoyed this book, please review it here so that other readers will be able to find it:
Barnes & Noble Link: B&N Review
Amazon Review Link: Amazon Review
Goodreads Review Link: Goodreads Review

To be added to Cheree's email list for notification of book releases, please send her an email at chereelalsop@hotmail.com

DAYLIGHT

REVIEWS

The Werewolf Academy Series

If you love werewolves, paranormal, and looking for a book like House of Night or Vampire Academy this is it! YA for sure.
—Reviewer for Sweets Books

I got this book from a giveaway, and it's one of the coolest books I have ever read. If you love Hogwarts, and Vampire Academy, or basically anything that has got to do with supernatural people studying, this is the book for you.
—Maryam Dinzly

This series is truly a work of art, sucked in immediately and permanently. The first line and you are in the book. Cheree Alsop is a gifted writer, all of her books are my complete favorites!! This series has to be my absolute favorite, Alex is truly a wonderful character who I so wish was real so I can meet him and thank him. Once you pick this book up you won't put it down till it's finished. A must read!!!!!
—BookWolf Brianna

Listed with Silver Moon as the top most emotional of Cheree's books, I loved Instinct for its raw truth about the pain, the heartbreak, and the guilt that Alex fights.
—Loren Weaver

Great story. Loaded with adventure at every turn. Can't wait till the next book. Very enjoyable, light reading. I would recommend to all young and old readers.

—Sharon Klein

The Silver Series

"Cheree Alsop has written *Silver* for the YA reader who enjoys both werewolves and coming-of-age tales. Although I don't fall into this demographic, I still found it an entertaining read on a long plane trip! The author has put a great deal of thought into balancing a tale that could apply to any teen (death of a parent, new school, trying to find one's place in the world) with the added spice of a youngster dealing with being exceptionally different from those around him, and knowing that puts him in danger."
—Robin Hobb, author of the Farseer Trilogy

"I honestly am amazed this isn't absolutely EVERYWHERE! Amazing book. Could NOT put it down! After reading this book, I purchased the entire series!"
—Josephine, Amazon Reviewer

"A page-turner that kept me wide awake and wanting more. Great characters, well written, tenderly developed, and thrilling. I loved this book, and you will too."
—Valerie McGilvrey

"Super glad that I found this series! I am crushed that it is at its end. I am sure we will see some of the characters in the next series, but it just won't be the same. I am 41 years old, and am only a little embarrassed to say I was crying at 3 a.m. this morning while finishing the last book. Although this is a YA series, all ages will enjoy the Silver Series. Great job by

Cheree Alsop. I am excited to see what she comes up with next."

—Jennc, Amazon Reviewer

The Galdoni Series

"This is absolutely one of the best books I have ever read in my life! I loved the characters and their personalities, the storyline and the way it was written. The bravery, courage and sacrifice that Kale showed was amazing and had me scolding myself to get a grip and stop crying! This book had adventure, romance and comedy all rolled into one terrific book I LOVED the lesson in this book, the struggles that the characters had to go through (especially the forbidden love)...I couldn't help wondering what it would be like to live among such strangely beautiful creatures that acted, at times, more caring and compassionate than the humans. Overall, I loved this book...I recommend it to ANYONE who fancies great books."

—iBook Reviewer

"I was not expecting a free novel to beat anything that I have ever laid eyes upon. This book was touching and made me want more after each sentence."

— Sears1994, iBook Reviewer

"This book was simply heart wrenching. It was an amazing book with a great plot. I almost cried several times. All of the scenes were so real it felt like I was there witnessing everything."

—Jeanine Drake, iBook Reveiwer

"Galdoni is an amazing book; it is the first to actually make me cry! It is a book that really touches your heart, a romance novel that might change the way you look at someone. It did that to me."

—Coralee2, Reviewer

"Wow. I simply have no words for this. I highly recommend it to anyone who stumbled across this masterpiece. In other words, READ IT!"

—Troublecat101, iBook Reviewer

Keeper of the Wolves

"This is without a doubt the VERY BEST paranormal romance/adventure I have ever read and I've been reading these types of books for over 45 years. Excellent plot, wonderful protagonists—even the evil villains were great. I read this in one sitting on a Saturday morning when there were so many other things I should have been doing. I COULD NOT put it down! I also appreciated the author's research and insights into the behavior of wolf packs. I will CERTAINLY read more by this author and put her on my 'favorites' list."

—N. Darisse

"This is a novel that will emotionally cripple you. Be sure to keep a box of tissues by your side. You will laugh, you will cry, and you will fall in love with Keeper. If you loved *Black Beauty* as a child, then you will truly love *Keeper of the Wolves* as an adult. Put this on your 'must read' list."

—Fortune Ringquist

"Cheree Alsop mastered the mind of a wolf and wrote the most amazing story I've read this year. Once I started, I couldn't stop reading. Personal needs no longer existed. I turned the last page with tears streaming down my face."

—Rachel Andersen, Amazon Reviewer

"I just finished this book. Oh my goodness, did I get emotional in some spots. It was so good. The courage and love portrayed is amazing. I do recommend this book. Thought provoking."

—Candy, Amazon Reviewer

Thief Prince

"I absolutely loved this book! I could not put it down. . . The Thief Prince will whisk you away into a new world that you will not want to leave! I hope that Ms. Alsop has more about this story to write, because I would love more Kit and Andric! This is one of my favorite books so far this year! Five Stars!"

—Crystal, Book Blogger at Books are Sanity

". . . Once I started I couldn't put it down. The story is amazing. The plot is new and the action never stops. The characters are believable and the emotions presented are beautiful and real. If anyone wants a good, clean, fun, romantic read, look no further. I hope there will be more books set in Debria, or better yet, Antor."

—SH Writer, Amazon Reviewer

"This book was a roller coaster of emotions: tears, laughter, anger, and happiness. I absolutely fell in love with all of the characters placed throughout this story. This author knows how to paint a picture with words."

—Kathleen Vales

"Awesome book! It was so action packed, I could not put it down, and it left me wanting more! It was very well written, leaving me feeling like I had a connection with the characters."
—M. A., Amazon Reviewer

The Small Town Superhero Series

"A very human superhero- Cheree Alsop has written a great book for youth and adults alike. Kelson, the superhero, is battling his own demons plus bullies in this action packed narrative. Small Town Superhero had me from the first sentence through the end. I felt every sorrow, every pain and the delight of rushing through the dark on a motorcycle. Descriptions in Small Town Superhero are so well written the reader is immersed in the town and lives of its inhabitants."
—Rachel Andersen, Book Reviewer

"Anyone who grew up in a small town or around motorcycles will love this! It has great characters and flows well with martial arts fighting and conflicts involved."
—Karen, Amazon Reviewer

"Fantastic story...and I love motorcycles and heroes who don't like the limelight. Excellent character development. You'll like this series!"
—Michael, Amazon Reviewer

"Another great read; couldn't put it down. Would definitely recommend this book to friends and family. She has put out another great read. Looking forward to reading more!"

—Benton Garrison, Amazon Reviewer

"I enjoyed this book a lot. Good teen reading. Most books I read are adult contemporary; I needed a change and this was a good change. I do recommend reading this book! I will be looking out for more books from this author. Thank you!"

—Cass, Amazon Reviewer

Stolen

"This book will take your heart, make it a little bit bigger, and then fill it with love. I would recommend this book to anyone from 10-100. To put this book in words is like trying to describe love. I had just gotten it and I finished it the next day because I couldn't put it down. If you like action, thrilling fights, and/or romance, then this is the perfect book for you."

—Steven L. Jagerhorn

"Couldn't put this one down! Love Cheree's ability to create totally relatable characters and a story told so fluidly you actually believe it's real."

—Sue McMillin, Amazon Reviewer

"I enjoyed this book it was exciting and kept you interested. The characters were believable. And the teen romance was cute."

—Book Haven- Amazon Reviewer

"I really liked this book . . . I was pleasantly surprised to discover this well-written book. . .I'm looking forward to reading more from this author."

—Julie M. Peterson- Amazon Reviewer

"Great book! I enjoyed this book very much it keeps you wanting to know more! I couldn't put it down! Great read!"

—Meghan- Amazon Reviewer

"A great read with believable characters that hook you instantly. . . I was left wanting to read more when the book was finished."

—Katie- Goodreads Reviewer

Heart of the Wolf

"Absolutely breathtaking! This book is a roller coaster of emotions that will leave you exhausted!!! A beautiful fantasy filled with action and love. I recommend this book to all fantasy lovers and those who enjoy a heartbreaking love story that rivals that of Romeo and Juliet. I couldn't put this book down!"

—Amy May

"What an awesome book! A continual adventure, with surprises on every page. What a gifted author she is. You just can't put the book down. I read it in two days. Cheree has a way of developing relationships and pulling at your heart. You find yourself identifying with the characters in her book...True life situations make this book come alive for you and gives you increased understanding of your own situation in life. Magnificent story and characters. I've read all of

Cheree's books and recommend them all to you...especially if you love adventures."

—Michael, Amazon Reviewer

"You'll like this one and want to start part two as soon as you can! If you are in the mood for an adventure book in a faraway kingdom where there are rival kingdoms plotting and scheming to gain more power, you'll enjoy this novel. The characters are well developed, and of course with Cheree there is always a unique supernatural twist thrown into the story as well as romantic interests to make the pages fly by."

Karen, Amazon Reviewer

When Death Loved an Angel

"This style of book is quite a change for this author so I wasn't expecting this, but I found an interesting story of two very different souls who stepped outside of their "accepted roles" to find love and forgiveness, and what is truly of value in life and death."

—Karen, Amazon Reviewer

"When Death Loved an Angel by Cheree Alsop is a touching paranormal romance that cranks the readers' thinking mode into high gear."

—Rachel Andersen, Book Reviewer

"Loved this book. I would recommend this book to everyone. And be sure to check out the rest of her books, too!"

—Malcay, Book Reviewer

The Shadows Series

"This was a heart-warming tale of rags to riches. It was also wonderfully described and the characters were vivid and vibrant; a story that teaches of love defying boundaries and of people finding acceptance."
—Sara Phillip, Book Reviewer

"This is the best book I have ever had the pleasure of reading. . . It literally has everything, drama, action, fighting, romance, adventure, & suspense. . . Nexa is one of the most incredible female protagonists ever written. . .It literally had me on pins & needles the ENTIRE time. . . I cannot recommend this book highly enough. Please give yourself a wonderful treat & read this book... you will NOT be disappointed!!!"
—Jess- Goodreads Reviewer

"Took my breath away; excitement, adventure and suspense. . . This author has extracted a tender subject and created a supernatural fantasy about seeing beyond the surface of an individual. . . Also the romantic scenes would make a girl swoon. . . The fights between allies and foes and blood lust would attract the male readers. . .The conclusion was so powerful and scary this reader was sitting on the edge of her seat."
—Susan Mahoney, Book Blogger

"Adventure, incredible amounts of imagination and description go into this world! It is a buy now, don't leave the couch until the last chapter has reached an end kind of read!"
—Malcay- Amazon Reviewer

"The high action tale with the underlying love story that unfolds makes you want to keep reading and not put it down. I can't wait until the next book in the Shadows Series comes out."

—Karen- Amazon Reviewer

". . . It's refreshing to see a female character portrayed without the girly cliches most writers fall into. She is someone I would like to meet in real life, and it is nice to read the first person POV of a character who is so well-round that she is brave, but still has the softer feminine side that defines her character. A definite must read."

—S. Teppen- Goodreads Reviewer

Never stop dreaming!

Made in the USA
Las Vegas, NV
10 January 2021